Dare to Risk All

by

Joyce M. Holmes

Dare to Risk All

COPYRIGHT © 2015 by Joyce M. Holmes

Cover Art by *Tina Lynn Stout*

The Wild Rose Press, Inc.
PO Box 708
Adams Basin, NY 14410-0708
Visit us at www.thewildrosepress.com

Publishing History
First Champagne Rose Edition, 2015
Print ISBN 978-1-62830-792-4
Digital ISBN 978-1-62830-793-1

Published in the United States of America

Ben crossed the room to the computer table. From where she sat, Tessa caught a whiff of a sensuous blend of spice and citrus as he passed her desk. She swallowed. Hard.

"I take it this was Ed Hardy's computer, and now it's for my use?" he asked after a moment.

"I guess," Tessa agreed. Needing to concentrate on something other than how sexy Ben smelled, she dug in her drawer for her appointment book to see what she had on her schedule for the day. Morris wanted her to clean up any outstanding work by the end of the week, leaving her free to focus on new accounts with Ben. She had been developing some ideas to pitch for spec work, which were almost in the final stages and wouldn't take long to finish once her computer was back up and running.

Ben walked over to her desk, folded both arms across his chest, and gazed down at her. "Ya know, this polite stranger thing is getting pretty old." When she looked up, he braced his arms on the edge of the desk and leaned in. "Are we talking to one another or what?"

Tessa dropped the book and flattened into her chair. That now familiar breathless feeling constricted her throat. His stance, his closeness, gave her an exhilarated, restless sensation. Her body reacted to the message she read in his eyes, little jolts of desire mingling with spurts of resentment. The treacherous way her body responded to him embarrassed her, and if she read his smug expression correctly, he knew exactly what effect he had on her.

No matter what or how she actually felt, her pride demanded that she prove this impertinent man wrong.

Praise for Joyce M. Holmes

Ms. Holmes won a 2012 RONE Award with her first published book, *Show No Weakness*. It also was a finalist in the Chanticleer Book Reviews' 2013 Chatelaine Blue Ribbon Writing Competition.

Dedication

In memory of Dexter, and to Sasa and Maddie.
Adorable Yorkshire terriers, all.
And, of course, my own little Roxy, only half Yorkie,
but 100% adorable. She owns my heart.

Chapter One

"Today's your lucky day, Tessa Leigh."

Tessa Caldwell rolled her eyes as she slipped into the chair beside Janey Kent and neatly lined up her notepad and two pens on the conference table in front of her. "Didn't your mom ever tell you not to count your chickens?"

"I feel it in my bones." Janey reached a hand behind her head, groping for the pen she kept stabbed through the knot of dark hair at the base of her neck. Then she helped herself to a couple pieces of paper from Tessa's notepad. "This day is yours for the taking. So is Ed's job."

"You and your bones, Janey." A male voice chuckled from behind them. Travis Spellicy, one of Tessa's favorites amongst the competitive marketing group she worked with, dropped into the empty seat on the other side of Tessa. "But, I agree with her this time, Tessa. No one's in a better position to take Ed's place, and Montgomery'd be a liar if he said you didn't deserve it."

"Thanks for the vote of confidence, guys. We'll have to wait and see."

Tessa had high hopes of getting the senior account executive position. Her work merited a promotion, even though her boss likely wouldn't see it that way. Morris Montgomery's archaic and chauvinistic opinion that

1

females were an inferior species, with no place in the so-called macho world of market sales, was legendary around the agency. As a result, she'd become a world expert at being passed over for promotion.

Not one of the other junior executives—who all happened to be male—had as much experience or seniority as Tessa, not that it had stopped Morris from promoting them ahead of her in the past. She doubted it'd be a factor again this time, despite her dedication and growing list of accomplishments.

After she came up with the perfect pitch to land the lucrative Lavender & Satin hand lotion account, her boss had no choice but to present her with the company's annual performance award, along with the bonus Pacific Coast cruise. She'd logged plenty of extra hours to earn the trip, and achieving that fairly lofty goal should count for something.

She closed her eyes against the mounting pain. It had been nearly five months now, and she'd promised herself not to dwell on the cruise any longer. Or the man she'd met on it. She had wallowed in memories of Ben Dunham for far too long, even after it became painfully clear he hadn't given her—or their time together—a second thought. And she wasn't about to go there now. She refused to think about him, to ache for him, and silently berate him for not caring about her. It was over, ancient history, and she needed to move on.

Travis's elbow jostled her back to reality, as he adjusted his glasses and flipped his notebook to a fresh page. "I hope this meeting doesn't take too long. I have a ton of ad time to buy today."

Janey gave an unladylike snort. "Since when are

the monthly staff meetings anything except long and tedious? We are talking about Morris the Monotonous, aren't we?"

As though on cue, Morris Montgomery entered the boardroom, and a hush fell around the table. In his late fifties, Morris had the well-fed roundness of a man who enjoyed the finer things in life.

"Good morning, staff," his voice boomed out. "There are a substantial number of items on the agenda this morning. First, however, I feel compelled to address a subject most certainly foremost on the minds of each and every one of you." His weighty pause for effect had Tessa barely managing to stifle an exasperated sigh. "As you know, Ed Hardy has embarked on a much deserved retirement, and it is incumbent upon me to name his replacement. Traditionally, our practice has been to promote from within our own ranks."

He smiled and waved a beefy hand in front of his face in an expansive gesture. "Without intending to keep you in suspense for any longer than necessary, I feel the existing situation is somewhat dissimilar to previous vacancies, so please bear with me while I explain my plans to fill the position."

As usual, her boss continued to move at his own plodding pace. This time the sigh refused to be denied, and Tessa swallowed it down with an audible breath. Janey reached over to give her fingers a reassuring squeeze. Travis plucked his glasses from his nose and began vigorously polishing the lenses, a sure sign he was worried or needed to think. His nervousness on her behalf would've touched Tessa, if she hadn't been so preoccupied with her own case of jittery nerves over the direction Morris seemed to be heading. She deliberately kept her face impassive and hoped for the best.

Morris puffed his chest out further. "As you will recall, last fall, Tessa received the company incentive bonus, and her work over the years has been exemplary. However, after a judicial assessment of the agency's recent rate of progress and potential for sustained growth, I have arrived at the decision to allocate this position jointly between two employees for the foreseeable future."

A chorus of surprised voices sounded around the room, although the announcement came as more of a disappointment than a shock to Tessa. Some vague rumors had circulated about the possibility of more than one employee taking on Ed's position because of the agency's recent rapid expansion. If she understood Morris correctly, she had the promotion, but she'd be sharing it with another colleague. A male colleague, to be more accurate.

"I would like all of you to welcome the newest addition to our team. He is a talented young man, and I predict we will see some highly innovative productivity from him in the coming years." Morris crossed to the boardroom door and opened it with a flourish.

Every muscle in Tessa's body stiffened, and her heart seemed to take an extra beat when she saw who stood in the doorway, but she allowed no trace of recognition to cross her face. Taking short, careful breaths, she watched in horrified fascination as Ben Dunham entered the room.

Captivating, disturbing, blatantly masculine, he exuded the same barely leashed energy she recalled from the three days spent with him on the cruise last fall. His sandy brown hair was beautifully styled and naturally streaked with varying shades of blond, just as she remembered it. His custom-tailored dove-gray suit showcased his impressive physique to perfection. He looked so incredible she practically shivered with delight.

Morris's chubby fingers smoothed the strands of hair trailing over his balding head. "Everyone, this is Benjamin Dunham. He has been with Montgomery Group in Vancouver for the past five years, and we have managed to persuade him to relocate to Calgary and take on the responsibilities of senior account executive. In conjunction with Tessa, of course," he added in apparent afterthought.

Ben halted a few feet from Tessa's chair, and she rose to her feet, sliding nervous hands down the front of her skirt. For an instant, they stood frozen face-to-face, outside of time together, cut off from the others, the air between them tangible and electric.

Ben took a step toward her. Instinctively she stepped back and stared with disbelief into the face that had haunted her for months. Those same iridescent sea-green eyes with flecks of gold and swirls of gray, surrounded by long, thick, dreamy lashes. The slight jog to his nose, as if it had been broken, a trivial flaw that saved his features from absolute perfection.

Neither of them smiled as they continued to watch each other. She could see memories of their one night together reflected in those extraordinary eyes.

Memories of his hands roaming her body, of his mouth searing hers, of the two of them reaching peak after shattering peak together, while thunder crashed and white-hot lightning forked its way across the storm-tossed night sky outside.

She tried to push the images from her mind and keep her manner professional. Then he offered her his hand, and her heart fluttered. A treacherous excitement began rising in her system as reality sank in—this was Ben, standing right in front of her. And this time they didn't have to say goodbye after three days.

She had an irresistible urge to reach out and touch his face. Her fingers itched to lose themselves in that crisp beach-sand hair, to wander across his chest, slide over the wide breadth of his shoulders and...

Stop thinking like that!

She forced herself to shake hands with him, uttering polite noises as though he were a complete stranger. Try as she might, she couldn't get her lips to form the smile of welcome she knew would be the courteous thing to do.

"We've already met." He continued to hold their handshake. His eyes were playful, with green turbulence just beneath. "Remember me?"

She realized with a start that she hadn't replied. The intoxicating scent of his cologne robbed her of breath, and his huskily seductive voice reverberated inside her, leaving her shaken and vulnerable. He was leaning in too close, and she had to jiggle her hand lightly to free it from his grip.

"Of course I do. We met on the cruise last fall." She hid behind an ultra-professional tone.

"That is correct." Morris's loud voice startled Tessa. She'd forgotten anyone else was in the room. "The Vancouver branch awarded Benjamin the cruise as well, last year, so the two of you have already had the opportunity to become acquainted. That should facilitate your working relationship."

Not bloody likely, Tessa thought with a sinking feeling of despair. How could she possibly maintain a businesslike relationship with Ben after the intimacy they'd shared?

"If you would be seated, I will introduce Benjamin around the table, and we can proceed with today's agenda."

Morris took the large leather chair at the table's head, while Ben backed into a vacant seat at the other end. Tessa turned away from him and sank into her chair between Janey and Travis.

Morris's decision to hire Ben hadn't fooled her in the least. No question, Ben had the qualifications for the job. It wasn't a big stretch to imagine how successful he'd be pitching a campaign. With his salesman's good looks and air of extreme poise, women would likely hang on his every word, and even men would be attracted to all that casual charm.

He'd also gotten the position because he gave it the proper window dressing. Although Tessa had never managed to shake her resentment, over the years she'd become resigned to the fact she lost marks with Morris because she didn't have what he considered the proper account executive image. Image meant everything in this business, and Ben nailed that persona precisely, right down to his Italian leather loafers. Young, aggressive and macho, he had the total package, and was exactly the type Montgomery Group sought. Exactly the type she could never be.

Tessa found it difficult to concentrate on the rest of the meeting—although she studiously avoided looking Ben's way, he occupied all her thoughts. She tuned out the buzz of conversation flowing around her as she struggled against the memories rushing vividly into her mind.

Memories of Ben's shameless flirting as he taught her how to use a golf simulator, of spirited conversations during long walks along the ship's deck, the way she hadn't been able to take her gaze off his incredible body while they swam in the pool the afternoon the storm struck. Ben's unexpected compassion when he noticed her fear of thunder. Making love half the night while the storm raged outside. Waking up in his arms and making love again...

Enough already!

She had convinced herself to forget Ben and that magical time together, and having almost succeeded— here he was, back in her life in a big way. Panic rose in her, and fighting a ridiculous urge to burst into tears, she scowled at the tabletop.

Sensing Ben's eyes on her, she risked a glance his way and caught him studying her, using the same look of frank, level-eyed admiration he'd used back on the cruise. His gaze contained a hunger she could plainly see, yet failed to understand. Men didn't tend to look at her that way.

She remembered how he'd called her a 'damn fine-looking woman' the day they'd met, and how she'd initially thought he'd been mocking her for his own perverse reasons. Because, without a doubt, she'd never win any Damn Fine-looking Woman awards.

Ben smiled, and his smile still had the strange ability to make her want to fling herself at him and kick him, both at the same time. With enormous effort, she pulled her gaze away from his and didn't allow herself to look his way again.

When the meeting ended, Janey haphazardly tucked her pen back in her hair and turned to Tessa. "Hey, hon, do you want to go somewhere to talk?" Janey obviously sensed her distress even if she'd have no clue about the actual complexity of the situation.

"In a bit," Tessa mumbled, pretending to an occupation with collecting her notepad and pens to avoid meeting her friend's compassionate gaze. "I have a couple of things I need to do first." Like get the heck out of there and compose herself. And then she had to figure out how to deal with a scenario she had fantasized about for months—meeting Ben Dunham again.

Her heart raced, and her breath came way too fast as she rose to her feet. She glanced rapidly around, afraid her face might betray her, but no one seemed to notice. She swung away from the table and narrowly avoided slamming into Ben.

"We have to talk," he said quietly after a circumspect glance over his shoulder.

To give herself an extra moment to shore up her composure, she silently studied him. He was an extremely handsome man, no denying it. With those confident, arrogant manners, he could probably charm the spots off a leopard, and Tessa was certain he took full advantage of that engaging grin of his. But if he wanted to resume what they'd started back on the cruise, she'd have to set him straight. Her aberrant behavior on that last night was definitely a one-time thing, and she didn't intend to do anything to put herself in a precarious position at work.

Dallas Christopher, Montgomery Group's red-haired vamp of a receptionist, sidled up to them before Tessa could gather enough of her wits to formulate an appropriate response. Dallas had the kind of body men seemed to have trouble keeping their hands off, and that appeared to suit Dallas just fine. Self-centered, materialistic, and eternally restless, she rarely acknowledged other women but always smiled brazenly at any man who looked her way.

"Welcome to Calgary, Ben, and to our firm," she cooed and shook his hand. In Tessa's opinion, she held his gaze and his hand a mite longer than necessary. He didn't seem to mind, though. There was no mistaking the naked appreciation in his eyes as he ran his gaze over Dallas's tall, curvy body.

Dallas gave him a saucy grin. "Well, hey, handsome. You've just made things way more interesting around here." Tessa almost gagged when Dallas coyly covered her slash-of-scarlet mouth. "Wow, did I say that out loud?"

Seriously? Who did the woman think she was fooling?

The sound of Ben's delighted laughter shocked Tessa and hurt her feelings. Dallas was as blatantly sleazy as a person could get, and Tessa couldn't believe how taken with her Ben appeared to be. Their preoccupation with their mutual admiration made it painfully easy for her to slip out of the room unnoticed. So much for thinking Ben might want to resume their relationship, more likely he'd intended to make sure Tessa had no misconceptions about what had transpired between them. It had been an opportunistic fling and nothing more.

Which was exactly what Tessa wanted, wasn't it? She'd already decided not to become involved with Ben again—or at least her head was trying hard to convince her body of this. She just hadn't been prepared for how badly it'd hurt to see him show such a flagrant lack of interest in her while making goo-goo eyes with that tacky Dallas.

His reaction to Dallas proved that Ben Dunham was merely another handsome man accustomed to trading on his sexual appeal to get what he wanted. The same type of man as Colin Barry, the charming snake who'd broken Tessa's heart without a qualm a few years back. Ben was obviously a player, just like Colin, and he'd already had her, so now he intended to target new territory.

Tessa walked slowly back to the cubicle she called her office, her mind spinning, her pride smarting, and her heart aching. Safely hidden behind the pseudo-wall dividers, she slouched low on her spine and leaned her head against the back of the desk chair. What in heaven's name was she going to do? It hadn't taken more than a few seconds around the man to realize she wasn't over him in the slightest. Not that she'd ever completely fooled herself into believing she was.

Although she'd known from the start she'd never forget Ben, she hadn't realized how the memories would haunt her. Whenever she thought about their time together, her entire body tingled and tensed with a special type of bittersweet nostalgia. She remembered clearly how he had made her feel special and attractive, the way he'd touched her and kissed her with such aching tenderness.

He had roused her long suppressed and tightly

controlled sexuality, and she had yet to find a way to lull it back to sleep. For the most part, she'd learned to ignore it because she had no time to pine after someone who clearly belonged in her past. Her ambitions were important to her, and she always put her career ahead of her personal life. Not that she didn't have a personal life. Well, okay, she didn't have *much* of one, which, in her opinion, simply made it easier to keep her professional goals clearly in sight.

Janey poked her head into the cubicle. "Hey, you okay?"

Tessa nodded, freeing herself from the tangle of memories. "I'm fine, really," she lied. "I half-expected Mr. Montgomery to pull a stunt like this." At least that much was the truth.

"Doesn't mean it doesn't suck the big one." Janey plopped into the spare chair. "Whaddaya think of that new guy? Talk about a walking aphrodisiac, eh? He should come with a warning label or something. It sure didn't take Dallas long to sink her fangs into him."

Tessa amazed herself by faking a believable indifference. "He'll have no problem handling her. He can charm the rattles off any old snake."

Janey leaned forward, visibly intrigued. "That's right! You met him on the cruise. Did you guys spend much time together?"

"Um, yeah, we hung out quite a bit." Tessa straightened in her chair and clasped her hands together on the desk. She usually confided in Janey about everything but didn't know if she could have this conversation with anyone, even her best friend.

Janey's eyebrows hiked a little higher, pulling her eyes wide open. "Ah! Tell me everything! What kind of a guy is he? Did you get along well?"

"You might say that." Tessa's gaze went to the office entrance—although the cubicle walls might be taller than standard, they still allowed for zero privacy—then back to Janey's avid face. Her voice dropped about three levels. "We, uh, you know..." In her mind, she called what they'd done *making love*. Realistically it had been nothing more than having sex. Sizzling, bone-melting sex with a stranger—a gorgeous, hotter than hot, stranger—but merely sex with a stranger, nonetheless. Somehow, she couldn't form those callous words. She winced and gave a quick shrug. "We, uh, spent the last night together."

"Are you *kidding* me?" Janey's voice rose in a disbelieving squeal. "You slept with the man?"

Tessa flapped a hand frantically to shush her. "Keep your voice down. I didn't plan it. It just happened. A huge thunderstorm hit, and I had my typical bad reaction, so Ben kindly saw me to my stateroom." She shook her head, trying to dislodge the images that came into focus, racing furiously across her mind. "Things just got out of hand."

She relayed to Janey how she'd decided to skip dinner and hide under her bed covers, cowering from the gathering storm, until Ben knocked on her door and insisted she join him. After the meal, he suggested they go on deck to view the play of lightning in the distance. Nearly panicked at the idea, yet not knowing how to get out of it without revealing her irrational fears, she'd reluctantly agreed.

In no time, Ben had figured out something was wrong. Jumping and whimpering whenever a shaft of lightning exploded against the black skies might have given her away. Or maybe it was the way she held both palms tight against her ears to muffle the nightmarish roar of thunder. A stupid, ridiculous reaction, but her breath-stealing, stomach-wrenching panic had moved her beyond the ability to fake normalcy.

With a tenderness and concern that rocked her, Ben had wrapped a protective arm around her and escorted her to her stateroom. As they entered, a huge crash of thunder vibrated through the room, the wind gusted and rain hit the window hard, and she'd clung to him. The storm suddenly seemed everywhere at once, raging outside, pounding the ship; raging within her, swamping her senses, destroying her defenses. Although safe from the storm outside, she'd begun to lose her hold on reality as the storm continued to build inside her...

The details dried up and she faltered, then grew silent. She couldn't share how incredible it had been to make love with Ben. And she didn't admit how shaken she'd been the next day, when they'd said goodbye. Or that he'd asked her to spend the rest of the week with him in San Francisco, and when she had to decline, how he'd held her as if he couldn't bear to let her go. When he lowered his head to search out her mouth with his, there had been a desperate hunger in his kiss. She'd caressed his face, stroked his hair, willing her fingers to remember the touch and feel of him, doubtful she'd ever see him again.

An episode that scarcely begun had ended and she'd only then started to realize how deeply it affected her, leaving her to wonder how a man she had known for three short days could cause her such turmoil.

She'd briefly considered asking Ben to call her

when he got home. By plane, Calgary wasn't that far from Vancouver, so they could find a way to get together. Then she recalled his words from their first dinner together when she'd asked about a wife or girlfriend. *Serious relationships aren't my style.* If Ben wanted more, he would've suggested they continue their budding relationship. But for all his sweet and tender gestures, he hadn't said anything of the kind, hadn't asked to exchange phone numbers or email addresses, nothing. And her innate insecurities wouldn't allow her to initiate a conversation he might not be interested in having.

So, as suddenly as that, the best thing ever to happen to her abruptly ended. Not once in the following months had she heard from him. Now, inexplicably, he was back in her life, and it felt so surreal, she didn't know what to do.

What to feel.

Janey swiveled back and forth in the chair, barely able to contain her glee. "Sweet little straight-laced Tessa Leigh doing the dance with no pants with a complete stranger. I'm speechless."

"No, speechless is when you are no longer able to speak. Which would be such a good idea at the moment." Tessa closed her eyes and massaged her temples, where a stress headache rapidly built.

"That explains why you two were having eye-sex all meeting."

Tessa's eyes popped open and she glared at Janey. "We were not. I barely looked at him."

Janey grinned unrepentantly. "Yeah, but honey, when you did, mmm-mmm. And he sure looked at you, all right. Like he was eating sugar with a spoon. So, tell me. Was he worth it?"

That was the million-dollar question, for which Tessa had no definitive answer. "Then yes, now no." A long, dragging groan rattled up her throat. "Honestly, Janey, I don't know how to deal with this. I never expected to see the man again. Now, thanks to that low-down Mr. Montgomery gypping me out of my promotion, I'll have to work closely with him on a regular basis. It's incomprehensible."

"You can't mean you don't intend to carry on with Ben?" Janey's eyebrows waggled significantly. "He is some cute."

"No," Tessa blurted much too loudly, and her gaze skittered over to the cubicle entrance. "No," she repeated in a more muted tone. "What happened on that cruise was a fluke. We haven't even spoken since. Besides, I'd be crazy to. You know Mr. Montgomery frowns on fraternization amongst colleagues."

Janey wrinkled her nose and gave an offhand flip of her wrist. "That old fart hasn't had sex for so long, he resents anyone else getting any."

Any other time, her friend's irreverent words would've had Tessa in giggles. This time, she found herself fighting back tears. She slumped forward, dropping her forehead to the desktop, and took a couple of calming breaths. "No one else is going to hear about this, right?" she asked, her words muffled against the stained laminate.

"No one? Not even Trav—"

Tessa shot upright. "Not Travis. Not anyone." To compound her growing humiliation, her voice cracked, and she put a hand to her trembling lips.

Janey leapt from her chair and scooted around to

perch on the desk's edge next to Tessa. "I had no idea when I said today would be your day, that this would happen. I'm so sorry, sweetheart. My bones usually know better." She rubbed Tessa's shoulder. "Come on, how about we check out your new digs? Maybe that'll cheer you up."

It couldn't possibly make her feel any worse, Tessa thought miserably, as she followed Janey down the hall.

****

Dallas Christopher had bold eyes and a brightly painted mouth. An absolute stunner, her tall, dazzling body was almost calculated to arouse desire.

She gave Ben a sly appraisal from under long lashes. "I bet women simply can't refuse your charm," she purred, rubbing talon-tipped fingers along his arm. "I sure find you hard to resist."

Ben glanced down at Dallas's hand on his jacket sleeve, then flashed a dry smile. "Feel free to try." He'd always considered skin-deep plenty deep enough, but to his surprise, although his hormones were aroused, his interest wasn't. He didn't have time to waste on a meaningless flirtation, and it irritated him to have allowed this woman to sidetrack him from his conversation with Tessa. Now, he had no clue where the hell Tessa had disappeared to.

Dallas giggled, his sarcasm evidently not fazing her. Her laughter turned to annoyance when a tall, thin man with horn-rimmed glasses joined them. Ben searched his mind for a name to put to the face—Travis Spellicy, the account traffic coordinator.

"Down, girl," Travis growled at Dallas. "No flirting in the workplace."

Dallas wrinkled her nose and shot him a venomous

glare. "Spoilsport."

Travis met her scowl without blinking. "Shouldn't you be working or whatever it is you do around here?"

Dallas fell into a pout, her hand rhythmically squeezing Ben's arm. "See you around, Ben."

They both watched as she sashayed out of the boardroom with an exaggerated sway to her shapely hips. "She's a rather receptive receptionist, isn't she?" Ben noted as he glanced over at Travis.

Travis took his glasses off and rubbed the little red indents on the sides of his nose. "Watch out for her. She eats men like you alive. You look up piranha in the dictionary, you'll find her."

Ben laughed, recalling the countless number of *Dallases* he'd been with over the years. "She doesn't look all that dangerous."

"Believe me, she is." Travis peered at the lenses of his glasses, flicked at a piece of dust and settled them back on his beaky nose with a frown. "She's a wild sexpot who can't keep her body off the men."

"With a body like that, I can't imagine the men complaining," Ben joked.

Travis gazed in the direction Dallas had gone, his frown deepening. "Myself, I don't see the attraction." He turned back to Ben and said gruffly, "Montgomery asked me to show you the ropes and get you settled in your new office. I'm Travis Spellicy, by the way, in case you didn't catch it earlier."

Ben took Travis's offered hand. "I remembered." He smiled at the other man, and Travis didn't make much effort to reciprocate, which had Ben wondering if he'd inadvertently taken the promotion this man expected to get. Ben had never felt comfortable with the way Morris Montgomery insisted he not contact anyone at the Calgary office prior to this morning's meeting. All the secrecy had him concerned things weren't on the up and up.

Morris had also not given him any indication he'd be sharing the position with Tessa Caldwell. Not that he minded working in partnership with her. Or doing other stuff with her, if she were so inclined.

He had tried to think of Tessa as just another pleasant interlude, a delicious memory, but the woman had woven some sort of spell around him. She wasn't anything like the type he usually went for—he generally preferred his women tall and curvy, not featherweights with a pixie cap of blonde hair. Despite this, he found Tessa to be a dangerous combination of delicate and desirable. The arousing image of her slim hips with that tantalizingly rounded backside and the saucy tilt to her small breasts had continued to play at the edge of his mind for months, and he hadn't dared to hope he'd ever lay eyes on her again.

When the opportunity to work in Calgary arose, he'd jumped at the chance to transfer. Montgomery Group's Vancouver branch was much larger than Calgary's, and he could languish there for years without cracking a senior position. Far better to be a big fish in a small pond.

Of course, transferring to Calgary meant seeing Tessa again, which was one of those good thing/bad thing scenarios. Being near her filled him with an almost painful expectation, an unnerving touch of excitement, and this could only lead to complications. As much as he wanted Tessa, his attraction to her was a bad idea on way too many levels. His number one priority had to be establishing a name for himself in Calgary. If not, the sacrifices he'd made to transfer here would've been for nothing.

He rubbed the bridge of his nose. The biggest sacrifice had been leaving his mother behind in Vancouver. They'd experienced more than their fair share of family trauma in the past and had developed a tight bond as a result. They would miss each other, but he'd promised to keep in close contact, and he always kept his promises to her. She'd spent enough years living with broken promises—and a whole lot worse— while his alcoholic father was alive.

Ben abruptly cut those painful memories off with brutal precision. He didn't often visit that particularly nasty back corner of his mind, and he sure wasn't about to go there now. "I gather my arrival this morning came as a surprise to everyone," he said to Travis, hoping the other man might enlighten him.

"You could say that. We all thought Tessa Caldwell had the promotion cinched. She's the most qualified for the position."

Ben recognized the impatient censure in the other man's tone and realized it wasn't Travis's toes he had inadvertently stepped on, but Tessa's. That might explain her standoffish reaction. He rested a haunch on the edge of the conference table. "I had no idea. No one told me I'd be sharing the position. I feel as if I owe Tessa an apology, even though I was as misled as she was."

Travis pushed a lock of dark hair off a steeply sloped forehead. "I'm not surprised. Montgomery has a way of setting his staff up like that. He believes a harmonious organization is a complacent one, so he encourages competition between the employees. Keeps everyone sharp. You never know who's on the way up and who's on the way out."

"And you figure Tessa should be on the way up?"

"In a word, yes." Travis's sharp hazel eyes scrutinized Ben from behind his glasses. "Tessa's about as sweet as they come, and in this business that's a character flaw. Just don't go and make the mistake of thinking she has more air than brains under that blonde hair. It's a total misconception. She's bright and talented, and she'll go far if given half a chance."

"You're totally preaching to the choir. Tessa really impressed me last fall with her quick mind and intuitive grasp of the advertising business." Nearly as much as she'd impressed him with her supple little body and sweet-tasting lips.

"Come on," Travis said, interrupting his thoughts before they became too X-rated. "I'll show you around. Montgomery's going to want you on track by tomorrow."

Ben struggled to rein in his impatience while Travis gave him an abbreviated tour of the place. Although he looked for Tessa around every corner, he found no sign of her, not even in the cubicle Travis pointed out as being Tessa's office. Pausing in the entranceway, Ben surveyed the small area with a keen eye. Evidence of Tessa's creative side showed in the whimsical touches she gave to the otherwise nondescript area. A silk plant, a cross-stitched poem, and a candy dispenser all sat on a battered filing cabinet. A large, framed landscape photo hung from one of the cubicle walls.

A smaller photo on her otherwise sparse desk

captured his attention, and he took a few quick steps into the room to examine it. It was a shot of Tessa and another young woman Ben assumed must be her sister. They shared the same small features and fine bone structure, but whereas Tessa looked like an earthbound angel with hair like a sunny halo around her head, the other woman could never be considered innocent-looking. Her heavily made-up eyes were sensual and sultry, her lips a provocative pout. Her honey-blonde hair hung long and sleek, in graceful curves over her shoulders. In short—a beautiful, sexy woman.

Ben appraised and dismissed her, his gaze returning to dwell with pleasure on Tessa's image. Beside her provocative sister, she looked more fragile and ethereal than ever, elegant and exquisite, with large blue eyes full of sweetness and candor. She had an intriguing sprinkle of freckles bridging a short, straight nose, and a delicate, proud chin. Her heart-shaped mouth had his mind reliving the velvet warmth of her kisses.

The hand that returned the photo frame to Tessa's desk held a slight tremor, and his reaction annoyed him. Why, out of all the countless women he'd known, could he not forget this particular one? Sure, the sex had been great, but that's all there was to it—great sex. He'd had great sex plenty of times and never gave it a passing thought. So why, exactly, was this dainty little flower causing him such strife?

Probably because she was much more than a lovely bit of charming fluff. She was sweet and vulnerable, true, but she was also smart and spirited. Not someone to play around with and then forget. She was too real, too honest, for that.

In fact, she was exactly the type of female he'd be smart to avoid. Tessa was the marrying kind, and genetics told him he wasn't husband material. He had doubts whether he'd make very good boyfriend material either. It was much better, much safer, to maintain the role of carefree playboy, to stick with women who wanted what he wanted—physical satisfaction without investing in any bothersome emotions. That, most definitely, didn't include Tessa Caldwell.

He tersely turned his back on Tessa's office and nodded his head at Travis. "How about showing me where my office is?" He spoke brusquely, so his emotions wouldn't show in his voice.

Chapter Two

One of the perks of being a senior account executive was getting an actual office. A spacious room with real walls, a door and a window with a view, and Tessa had long coveted one all to herself. Morris shot that prospect down when he informed them at the meeting that she and Ben would share the space. Ben would use Ed Hardy's large walnut desk while she had to make do with her old chrome-and-laminate one, which the maintenance personnel would move into its new location tomorrow.

"This is great," Janey said as she spun in a slow circle in the middle of the room. "It's so huge, you won't even notice you have a roommate."

"I'll know he's here, all right. I couldn't possibly be in the same room as the man and not be aware of him."

Janey stopped spinning and drilled Tessa with a narrowed gaze. "You care about him that much?"

Tessa stalked over to the window, raking her hair back with her fingers as she watched, without really absorbing, the activity on the busy street seven floors below. "Even though I've tried like the dickens to put Ben out of my mind, I think about him all the time." She not only thought about him, she could feel his skin against hers, could hear him breathing in her ear. Deep in the night, she still reached for him, aching with need.

But the cruise had been a fantasy; it wasn't real anymore. And judging by the way she'd left Ben drooling all over Dallas Big-boobs Christopher, it had never been real to him.

Janey joined her at the window. Instead of looking out, she kept her gaze fixed on Tessa's face. "I remember the way you acted after you returned from the cruise, ready to jump down everyone's throat. At the time, I thought it was unlike you, but now I understand. You were nursing a broken heart."

Tessa forced a smile. "This is called animal magnetism, pheromones or whatever. My heart was never involved."

Janey tilted her head to one side. "Do you honestly believe that you, Tessa Leigh Caldwell, could sleep with a guy and not get emotionally involved? Especially when you hadn't slept with anyone for so long, you were practically a born-again virgin."

Hysterical laughter welled up in her throat, and she swallowed it back with difficulty. "Yeah, well, can you blame me? Look what happened when I got emotionally involved with Colin."

Janey's warm eyes turned cold, and she came as close to looking hateful as was possible for her. "Colin Barry was an egotistical, immature jerk. He didn't appreciate how good he had it with you."

Tessa waved her hand, brushing back the remnants of bitterness and pain. "No, he knew, all right. But when he met my sister, he saw how much more she had to offer. Attractive men such as Colin Barry and Ben Dunham look right through the likes of me. They want to be with desirable women like Lauren, or even that sleazy Dallas. Not sexless, curveless, me."

Tessa figured herself to be one of the least sexy women in the city—make that the entire province—and her sister was, well, Lauren was gorgeous and flamboyant, in constant motion like a fluttering butterfly, and she drew men to her without effort. Tessa, on the other hand, was prone to being called cute. Not striking, not pretty, never beautiful—just plain-vanilla *cute*.

Besides the obvious differences in looks, Tessa and her younger sister were as unalike as night was from day in every other possible aspect. She'd always been the quiet, responsible one, while Lauren was all flash and flirt with a constant stream of males sniffing around her. Though Tessa loved her sister dearly, she wasn't blind to Lauren's human frailties. Lauren needed parties and fancy clothes, and she craved constant male attention. She had to have people to take care of her. And from the time they were little girls, after their mother died and their father turned to his work for consolation, Tessa had tended to be the one who handled the 'taking care of' part.

In fairness to her sister, Lauren hadn't tried to steal Tessa's lover away from her, it had just happened. The affair between Colin and Lauren had burnt out almost as fast as it flared up, and they'd both moved on without much fuss and no apparent regrets. Tessa had been the only one left hurt and broken-hearted. But she had learned a valuable lesson in the process. It made her wary of leading with her heart, instead of her head. And her sister's long string of shallow liaisons had made her even more leery of basing a relationship on a physical attraction.

Colin was the last serious relationship she'd had,

and she swore she would avoid men like him at all costs, forever and always. And Ben Dunham, unquestionably, fit in that category.

"Tessa." A hand waved in front of her face. "You look a million miles away. Did you hear me?"

Tessa blinked. "What did you say?"

"I said you should thank your lucky stars you didn't waste yourself on the likes of Colin Barry. The jury's still out on Mr. Ben Dunham. I have a notion he's interested if you are, but only you can decide if he's right for you."

Tessa gave her friend a hug. "Thanks for being so sweet and understanding. Let me assure you, Ben is the exact opposite of the right man for me."

All she had to do was convince her susceptible heart and traitorous libido of that.

****

The office door stood open, and the sound of female voices reached them before they entered the room. Ben's pulse quickened along with his footsteps. Finally, he'd found Tessa.

She stood by the window with the woman who had sat next to her during the meeting, an attractive brunette in her late thirties with generous features and dark eyes. As he entered the office with Travis, Tessa abruptly ended her sentence, giving Ben the impression he'd been the topic of conversation.

Eager curiosity etched across the face of the other woman—Jane *Something*—as she hurried across the room toward them.

"Hi, Ben." She extended her hand. "Jane Kent. I'm one of the creative directors here. Welcome to the company."

Ben returned her friendly smile as he shook her hand. She had a firm, no-nonsense handshake, and Ben detected a glint of knowing in the dark depths of her eyes. His intuition told him she was privy to what went on between Tessa and himself on the cruise. He also had the gut feeling Jane approved of him. Here was a possible ally, and judging by the tight expression on Tessa's face, he needed all the friends he could get.

"Thanks, Jane. I look forward to working with you." He zapped another glance Tessa's way. Her teeth busily worried her bottom lip, and she wouldn't make eye contact. "With all of you."

"Come on, Trav." Jane snagged Travis by the elbow and propelled him toward the door. "Let's leave these two to sort out their new office space. Catch up with you later, Tess," she called breezily before disappearing through the doorway.

With Jane and Travis out of the room, Ben and Tessa stood in silence, an uncomfortably guarded air suspended between them. Ben searched for something appropriate to say. What exactly does a person say to the woman he'd made earth-shattering love with, then hadn't seen for months, only to unexpectedly show up to steal, albeit inadvertently, the promotion she had her heart set on? Not surprising, he couldn't think of a single blasted thing.

She looked even better than in his memories. Her hair had grown since last fall, the longer lengths in the front almost reaching her chin, and Ben found himself wanting to run his fingers through that silky blonde cap to see if it felt as soft as he remembered. Her navy-blue skirt hugged slim hips, and her delicately curved upper body was encased in a sweater set the same color as her eyes, which at the moment were a very frigid blue.

"I meant what I said," he finally blurted, desperate to fill the conversational chasm. "It'll be great working with you." He tried for a smile, hoping she'd return it, but her face remained neutral, unsmiling, not giving him anything.

Tessa crossed her arms over her chest and leveled her gaze at him. "Why did you transfer here? I would've thought you'd consider this slumming."

Her blunt words wiped the smile off his face. "What the hell kind of thing is that to say?"

"What did you expect after all these months? For me to fall willingly into your arms?" Her voice was horribly steady, unrecognizably controlled. Her aloofness disturbed him, and the fact that he let it get to him, disturbed him even more.

He moved toward her, his arms out. "I'd settle for a hug."

"Please don't touch me." The frigid resolve in her voice stopped him mid-stride. She had a withdrawn look about her, as though she was speaking to someone she hardly knew and would rather not become better acquainted with.

The urge to annoy her, to disturb that icy calm was the strongest emotion Ben recognized amongst the seething mass of feelings erupting within him. He stepped forward. She backed up. He took another step. This time she didn't move, and he rapidly closed the gap between them. As he reached her, she deliberately turned away, so he cupped a hand on her shoulder and pivoted her around to face him. Sliding his hand down her arm, he captured her fingers. With his other hand, he brushed the hair from her face and lowered his mouth to her ear.

"Hey, cutie, I'm disappointed you're not happier to see me."

He crooked a finger under her chin and studied her lovely, fine-boned features. A multitude of emotions flashed through the eyes staring back at him, just not the desire he longed to see.

She folded her fingers around his wrist, yanking his hand away from her chin. "That's not fair. We both know who's stronger. If you were a gentleman, you'd back off."

Despite knowing better, the need to ruffle her composure, to break down her defenses, ran strong. "I've been accused of many things, being a gentleman was never one of them. Besides, whoever said life was fair?"

She used her free hand to tug the captured one from his grasp. Her fingers felt small and fragile compared to his, bringing sharply into focus his height compared to her smallness. Appalled by his behavior, he jerked back with both hands up in surrender.

"I'm sorry, really, really, sorry. I'll never do that again, but please don't continue to ignore me."

"There's nothing to say."

Her abrupt words were meant as a dismissal; however, he had no intention of being dismissed. He wanted to know what was going on, and he bloody well intended to find out. "The hell there isn't. Five months ago, we couldn't get enough of each other, and now you're standing there, staring at me like I'm some dude you vaguely remember from the bus stop."

His voice had risen, and as soon as he realized it, he clamped his mouth shut. A sick sensation cramped his belly while a twinge of apprehension escaped from a shadowy place in the back of his mind. He hooked a finger in his tie to loosen it, then unbuttoned his collar and resumed speaking in a calmer tone. "Why are you so willing to write me off? Am I too much of a challenge?"

She shifted her weight, thrusting out one slim hip, a small, provocative movement. "Get real."

He raised a cynical eyebrow, forcing his words into a taunt she couldn't ignore. "Oh, I'm totally real. And I'm not going anywhere, so you damn well better get used to it."

He didn't understand why he bothered to engage in this verbal sparring with her. He usually got along famously with women. They tended to like him. A lot. That wasn't conceit talking; it was fact.

Fact and dedicated effort. Years ago, when he realized how risky it'd be for someone with his genetically substandard background to engage in anything deep and meaningful with a woman, he'd cultivated a charming, devil-may-care façade. A long string of superficial relationships, offering nothing more than physical release, proved he'd accomplished his goal. Impressing people was his specialty, he made his living from it, yet Tessa didn't seem at all impressed. Far from it. Her expression showed equal parts pity and scorn.

She hoisted herself to the desktop and swung her legs back and forth. With the experienced eye of a connoisseur, he took a moment to admire those exceptional legs. Very nice.

"Okay, Ben, you tell me. What do you see happening? After all this time without a word, you suddenly show up and want to be my boyfriend?"

He glanced at her, then away, lifting one shoulder in an uncomfortable half-shrug. His throat worked on a hard swallow. "I, this...okay, see..." He mentally gave himself a sharp kick in the ass. *You're not a coward, so spit it out already.* "My life doesn't really have room for romantic interests right now."

"I thought as much."

"If we plan to spend the foreseeable future working in close proximity, couldn't we at least be friendly? Hell, I'd settle for mere politeness. I'm not into the whole cold war thing. Come on, Tess, please." He hated wheedling as much as he hated stumbling over his words, but he couldn't seem to help himself.

Those superb legs of hers moved back and forth, back and forth, beguiling him into remembering how they felt wrapped around his back, moving in rhythm with him. With extreme effort, he banished the erotic image and forced his gaze from her legs to her face. Bright, hot spots of anger reddened her cheeks, and her eyes snapped clear angry blue.

Ben stuck his hand in his pants pocket and rattled his change. "Okay, I get that you're mad, but I seriously have no clue what I did to upset you."

"Really?" she fired back, her voice turning shrill. "I'd think it should be blatantly obvious, but if you need it spelled out, I can do that." She took in a deep breath, though it didn't appear to calm her. "I am *so* angry because you stole my job. I deserved that promotion. All to myself!"

"Tessa, I didn't take your promotion." He rubbed a hand hard over his face, then shook his head, unable to control his mounting frustration. "I didn't even know you were up for the promotion or that we'd be sharing it. Montgomery forgot to mention that little detail when he offered me the job."

Her face creased with thought, and he could see the answer hadn't satisfied her. "Why did you accept it? You told me you loved your job in Vancouver. You even made fun of Calgary. Referred to it as Cow-town, or something equally rude. Why in the world did you have to come here?"

He couldn't quite figure out why he felt like such an asshole about the situation. What, exactly, had he done wrong? He got the position because he was good at his job. It hadn't hurt to have Morris extol his talent and tell him how far he could go with the agency. He'd eaten up the praise and liked the taste. He saw now that Morris had played him a tune, and it was humiliating to realize how readily Ben had danced for him.

"I came here because it was a wise career decision," he said, trying to convince both of them. "I'm sorry you feel cheated, but I've as much right to this position as you do. Morris tricked me, too, but I'm not angry about it. I have no problem sharing the promotion. I'm thinking you don't have a real problem with it either. Something else is bugging you."

"There is one other thing, now that you mention it." She paused, and her legs stopped swinging. "It's been almost five months since we last saw each other. Not once did you call, drop me a text, nothing. Not even to let me know you were moving here. What kind of a person does that to someone they've been intimate with?"

Guilt rocked him back on his heels, and he wanted to explain how he'd fought with himself not to phone her. They'd never discussed continuing their friendship, and as much as he'd missed her and often thought about her, it'd be pointless trying to carry on a long-distance relationship. He'd be the first to admit to having a short attention span when it came to women, and he figured her hold over him would eventually fade. Judging by his feelings at the moment, she continued to appeal to him as much now as she had the day they'd met.

He struggled to sort through his thoughts, to make some sense out of this mess. "Sorry," he said finally. "I didn't think—"

She slapped the desk with the flat of her hand, a sharp sound that made him flinch. She might look like a delicate kitten, but the woman had claws. "Damn straight, you didn't think. We had sex, Ben, more than once. Did it never occur to you I could be pregnant?"

A chill skated down his spine, and his gaze slid to Tessa's slim midsection. He saw no evidence of a baby bump, which meant zippo because he had no idea when a woman started to show. "We used protection." He *always* used protection.

"That kind of protection has been known to fail. Maybe you didn't care enough about me to keep in touch, but did you not even care to find out whether you might become a father?"

He had a sudden sense of being in a car without brakes, hurtling down a steep hill, with a sharp bend looming nearer. "You aren't? Pregnant. Are you?"

"No, I'm not, actually. That's not the point, is it?"

Exasperation immediately overrode his relief. "No, it's not the point; however, I refuse to take all the blame here. There were two adults in your cabin that night. When one of us tried to stop—twice, as I recall—the other one had the most delectable way of convincing him to change his mind. Ring any bells?"

She crossed her legs, one pump dangling off her toes. "Isn't that just like a man?" Bitterness sharpened her words as her voice picked up speed. "Behave shabbily, then twist things around and make me out to be the one in the wrong."

He held out his hands, searching for something, anything, to defuse the situation. "No one's wrong here, and I don't want to argue." Shamelessly he switched gears, turning on his most engaging smile. "Look, if we call this our first fight, we officially get to have make-up sex. Just tell me where and when. I'll bring whatever sort of protection you want."

"That is so not funny."

Ben ditched the smile and tried for an appealing look. "I'm dead serious."

Tessa straightened, locked her knees tightly together, and stared. She blinked once, then exploded. "You're outrageous, Benjamin Dunham, and I wish you'd go someplace else and complicate the hell out of someone else's life."

She confused him, knocked him off balance with her animosity. Of all the little reunion scenarios he'd played out in his mind—most of them rather erotic— never once had he imagined reality turning out this way.

Her open hostility exasperated him, and his fists involuntarily bunched at his sides. Scared of himself, of the anger, he carefully relaxed his fingers.

Never, ever, make a fist when you're angry.

"I'm not inclined at this moment to make your life any easier," he told Tessa coldly. "And for today only, this is my office, so I suggest if you can't bear to be around me, you should leave."

That snapped her mouth shut. She hopped off the desk, nearly losing her balance because of her loose shoe. He grabbed her arm to steady her. She inhaled sharply, and he let go so quickly she stumbled backward. This time, he let her set herself right without offering any help. She shot him a dirty look and stomped off, her sassy little rump swishing from side to side as she stalked out of the room, slamming the door behind her.

Muttering a string of colorful curses he didn't normally indulge in, Ben went over to his desk and collapsed into the leather chair. A need for distraction had him examining his surroundings for the first time. It was an attractive office, comfortable and functional, with good artwork hanging on the walls and a large window adjacent to his desk. A roomy leather couch lounged beside the window, and an elaborate computer station was set on a long table on the opposite wall. There'd be plenty of room for Tessa's desk at the far end facing his desk.

A muscle ticked at the side of his jaw, and he sank deeper in the chair to stare moodily out the window. He would've thought he had more pride than to chase after a woman who lacked interest. Keeping his distance with Tessa would be the smart thing to do, but Ben enjoyed a challenge. Despite knowing better, he found himself seriously considering doing the dumb-ass thing.

****

Tessa left the Sunnyside C-train station and briskly walked in the direction of the rambling old Victorian-style house she shared with her sister, Lauren. The same house they'd grown up in and the only place Tessa had ever called home. Night was settling in, and Tessa drew her collar up for protection against the late February chill.

She sighed, and her breath became a white cloud in the cold air. She'd felt such a profound relief, when the workday had finally ended and she hadn't had to lay eyes on, or speak to, Ben again after that uncomfortable confrontation in *his* office. If talking to him for five minutes could leave her so rattled, she wondered how she'd endure working in the same room with the man every single day.

She had been annoyed with him for suddenly appearing in her life without any warning after those long months of silence. And angry with him for not offering a proper reason why he hadn't contacted her. But it didn't come close to her fury with herself and her traitorous body for wanting him anyway.

As she crossed the street and turned the corner onto her block, her gaze automatically went to the old house on the opposite corner. It looked shabby and lonely. Memories of the dear old lady who had lived there up until a couple of months ago made Tessa melancholy. Doris Pidlasky. Mrs. P, as Tessa had affectionately called her for as long as she could remember.

When Tessa's mother died unexpectedly from a rare virus that attacked her heart, Doris had stepped in and helped raise nine-year-old Tessa and seven-year-old Lauren. Her own children had already grown and left home, and Doris had welcomed the little girls as if they were part of her own family.

In many significant ways, Tessa felt closer to Doris than she did to her own father. Dr. Ellis Caldwell was a hardheaded, no-nonsense man, who held strong views and didn't have much patience with what he considered frivolous female sentiments. He had a knack for making Tessa feel guilty, embarrassed, whenever she didn't meet his high standards. She'd learned at a young age to smile and be agreeable even if she felt miserable. It was much easier than facing her father's disapproval.

Not that he'd been around that often, anyway, as she grew up. He'd directed most of his focus and energy on his surgical practice, more than ever after his wife had died. When Tessa needed a shoulder to cry on or someone to offer advice, she'd turned to Doris, and the bighearted woman never once let her down.

In the past few years, as Doris grew increasingly frail and absentminded, and with the Pidlasky offspring living in different cities across the country, Tessa had willingly taken on most of her care. Then, one day out of the blue, Doris's daughter came for a visit and when she left, she took Doris with her. Diagnosed with Alzheimer's, poor Doris now lived in an extended care facility in British Columbia's lower mainland, no longer able to live on her own.

Tessa phoned her once a week, but the last time she'd called, Doris seemed confused about who Tessa was, which absolutely broke Tessa's heart. She missed her dear friend greatly, and she hated the way the house sat unsold because Doris's children were asking too much money for it. Doris would hate it, too. The generous old lady would rather have given the place away to a needy family than see it remain empty.

With one last, lingering look over her shoulder, Tessa continued on her way. The lights were on at home, and Lauren's late model Corvette crouched, sleek and powerful, on the street behind Tessa's elderly Honda. None of the old houses on the block had garages, a fact Lauren bemoaned every time she had to scrape frost or clean snow from her beloved Corvette's windshield.

Tessa climbed the narrow steps to the wrap-around porch and reached into the mailbox. Of course, the day's mail still waited inside. Lauren didn't bother herself with such trivial details as checking the mailbox. That's what she had assistants—and Tessa—for.

A quick shuffle through the envelopes revealed nothing more interesting than bills. That's all she ever got, bills and junk mail. At least Lauren received invitations in the mail. Invitations to art gallery shows, to parties and restaurant openings. Not that Tessa envied Lauren's freewheeling lifestyle. Still, there was no confusing which Caldwell sister had the active social life.

"Hello," she called after unlocking the front door. Milo came barreling down the hallway, claws clicking like tiny castanets on the hardwood floor. That's saying a six-pound Yorkshire terrier could actually barrel.

"Hey, baby," she cooed, putting the mail on the hall table so she could bend down and scoop the little guy up. "Did you miss me?" Milo squirmed ecstatically, trying to catch her face with his quick pink tongue. "Enough already." She giggled and set him back on the floor. "Has Lauren fed you?" she asked as she hung up her jacket and put her winter boots on the tray in the closet. Not likely, if she knew her sister—which she did.

The little pooch had finally gotten tired of crossing

his hind legs and learned how to use his doggy door, so at least that wasn't a problem when Tessa had to work late. But he didn't like the dry dog food she left out for him, preferring to wait for something canned and extravagant.

Tessa found Lauren in the kitchen, fixing a cup of hot chocolate.

"Hi, Sis," Lauren greeted her with her usual vivacious smile. She gave the chocolate one final stir, then licked the spoon and put it in the sink. "I swear it's going to snow again. My poor skin can't take much more of this cold, dry weather."

Lauren's skin looked as dewy fresh and beautiful as ever. Tessa had much-hated freckles, while Lauren's complexion was creamy and flawless. Under the skillful guidance of her agent, Anthony deAglo, Lauren had established a formidable name for herself as a freelance photographer, although with her natural beauty and grace, she could've been equally successful as a model in front of the camera.

"I wouldn't mind more snow." Tessa happened to love the cold weather, just as she loved the warm weather and the rainy weather—as long as there weren't any thunder and lightning. And since the cruise, she might possibly even tolerate thunderstorms now that she had an entirely new and enthralling set of memories to associate with them.

Exhaling abruptly, she forced her mind away from that thought and any others that might follow. "Did you feed Milo?"

"I just got home." Lauren spoke like a little girl explaining why she didn't have all her chores done. "I'm freezing, and I needed something to warm me up."

Tessa popped the top off a small can of dog food, then scooped a few spoonfuls into Milo's bowl and set it on the floor by her feet. Milo dipped headfirst into the bowl, leaving only the wagging stub of a tail showing as he quickly lapped up his dinner.

"I wasn't criticizing," she explained. "I just wanted to know." Technically, Milo was Lauren's dog. No, technically, he belonged to an old boyfriend of Lauren's, at least a dozen old boyfriends back. Tessa had long forgotten the guy's name. Lauren had bought the puppy for the boyfriend who promptly returned him to her a week or so later when they split up. That was four years ago, and Tessa had been taking care of Milo ever since. Not that she minded. She was madly in love with the little fellow, and he returned her devotion many times over.

She took a container of leftover Chinese food from the fridge and spooned some onto a plate. "Do you want any?" she offered Lauren. Lauren wrinkled her nose and shook her head, so Tessa popped her plate into the microwave and put the rest back in the fridge.

They discussed Lauren's most recent romantic crisis while Tessa ate her Kung Po Gai Ding and Lauren sipped her hot chocolate, then Lauren had to rush off to get ready for her evening engagement. It wasn't until after she had left, that Tessa realized she hadn't had a chance to tell her sister about her new promotion. Or the fact that her most recent lover had unexpectedly shown up to share that promotion with her.

****

"Morning, Tessa," Ben and Travis chorused as she came down the hallway toward them the next morning.

41

She had arrived at least twenty minutes early, so why was Ben already at work? Sharing small talk and coffee with Travis in the hall outside their office. *Brownnoser*. And he'd effectively stolen the advantage of being the first to settle into the new office.

Ben's gaze moved coolly, shamelessly, over her body in a deliberately appreciative manner. His sensuous mouth curved into a smile that made her legs go rubbery and had her wishing she'd chosen a pantsuit instead of the curve-clinging wool dress.

Not that she had any actual curves worth clinging to.

"Morning." She smiled pleasantly at Travis first, then nodded briefly in Ben's direction and turned her back on him, hoping he wouldn't follow her into the office.

He did. And he closed the door behind him.

She went to her desk, using it as a barrier between them to help cope with his presence. Her temper tended to subside as quickly as it flared, and yesterday's outburst already shamed her. After careful consideration, she realized she'd behaved unreasonably toward Ben. Because he was right—he had offered to stop before they'd made love, and she had been the one to convince him otherwise.

Despite not feeling very logical right now, common sense told her she shared in the responsibility for what had happened between them. She needed to put aside her personal feelings and concentrate on work. Because there was no room for personal feelings at the office. Not irritation, or resentment, and definitely not regret or any residual and unwanted desire.

She'd never be oblivious to the attraction of Ben's sea-deep green eyes and flashing smile, but as far as she was concerned, that would be the extent of it. What had happened on the cruise was attributable to the circumstances, the romantic setting. Nothing more. Trying to continue with that type of behavior here at the workplace would be a recipe for disaster, or at the very least, she'd run the risk of losing her job. She'd always managed to keep her career goals clearly in sight. Now should be no different.

Ben shrugged out of his suit jacket and hung it across the back of his desk chair. He paced restlessly around the room, then moved to the window and stood in front of it with his hands in his pants pockets. Tessa surreptitiously watched his every move, enjoying and appreciating his casual grace and masculine beauty. As she grew aware of the direction her thoughts had headed, she irritably stopped herself and focused on her desktop instead. The photo of her and Lauren lay face down in the middle of her desk, and she placed it in its usual spot at the far left corner.

"The fellow who moved your desk and filing cabinet said something about hooking up your computer later this morning."

"That'll be fine," Tessa muttered as she reached out and nudged the picture frame a fraction of an inch to the right.

Ben crossed the room to the computer table. From where she sat, Tessa caught a whiff of a sensuous blend of spice and citrus as he passed her desk. She swallowed. Hard.

"I take it this was Ed Hardy's computer and now it's for my use?" he asked after a moment.

"I guess," Tessa agreed. Needing to concentrate on something other than how sexy Ben smelled, she dug in her drawer for her appointment book to see what she had on her schedule for the day. Morris wanted her to clean up any outstanding work by the end of the week, leaving her free to focus on new accounts with Ben. She had been developing some ideas to pitch for spec work, which were almost in the final stages and wouldn't take long to finish once her computer was back up and running.

Ben walked over to her desk, folded both arms across his chest, and gazed down at her. "Ya know, this polite stranger thing is getting pretty old." When she looked up, he braced his arms on the edge of the desk and leaned in. "Are we talking to one another or what?"

Tessa dropped the book and flattened into her chair. That now familiar breathless feeling constricted her throat. His stance, his closeness, gave her an exhilarated, restless sensation. Her body reacted to the message she read in his eyes, little jolts of desire mingling with spurts of resentment. The treacherous way her body responded to him embarrassed her, and if she read his smug expression correctly, he knew exactly what effect he had on her.

No matter what or how she actually felt, her pride demanded that she prove this impertinent man wrong.

Chapter Three

"Could you back off? I don't want you sharing my personal space. I intend to do and say whatever is necessary to have a productive workday, and not a thing more." Her words sounded harsh even to Tessa, but with her body behaving in ways she had no control over, she forgave herself the overreaction.

Ben straightened, his thigh leaning casually against the desk edge, his posture disdainful and cocky. "Thank you for being so willing to grit your teeth and suffer my existence."

She ignored his sarcasm. "And I'd feel more comfortable if you'd stay on your own side of the office."

His amusement showed on his face. "My aim wasn't to make you feel comfortable."

She bit down on another surge of irrational anger. He wanted to goad her, and she was playing right into his hands. She ordered her mouth to smile and managed a reasonable facsimile. "What in the world did you do for amusement before you met me?"

He gave a mocking, yet somewhat tender grin. "I'm sorry, I heard you say 'What in the world', then I got lost in your lips and didn't catch anything else. Could you repeat it?"

"Eww. Could you be more annoying?"

"I'm just getting warmed up, thank you."

Feeling sulkier by the moment, Tessa changed the subject. "I'd like to know why you get the window view, and I'm stuck over here in the corner."

Ben swung around and looked at his desk, then back at hers. "I don't care about the view. If you want it, you can have it."

She didn't expect that. Besides, he was probably bluffing, and she was in just the mood to call him on it. "All right then, let's switch. If you're willing to help me, we could probably move the desks around by ourselves."

"Why move the desks? Unless you've become fond of this old relic, you can have mine, and I'll take yours."

He actually sounded sincere, and his unexpected cooperation caught her off guard. She told herself she was making something out of nothing because his sudden reappearance in her life had her unstrung. "Forget the whole thing. You can't see anything from your desk anyway, except the high-rise across the street. I'll stay here."

Raising his brow in a good imitation of innocence, he asked, "You sure? I wouldn't want you to think I have something you don't."

"I said I'd stay put." Now he had her sounding like a petulant little girl. She forced herself to calm down. No point letting the situation play on her nerves. It was far too late for that. Ben was here, and she needed to accept it.

Ben went over and dropped into the chair behind his desk. "Is there a man in your life? Is that why you're flashing the hands-off signal?"

Tessa rolled her eyes and sighed. Did he ever stop?

"No, I'm not involved with anyone. You're just not my type."

He leaned back, his Italian loafers up on the desk with ankles crossed, listening with a skeptical expression. "And what, exactly, is your type?"

She shrugged and picked up the appointment book. "Not you." She hoped her lack of interest would dent his male pride sufficiently for him to leave it be.

His feet dropped to the floor, and he sat forward in his chair, his back straight and tense. Tessa got the impression of strong emotion held under strict control. His mouth tightened, then he forced his lips into a smile that didn't reach his eyes. "You're not sure what your type is, yet you know I'm not it?"

"Yes." She was getting adept at this lying business. Not exactly an admirable attribute, although she didn't mind rattling his chain a little, in return for the way he so easily annoyed her.

Ben opened his mouth, then clicked it shut again as the phone on his desk began to ring. "Dunham," he said brusquely into the receiver. "Oh hi, Travis." He ran a hand through his hair and glanced at Tessa. "Yes, of course. The boardroom? I'll be right there." He hung the phone up, then lifted his suit jacket from the back of his chair, sliding his arms into it as he crossed the room. "We'll have to continue this captivating conversation later. I've a meeting to attend."

"What kind of meeting?" Tessa couldn't help asking.

"To go over some accounts, I imagine. I'm sure the idea is to put me to work."

She scooted out from behind her desk. As usual, her heels were somewhere underneath, but she didn't take the time to retrieve them. "Shouldn't I be at the meeting, too?"

Ben glanced down at her feet, and his mouth twitched. Tessa's toes curled under his scrutiny. Let him wear high heels that pinched the way hers did and see how long he lasted in them. Her face flamed, and she wished the earth would open up and swallow her—or better yet, him.

"Guess not. Travis said there's a meeting with Morris in the boardroom. He didn't mention anything about you accompanying me."

Could a person sound any smugger? Tessa clamped her teeth against some inspired retort like 'Screw you' and carefully arranged a show of indifference on her face. "They probably know I'm swamped with my own work. I've got loads of important stuff on the go."

Ben paused at the door, that annoying twitch playing around the corners of his mouth again. If he dared laugh, she'd kick his gorgeous butt, even if she had to climb on a chair to do it.

"If the stuff's that important, shouldn't you get at it?"

"*Shouldn't you get at it?*" Tessa sneered as she mouthed the words to Ben's retreating back, then stomped over to his desk to buzz Janey's office. After four rings, she got Janey's voicemail. Did that mean Janey was at the meeting, too? And Travis? Why wasn't she included?

Hanging the phone up, she instructed herself to stop taking everything personally. So what, if she didn't sit in on every single meeting, and big deal if she had to share an office with Ben. Plenty of other staff members shared offices without a problem, and there was no reason she and Ben couldn't manage to, as well. The senior exec position belonged to her. That's all that mattered in the big picture. She'd find a way to deal with the other little nuisance details.

A person had to make personal sacrifices to get ahead in her career, she'd learned that much from her father. Ellis Caldwell had become a highly successful surgeon by dedicating most of his waking hours to his profession. Tessa modeled her own ambition after her father's. If it worked for him, it would work for her.

She pulled her sketchbook out of her top drawer, deciding it'd be better to keep busy, than to sit and stew about not attending the meeting. She could rough out some ideas for the spec work on paper until the maintenance man showed up with her computer.

Her pencil began flying and flicking over the sheet. The image that appeared had no commercial value to it. It was personal, intimate, and revealing. A portrait of a man. A man with heavy brows over compelling eyes, a slight bend in the bridge of an otherwise perfect nose and—her pencil added a few more lines—a sensuous mouth with a little crease right in the middle of the full bottom lip.

Tessa sucked in her breath as she stared down at the sketch. After two shocked beats, she quickly began flipping the pages over, using the sheets of paper to hide what she'd drawn. She sank onto her elbows, her fingers on her forehead.

What was she thinking?

That was her problem. She wasn't thinking. Ever since she met Ben Dunham, the ability for rational thought seemed to have completely deserted her.

****

"I tried to get hold of you earlier. Were you in that meeting I wasn't asked to attend?" Tessa spoke to Janey over her shoulder as she retrieved her ham and cheese sandwich from the fridge in the break room.

Janey opened her lunch bag and began spreading out her meal on the table in front of her. "Uh-oh. Sounds like someone has her panties in a twist."

"I hate that expression, and you know it. Can you blame me for feeling ignored? Was I not made senior executive, too?" Tessa pulled out a chair and plopped herself in it.

"Settle down, honey. I asked Morris that exact thing, and he said this meeting was to get Ben online with some of our outstanding accounts and better acquainted with the other staff members. He said you already had a full plate with everything you needed to clear up."

"I'm not that busy."

Janey took a bite from the corner of her sandwich, chewed and swallowed, all the while contemplating Tessa with serious brown eyes. "If you don't like the treatment, you have to speak up. I've told you this before, and I can only repeat myself. As long as you let Morris take advantage of you, he will. That's how he operates."

What Janey said made sense. At least as much sense as all the other times she'd said it, but Tessa hadn't taken her advice then, and she doubted she'd do it now. Despite having a heart of gold, Janey had a spine of steel. No one got away with pushing Janey Kent around. Tessa, on the other hand, wasn't exactly the confrontational type. To put it mildly, she got ill at the mere whiff of dissension. Admirable or not, her instinct was to do whatever necessary to avoid conflict, rather than face it.

Growing up with a father who expected to have his rules followed without question, Tessa had discovered early the benefits of keeping her mouth shut and going with the flow. She sheepishly admitted she'd developed such a need to avoid confrontation that anyone with a strong personality could, and often did, dominate her.

And that thought segued into one about another person with a strong personality she'd like to avoid. She sank onto her elbows with a disheartened sigh. "What makes Mr. Montgomery think Ben Dunham is so wonderful?"

"You mean, besides the fact he could sell you a dead horse and you'd drag it away with a smile on your face convinced you'd just got the deal of a lifetime?"

Tessa grudgingly laughed at Janey's accurate portrayal of Ben's sales ability. She remembered the shoptalk she'd shared with him on the cruise, and how he'd constantly impressed her with his endless ideas and creative solutions. She had to concede, even more grudgingly, that he really was a grade-A salesman with extraordinarily persuasive words, capable of convincing anyone of practically anything. She was living proof of that. He'd easily convinced her to behave in a manner completely opposite to her usual cautious temperament.

But that was a whole other story. And she was finished talking about it.

"He's good, I'll admit that. He's also a guy." While Tessa, on the other hand, was a short, blonde female.

"He's definitely a guy," Janey agreed around a mouthful of bologna sandwich. She swallowed and continued. "I actually catch myself staring at him. Not only does he look yummy enough to eat, he has such impeccable manners."

"Impeccable?" Tessa almost choked on the absurdity of the notion. She could say several things about Ben's manners—cocky, arrogant, sardonic, outrageous, irreverent... Not one of those words were synonymous with impeccable. "Impeccably rotten, perhaps."

Janey arched a knowing eyebrow in her direction. "You two kidlings not getting along?"

Tessa picked at her sandwich, tearing off small pieces of bread and dropping them onto her napkin. "I wouldn't say that exactly."

They weren't *not* getting along. Ben just knew exactly what to do, what to say, to push buttons she didn't even know she had. And he didn't stop pushing until he provoked a response. Despite her dread of conflict, she seemed to have no trouble going head-to-head with him. The reason for this, it suddenly dawned on her, was because Ben treated her as an equal, as did Janey and Travis, neither of whom lacked in strength of personality. Although Ben tried his best to get to her and often succeeded, he never demeaned her or made her feel inferior.

This realization did nada to redeem him in her eyes. She didn't want to have any positive thoughts about him. She didn't want to consider the possibility he might be a decent guy under all that annoying posturing. It would be smart to remember those superb salesman skills of his and his capacity to tell a person exactly what they wanted to hear.

Janey covered Tessa's hand with hers, halting the relentless shredding of her sandwich. Tessa wasn't sure if she meant to offer support or simply because Janey couldn't stand to see good food go to waste. "After spending some time together again, how *do* you feel about him?"

"I feel nothing about him." Until she'd figured out his angle, she refused to admit to anything concerning Ben Dunham.

Janey stared at her, and Tessa had the feeling her friend saw right through her denial. Thankfully Janey didn't call her on it. "Is he wanting to, you know, pick up where you left off?"

"Janey! Be careful." Tessa darted a glance behind her, even though she knew they were alone, then motioned Janey closer. "Okay, for fun, let's say he's interested. Montgomery Group has a strict policy against dating, so why would I want to risk my future with this company for the opportunity to play around with a man who openly admits he doesn't have room for a woman in his life. Who, in his own words, doesn't do serious relationships? Besides, if he cared in the least about me, why didn't he bother to pick up the phone and, oh, I don't know, maybe mention the fact he was moving out here?"

"Umm." Janey nodded her head as she polished off the last of her sandwich. "Travis told me about that. Apparently, Morris made it a condition that Ben could have no contact with any of us before he came out. I guess the crafty old bugger wanted to keep everyone guessing until the last minute, afraid it would ruin the impact of his big surprise at the meeting."

That gave Tessa a moment of pause. She could see Morris doing exactly that, but still, if it had been important enough to Ben, he would've made an exception for her. After all, they did share a little history together. No, she couldn't accept that he'd kept silent at Morris's request as a reasonable excuse for not telling her. She didn't trust him, and she didn't trust his motives.

And, worse yet, she didn't trust herself.

****

Somehow that day went by, then another one. Then an entire week. Several times during the course of the workday, Tessa would turn toward Ben to ask a question or initiate a conversation, and then remembered she wasn't acknowledging his presence. It didn't take long to realize the difficulty of keeping silent. She *wanted* to talk to Ben, to share ideas and think out loud. Hard as she tried, she couldn't seem to hold on to her resentment.

Although she often felt the weight of those sea-green eyes boring down on her as she worked, Ben seemed to respect the fact that she wanted him to leave her alone. She couldn't help noticing he was more considerate than she'd expected. All necessary exchanges between the two of them had been courteous and professional. Ben treated her exactly the same way he did all his other coworkers, outwardly friendly, always in a civil business manner. Maybe, just maybe, he had given up the idea of pursuing whatever it was he'd planned to pursue with her. Which, it vexed Tessa to admit, came as both a relief and a disappointment.

They were both seated at their respective desks about ten days after Ben's arrival, when he softly called her name. With a mixture of dread and expectancy, she met his gaze.

"What?"

He rose, stretching, and stepped out from behind his desk. "We both know *what*, Tessa. Let's talk about how long, instead. Like, how long are you going to act as if nothing happened between the two of us?"

Her heart suddenly began beating faster than hummingbird's wings. He hadn't given up after all. He'd just waited until he'd lulled her off-guard.

"As far as I'm concerned, nothing of consequence did happen." The lie was so blatant, her voice croaked with dryness, but she forced herself to speak through it. It was vital to maintain the pretense that he didn't affect her. Recognizing his physical appeal was one thing; allowing it to go further was out of the question. "The best thing you can do for both of us is forget all about it."

He rested his backside against his desktop with his arms propped on either side. "You can't be serious? How can I pretend it never happened? How can you?"

He seemed pensive and sincere, and unexpected tears filmed Tessa's eyes. She forced herself to act busy, shuffling paper from one side of the desk to the other, then back again, doing whatever she could to avoid his earnest expression. She had almost learned how to cope with his irreverent behavior, and a part of her actually missed his silly jokes and flirtatiousness. This tender side of his personality, however, continued to confuse her.

"You'll have to figure that out for yourself because we've already had this discussion. What happened is over. Done. There won't be any repeats."

"Why not? I wanna be with you. And you wanna be with me."

She stopped her paper shuffle and glanced up

sharply. "Says who?"

He exhaled an exasperated, low laugh. "You trying to tell me there's no attraction? Because I damn well know you're as aware of me as I am of you. And any day now, you're going to give in and decide you've made us wait long enough."

She practically shivered from the tension of needing him and trying not to acknowledge it. She'd thought herself immune to the handsome face and smooth guy act—that was more her sister's department—but it was proving harder and harder to ignore the pull of this man. "I'm telling you that if there is an attraction, we won't be acting on it," she replied in her steeliest voice. Maybe if she insisted hard enough, they both might believe it.

Ben crossed his arms over his chest. "You've been spoiling for a fight since the day I got here, and you can throw all the attitude you want, it's not going to change the fact that there's unfinished business between us."

She swallowed hard and tried to steady her nerves. "You want to talk business? I'll talk business. This is how it's going to be—I do my work, you do your work. When necessary, we work together. That's all. Got it?"

When he pushed away from the desk and started in her direction, Tessa conveniently remembered a file she needed from the filing cabinet and grasped at this excuse to turn her back on him. As she searched the drawer, she could sense his presence directly behind her. Her fingers became all thumbs as she tried to sort through the folders, looking for the one containing the market research she wanted to review.

Without warning, Ben kissed the sensitive spot right below her ear, the press of his lips a warm and delicious spark of pure delight. The world spun and her breath caught. Pretending an elaborate disinterest, she closed the cabinet drawer, then turned to face him.

"What do you think you're doing?"

"Smelling your cologne and kissing your neck."

He was shameless and far too persistent, yet there was something about the man that appealed to a part of Tessa she never knew existed. A little place deep inside where she felt sensual and daring and desirable. It was all she could do not to wrap her arms around him and kiss that sexy mouth, to heck with the consequences. But she had too much self-control to give in to her impulses. Encouraging his touch would be a mistake from which she might not recover.

"Well, how about you don't do that? Don't you understand anything about personal space?"

Careful not to make body contact, Tessa inched away from Ben, giving herself a little more breathing room. Now all she had to do was figure out how to resume breathing.

She neatly sidestepped him, but before she could go any further, his hand reached out and fastened around her upper arm, his fingers as intimate a caress as his lips had proven to be moments earlier.

"Tessa, please," he said, his voice ragged, and suddenly they were standing close enough for her to feel the heat emanating from his body, the sensual pull between them even stronger than it had been on the cruise.

Even though he knew she wanted him and was likely counting on that attraction to win their sexual tug-of-war, she refused to give him the satisfaction of capitulating. She didn't need these emotions. They could only tangle her up and drag her down. Despite knowing this, it took more willpower than she'd ever needed to walk away.

"Where are you going?"

"Outta here," she replied without looking back. "If I stay any longer, I'll end up saying things we'll probably both regret." Or more likely, they'd end up doing something she'd regret. Something on that big old leather couch over there. That tempting, comfy-looking couch, which had no business being in the room to taunt her with possibilities.

"You can't just leave."

Tessa spun toward him. "Watch me. And while I'm gone, why don't you think about a few things. Like the concept of mutual consent and respect for another person's decisions. I don't ever want to have to tell you again to keep your hands and your...your...lips to yourself. Have I made myself clear?"

He smiled, but his eyes were inscrutable. "Crystal."

For no reason she could comprehend, the hot sting of tears returned to her eyes. "Good."

Unsure what to do next, Tessa went looking for Janey. She rapped on the partially opened door to Janey's office and stepped inside. "Hey, are you busy?"

Janey glanced up from her computer screen. Tessa's face must've betrayed her miserable state, because Janey frowned and instantly gave her all her attention.

"Is there a problem?"

Tessa slumped into the chair facing Janey's desk. "It's not work-related, but yeah, I have a problem." She crossed her arms around her middle and dropped her chin to her chest. "Actually, it's sort of work-related, because it's affecting my work."

"Let me guess. Ben, right?"

Tessa huffed out a frustrated sigh. "Ben. Right. You won't believe this. He kissed me. On the neck. Right in the office."

Janey leaned forward, a broad smile lighting up her face. "Aww, no fair. Why don't things like that ever happen to me?"

Tessa straightened in the chair and glared at Janey. "I'm serious. I don't know what to do about him."

"How about giving in?" Janey asked, and when Tessa snarled at her, she snickered unrepentantly. "Come on, the man's a walking dream, and you haven't had a date in at least six months." Janey continued to smile, while her eyes grew serious. "I know you don't think men are attracted to you, but they would be if you'd show a little confidence."

The naked desire Tessa had seen in Ben's eyes smoldered in her mind, leaving her tense and on edge. He was attracted to her, all right. For all the wrong reasons.

"I'm confident about knowing I should stay far away from Ben Dunham. He's a walking dream, I agree, and he's turning my life into a living nightmare. It's a game with him, an ego thing. He can't stand how I didn't fall into a Victorian swoon when he showed up here, so now he won't let up until he wins."

"Does he not understand the word 'no'? Or are you not saying it?" Janey asked, tapping her pen for emphasis.

Tessa closed her eyes, and the image of Ben's flashing white teeth and sea-green eyes mocked her behind her lids. She was saying no, all right, except her words lacked conviction, and Ben was intuitive enough to pick up on her mixed signals. He was like one of those big dangerous cats, and he could smell the scent of her imminent surrender.

"Tessa honey, I've known you far too long not to see there's something you're not telling me. I think you're letting him make you crazy. And you're making yourself crazy, too, by saying no, when you'd rather say yes."

As usual, Janey was right on the money. She was making herself crazy. And she didn't like the person she was becoming, snarling one moment, teary-eyed the next, always on the edge of losing control. That type of behavior was completely foreign to her character.

Her frustration mounting, she threw her hands up and let them drop to her sides. "What other option do I have? I have to say no. Mr. Montgomery would flip if he caught the slightest hint of impropriety, and there's no way I'm going to jeopardize this new promotion. I've waited too darn long and worked too darn hard for it. Besides, I've told you, Ben doesn't want a girlfriend. I've watched Lauren engage in one shallow, physical relationship after another, and I can't do it. I'm not made that way."

"No, you're not," Janey agreed. The phone began ringing and with an apologetic grimace, she scooped up the receiver. "Jane Kent." She mouthed a "sorry" and held up a finger to signal she'd only be a moment. "Oh, Bray, hi. No, I haven't been ignoring you, honey." She winked at Tessa. "I'm just one busy lady."

Braden Kent was Janey's cousin. He ran his own marketing agency, in Vancouver, although Tessa seemed to think it wasn't quite in the same field as

Montgomery Group. Janey had mentioned to Tessa that Braden's partner would soon go on maternity leave and had decided to stay home after the baby came. Braden wanted Janey to move to Vancouver and work with him.

Tessa couldn't imagine what she'd do if Janey moved away. She counted on her friend for everything from professional advice at work to emotional support in her private life. But she doubted she had serious cause to worry. A born and bred Calgarian, Janey had far too much going on in the community to consider leaving. Besides practically running the art department here at Montgomery Group, she had a hand in a number of worthy causes. She also dedicated a great deal of time helping her parents with the care and welfare of her teenage brother, Stevie, who had Down Syndrome.

Judging from the side of the conversation Tessa could hear, Braden hadn't given up on Janey yet. Tessa gave Janey a brief wave and left her to her phone call. She needed to get back to work. She couldn't hide from Ben forever. Although given her druthers, it was the preferred option.

****

He'd handled that one just swell, Ben thought with disgust. Instead of convincing Tessa to play kissy-face with him, he'd chased her right out of the room. He wasn't sure why she brought out a side of him usually kept safely buried. A vulnerable side that couldn't keep a handle on his emotions.

Instead of egging her on, he should do himself a favor and stay clear of her. His current agenda didn't include chasing cute little females. Making a name for himself at this agency needed to be his top priority.

Once he'd established his credentials in Calgary, he'd be free to pursue whatever sort of distraction caught his eye. And that didn't necessarily mean Tessa Caldwell.

He slid off his tie and undid the top two buttons of his shirt. Tossing the tie onto his desktop, he lowered himself into his chair, taking deep, slow breaths. Long ago, he'd taught himself not to lose his temper, never to lose control, and always remember anger was a weakness.

Ben knew all about the ugly repercussions of uncontrollable anger. No one could get angry quite like his old man; red-faced, arteries bulging in his neck, jaw muscles bunching. Totally irrational. Pour a little alcohol on that temper and it made for an explosive situation. And Ben had lived for fourteen years with the fallout of those outbursts. Those memories from his past made him burn with shame, as though he had been as guilty as his father. Because Ben hadn't taken the brunt of the abuse—his mother had. His sweet, gentle, loving little mother.

He tilted his head back and allowed his mind a rare journey back over the years. As a weird, twisted sort of punishment, he purposely dredged up some particularly painful scenes from his childhood. The raised voices, the sound of sobbing in the night, his mother with another bruise to hide the next morning.

Ben's childhood had been a never-ending cycle of abuse and regret, threats and apologies, cruelty and remorse. He never understood why his mother continued to live with an abusive husband. Why she put up with the cruel taunts, the drunken rages and violent threats that often became reality.

His sole goal as a young teenager, the one thing

that kept him going through all the ugliness, was the hope of rescuing his mother. The hope that one day he'd take her away and she'd never have to live with fear and pain again. Old resentments roiled in his gut as he closed his eyes and conjured up a vivid picture of his long-suffering mother. For years, he'd tried to convince her to leave his father, but she never would. She'd always made excuses for him.

He didn't mean it. It was my fault. I should know better than to antagonize him when he's drinking. He said he's sorry, he loves me and can't live without me. I can't leave him. He needs me.

And each time that he failed to help her, Ben had taken out his frustration and helplessness in terrible fits of rage, punching the mattress on his bed until he finally collapsed in an exhausted heap, crying his pain and guilt into his pillow. To this day, those outbursts shamed and frightened him. He had never once revealed to anyone what he'd done in the privacy of his childhood bedroom.

Ben pressed his fingers into his eye sockets until the pain drove away the memories. They were too wrapped up in misery and remorse and, unable to deal with them any longer, he thrust them aside.

He'd go find Tessa and apologize to her. Tell her she'd won. He'd leave her alone. It was for the best, for both of them. He couldn't take a chance with the emotions she awoke in him. He could never risk finding out what he might do if he became really angry, because he sometimes wondered, deep down where he didn't like to go, if the sickness lived inside him, too. If he could ever hurt a woman.

Figuring the most likely places to check for Tessa

would be Janey's office or the break room, Ben set off down the corridor in that direction.

"Hey, Ben," Dallas called from the other end of the hall. "Got a minute?"

"Sure." Ben turned back and headed toward Dallas as she continued in his direction, a sultry smile on her kiss-me lips. She was one prime piece of real estate, no mistaking it.

"I'm so glad I ran into you." Her voice held a flirtatious note and she made direct eye contact as she spoke, letting him see her interest, an interest Ben didn't share. Gorgeous hunk of woman or not, something about Dallas made him vaguely uneasy.

"What's up?"

"My favorite band is playing at a club downtown this weekend, and I'm dying to hear them. So what do you say?" She placed her hand on his forearm, squeezing a little tighter than necessary.

"Are you asking me out?"

Her laugh was overly confident. "No, silly, you're asking me out. And I'm saying yes." The laughter died, and she leaned toward him, caressing his shoulders, his biceps. She took his hands and settled them on her hips. "Damn, but you do things to me." Running her fingers back up his arms, she sidled in closer. "We could be so hot together."

With a quick glance around, Ben drew back. "What're you doing?"

"This." Dallas grabbed his face between her hands and before he could react, she kissed him. Her lips were wet, and her tongue pushed unexpectedly between his teeth, thrusting into his mouth. Shocked by her brazen audacity, he pulled away, and she grinned mockingly.

"Why'd you stop just when things were getting fun?"

He gasped. He—who was so accustomed to engaging in sexual innuendoes—actually gasped, then stammered like a little schoolboy. "We can't...you can't...do that."

"No?" Dallas narrowed the gap between them, once again pressing up against him. "How about this, then?" Both arms snaked around his neck, pulling him so close her breasts flattened against his chest and her hips ground almost painfully against him. Her mouth sought out his in a kiss that could only be described as ferocious.

Ben tore himself out of her embrace and scrubbed the side of his hand over his mouth. "What the hell, Dallas, are you crazy? We're standing in the middle of the damn corridor at work. It's amazing someone didn't see us."

The fingers of her right hand inched up and down the length of her left arm, a narcissistic, caressing gesture. Her gaze was riveted over his shoulder, and her grin turned nasty.

"Actually, honey, someone did see us."

Ben spun around, a sick feeling churning his insides. As he feared, Tessa stood in the hall, just outside Janey's office. Her eyes were huge and liquid with shock, her face betraying a world of hurt.

"Uh, Tess. Hi. If you're wondering, Dallas and I were horsing around, that's all. It wasn't what it looked like."

Despite trying his best to downplay the incident, Dallas didn't leave him much maneuvering room. She linked her arm through his in a proprietary fashion, her body pressed up close and uncomfortably personal. She gave a bawdy wink in Tessa's direction. "I don't know what it looked like, but it felt damn fine. This man sure knows how to use his lips."

Damn it to hell. This wasn't fair, and it wasn't the truth, yet how could he possibly deny anything when he probably had Dallas's blood-red lipstick smeared all over his guilty face?

Chapter Four

Tessa hated herself for feeling jealous, and she couldn't bear to watch Ben and Dallas together for another second. "If you two want to act like a couple of hormonal teenagers, it's none of my business." With an irritated huff, she stalked away from them.

"Hold up, Tessa," Ben called behind her, but she kept on walking. She needed time to gather her composure before she reached their office.

Ben started talking the instant he entered the room, trying to explain what needed no explanation. She recognized necking when she saw it, and Ben and Dallas had been in one heck of an intimate liplock when she walked out of Janey's office.

"I don't know what you thought you saw, but—"

"But what? Your lips just suddenly got vacuum-sucked to her face, is that it?"

"Funnily enough, it sorta was like that—"

"Stuff a sock in it, Ben. I'm not interested. Although, I must say, I'm not surprised. Dallas is always ready and willing, and I guess when I wasn't receptive, you simply moved on to easier pickings."

He had the nerve to smile. "There's no law against flirting. And I'm as red-blooded as the next guy."

She put the back of her hand to her forehead and rolled her eyes, trying to pretend none of this mattered. "Whatever. But I'll give you fair warning, Mr.

Montgomery doesn't look favorably on swapping spit in the hallways. In the future, you should try to use a little self-control. Oh, wait…I forgot…you aren't acquainted with that concept."

He pulled an innocent face and pressed a hand against his chest. "I tried not to kiss her, but it wasn't that simple."

Her possessiveness rose to temper-tantrum proportions. "Yes it is. It's very simple. You—just—don't—kiss—her." She painfully ground each word out from a tightly clenched jaw.

"Look, Tessa," Ben said. "You're the one who's been making it abundantly clear you don't want to be with me."

"That doesn't mean I want to watch you pawing at Dallas, of all people."

Just because she didn't want to want him, it didn't mean she wanted him with anyone else. And maybe, just maybe, she wanted him to want her. She had the presence of mind to realize those feelings were illogical.

Ben's tight smile developed into a full lopsided grin. "Oh, I get it."

Tessa warily crossed her arms around her middle. "You get what?"

He nodded his chin her way. "You're jealous."

She didn't want him to see how deep the cut went, refused to give him that satisfaction. "No! That's not what I meant. I am not jealous."

"Yes, you are. You're jealous of me and Dallas."

"That's ridiculous. As if I'd be jealous of you and anyone."

"I think you are. As touching as that is, you have

no right." His voice took on the exasperated tone of one speaking with a spoiled child. "Let me try to explain this with simple words." He held out a hand, palm up. With his other hand, he pretended to place something in his palm. "You have a piece of cake, you eat it and then it's gone." His hand closed into a fist, then opened again. "You can't get it back. You're familiar with that concept, right? You can't have your cake and eat it too, Tess. It doesn't work that way."

Swallowing the angry words trembling on her tongue, Tessa stomped over to her desk. For the rest of the afternoon, she made it blatantly obvious that as far as she was concerned, he had ceased to exist. But every move she made, every thing she did, she could feel those penetrating green eyes watching her, and she knew if she bothered to look his way, he'd be grinning.

****

"You should've seen them, Janey. It was disgusting. She was clinging to him like wet underwear, and he was lapping it up."

"Dallas has always been about as subtle as a broomstick across the knees. Someone should warn Ben that once she's had him, she'll dump him like yesterday's coffee grounds."

"It'd serve him right if she did," Tessa growled back.

Ben paused outside the break room and leaned in to listen to the voices coming through the open door. He shouldn't be eavesdropping. But what the hell, they were talking about him.

"Whaddaya mean, it'd serve him right?"

"He thinks he's so hot. Like he's God's gift or something. I turned him down, so he moved right on to easier conquests. He deserves anything Dallas dishes out and more."

"You sound awful bitter for someone who says she doesn't care about the guy."

Tessa not only sounded bitter, she sounded as though her feelings were hurt, and that was all Ben's fault. Instead of playing with her, back at their office, he should've explained how Dallas had waylaid him, then blindsided him with those kisses—kisses that almost gagged him. Hell, he had tried to explain, then she got on her high and mighty, and he hadn't been able to resist teasing her a bit.

He hadn't wanted to hurt her, but fair was fair, and she'd told him flat out she didn't want anything to do with him. So, what he did and who he did it with, was none of her business.

He gave a phony cough and stepped into the room. Tessa and Janey were in the process of putting on their winter coats, and they both stopped in mid-motion when they saw him.

"Hello, ladies. I hear it's a brisk one out there, so make sure you bundle up."

Tessa didn't answer, but Janey smiled his way. "We've just turned the calendar to March. Did you expect any different?"

Ben reached into the closet for his overcoat. "Back home, the spring bulbs are set to bloom."

Janey gave a melodious laugh and wrapped a warm scarf around her neck. "This is Calgary. We don't rush into spring here." She adjusted her scarf, tucked it into her coat, then started doing up her buttons. "Are you settling in okay, Ben?"

"Truthfully, I'm getting real tired of staying at that

shoebox-sized travel apartment, and I'd like to find my own place. Can either of you give me any pointers?"

"There's a vacancy sign on the apartment building down the street from Tessa's house," Janey promptly volunteered.

"Is that right?" Ben turned to Tessa. "What part of town do you live in, Tessa?"

She shrugged, implying where she lived was hardly information she'd care to share. She was obviously trying her best to keep her distance, which made him just as obstinately determined to thwart her efforts.

"She lives in Sunnyside. It's a great neighborhood full of big old houses, convenient to downtown. Right across the Tenth Street bridge," Janey told him, ignoring Tessa's laser glare.

"That sounds perfect. Could I get the address?"

"Why don't you take him there, Tess?" Janey's look of innocence intensified. "It's along your way."

"Could you, Tessa? I'll follow you with my car."

"I took the C-train today." Tessa spoke for the first time, her voice offhand and contrary.

"Perfect, then," Janey said. "Ben can give you a lift home." Tessa continued to glare at Janey, and Janey continued to act as if she didn't notice. She stepped out of her pumps and into a pair of boots. "I have to run." She wagged a gloved hand. "See you tomorrow. Good luck, Ben."

Ben sensed she meant more than good luck finding an apartment. If she meant good luck getting Tessa to help him, he needed all that luck and more. And if she meant good luck getting Tessa to warm up to him, he'd pretty much written that off as a lost cause.

Without Janey's presence to defuse the friction, an

awkward, electric tension developed and Ben hurried to break the silence. "You don't need to do this, but I'd appreciate the help. I'm going bonkers in that one-room apartment."

Tessa bit her lower lip, and it made him want to kiss it. He shoved his hands into his pockets to keep from touching her.

"That's fine, I'll show you where the apartment building is." Her agreement suggested cooperation, while her manner remained all business.

Ben drew on his gloves as they stepped outside. The meager late-day sunlight offered no warmth, and the wind had a knife-edge to it. Its chill instantly began to penetrate his layers of clothing. Huge, wet snowflakes whipped around in the breeze, melting as they touched the ground. Frozen gray and black snow lay in lumpy heaps along the sidewalk, as hard as the concrete beneath it.

"Cold, huh?" he said, glancing down at Tessa striding briskly at his side. Her cheeks and the tip of her nose were already turning an appealing pink.

"I hadn't noticed."

Her clipped answer didn't invite further conversation, and they continued in silence to the parking lot where Ben had his BMW parked. He started the engine and turned the heater on full, then climbed out to scrape the frost off the windows, his head lowered against the gusting wind.

"Why don't you wait in the car? It'll warm up in no time."

"I'm fine out here. It's a gorgeous day."

Ben glanced over to see if she was kidding. It didn't look like it. She seemed perfectly content to stand there in the wind and cold. That had to be what they called being acclimatized, he decided, as he brushed snowflakes from his shoulders with his gloved hand.

"Well, I'm freezing my butt off, and I can't believe it's trying to snow again."

"Spring is just around the corner." She was making conversation for the first time in hours—make that, days—and Ben was thankful she seemed to have abandoned her aloof act.

He smiled wryly and tried not to shiver. "Which means it's not here yet."

She turned her mittened hands palms up at her sides and drew the frigid air into her lungs. "Just breathe that fresh air."

Ben's breath climbed through the air like smoke. "I can't! My nose is too numb."

"Wuss." Her smile flickered on, then, as quickly, back off.

He opened the passenger side door for her. "Just get in the car, tough lady."

With the heater blowing full blast, he pulled out of the parking lot. The light snow grew heavier as the car moved slowly through the city's icy streets.

"Do you always take public transit to work?" he asked, just to have something to say.

Tessa shrugged. "Sometimes I drive." The words were short and clipped, and directed at the side window.

She continued to nix his every attempt at conversation, and it was a long, uncomfortable fifteen minutes before she indicated for him to stop in front of a brick low-rise apartment building situated on the corner of a residential block. Hedges ran along the building, feathered with fresh snow, and both the yard and the building appeared well maintained.

Ben could envision himself living there. And knowing Tessa lived in the vicinity was a definite selling feature.

"This is the place," she told him curtly, with her hand on the door handle. "The manager's name is Gordon Pincell. Feel free to use my name as a reference."

"Where are you going?"

"Home. I said I'd show you where the apartment building was. I have, so now I'm leaving." She started to open the car door.

"Wait." He reached across her and pulled the door closed on a draft of frigid air. "You know this apartment manager personally?"

"Mm-hmm. He went to school with me. With my sister, actually. Had a huge crush on her. Then again, what guy didn't?"

Ben recalled the picture of the two women on Tessa's desk, back at the office. Great-looking lady, no wonder she had lots of admirers. He imagined Tessa also had her fair share of admirers. That thought didn't seem to sit well, and with an irritable shrug, he turned back to the immediate task.

"Would you go in with me? Since you know the guy and all."

"Come off it, Ben."

"I'm serious. Please. I could use your influence."

She stared steadily at him for a moment, and her emotions played across her face as she assessed his sincerity.

"Okay," she said finally. "Just to introduce you."

They got out of the car and walked up the wide, heavily salted steps. Tessa pushed the manager's intercom button. "Hi, Gordon," she said to the tinny voice that came through the speaker. "It's Tessa Caldwell. I have someone here who'd like to discuss renting your vacancy, if you have the time."

"Sure, Tessa Leigh. I'll meet you in the lobby."

"Tessa Leigh, huh?" Ben grinned down at her.

The cold hadn't caused the pink stain on her cheeks this time, and its appearance nearly had Ben's good intentions taking a hike. He had to battle a strong urge to press his lips against one of those delicate cheekbones and drink in the sweet heat of her skin.

"Shut up," Tessa growled and reached for the door as the latch released.

****

The sun had disappeared while they were inside, swallowed whole by dense gray clouds. Snow fell heavier by the minute, thick and soft like cotton batting. Several inches already covered the ground, with no sign of letting up. Tessa and Ben's footsteps didn't make a sound on the white cushion of new snow. They paused on the sidewalk, under the weak luminescence of the street light.

"Thanks for your help," he told her with a grateful smile, hoping to smooth her ruffled feathers with good behavior. "I'm really pleased to have found an apartment at such short notice. I couldn't have done it without you."

"You're welcome," she replied with that annoyingly formal tone she'd assumed since witnessing the debacle with Dallas in the hallway. "I'll see you tomorrow."

Ben touched her arm as she turned to leave. For the briefest of moments, he debated asking her to join him for dinner to express his gratitude, then decided not to push it. "I'll drive you home."

Tessa glanced down at his hand, then up at his face. Her thunderous expression told him to remove his hand and to do it immediately, so he did. She wasn't in the mood to be riled, and for once, he didn't much feel like riling her.

"I only live down the block, and I'm capable of walking."

"Of course you're capable of walking, but I'll drive you anyway. This weather is ugly, and it's gotten dark." A muscle in her jaw flexed with annoyance, but she got into his car without arguing.

Leaving the engine to warm up, Ben brushed the snow off the car's roof and windows, then climbed back inside with Tessa. Beyond Tessa muttering her house number for him, they didn't talk as they inched down the snow-filled street. When he located the number on the other side of the street, Ben pulled a tight u-turn and drew up behind the Honda parked in front of Tessa's charming old white-with-green-trim house.

Watching Tessa in the light from the street lamp, he wasn't sure what to say to her, even though he definitely owed her something. Some kind of apology for what happened with Dallas and his ensuing shoddy behavior in the office.

As though aware of his scrutiny, she slowly turned and stared at him without expression. "Thanks for the ride." She reached for the door handle.

"Wait, please." He sighed, wondering where to

start. The beginning was usually a good place. "I owe you an apology. I believe I owe you several apologies. I'm sorry I never called you in the months following the cruise. Despite thinking I had good reasons at the time, you deserved better than that, and I'm sorry if you were hurt by my inconsiderate actions." She opened her mouth, and he put up a hand. "Let me finish. I apologize, too, for my behavior at the office, especially this afternoon. Even though you misread the situation between Dallas and myself, I shouldn't have teased you or hurt your feelings. So, I'm sorry. I'll try to do better."

She bit her bottom lip and swallowed hard, her unblinking eyes large and luminous. "Apology accepted," she said in a soft voice. Without another word, she left the car and walked directly up the front walk, not once looking back before disappearing into her house. An unaccountable wave of disappointment washed over Ben. A feeling of such intensity, it took several moments before he could throw it off. And the self-recriminations that followed lasted far longer.

What did he want from her anyway? What did he expect? Friendship? Something else, something more? What exactly? Good questions, for which he had no good answers. He understood why they shouldn't get involved. He'd already worked through all the reasons why he should leave her alone. He'd told himself repeatedly to stop chasing her.

Smiling grimly, he put the car in gear and eased away from the curb. How could he stop? It was a craving—to spend time with Tessa. Something about her stirred up his blood and made him forget why he should stay away. His desire for Tessa was so all-consuming that his instinctive need for detachment had practically deserted him.

It took no effort to remember how she felt in his arms, and his blood pumped hot and fast as the memory of their lovemaking flashed vividly through his mind. That was then, and this was now. Tessa might still be teasing and tormenting him, but she definitely wasn't doing it on purpose. Whatever inclination had possessed her to make love with him back on that cruise had passed, and she clearly had no interest in doing a repeat. He'd never forced his attentions on a woman, and he wasn't about to start now, no matter how badly he wanted her.

He smiled again as he made a left turn onto Tenth Street. That didn't mean he wasn't above using some subtle persuasion to get her to change her mind.

****

"Darn this old printer. That's the second time it's jammed this morning."

Tessa hated the unreliable printer and found it completely inconvenient the way the maintenance man had tucked it away under the table, giving them a roomier working surface up top, but making it difficult to reach when it jammed. Which it did with frustrating regularity.

Having her nerves permanently on edge didn't help matters. She was trying her best to set aside the feelings of anger, disappointment, and yes, drat it all, of jealousy, that had plagued her since she saw Ben and Dallas kissing in the hallway two weeks ago. She was doing all she could to maintain a polite professional relationship with Ben. After all, she was generally a polite person, completely capable of getting along with her coworkers.

And after his unexpected apology that had almost put her in tears, even Ben was cooperating. Or was he? This uncertainty, this waiting for the next shoe to drop, had Tessa wondering how far tight nerves could be stretched before they snapped like an over-used elastic band. She couldn't find fault with his behavior. He acted friendly, in an impersonal sort of way, went efficiently about his business, and was helpful and accommodating when they worked together.

Yet, every day it seemed he purposely, if subtly, touched her. Some part of his body—an arm, an elbow, a hip—made casual and fleeting contact with a part of hers. No more than that and never anything inappropriate. Just enough to keep her body primed and restless and convinced he was up to no good.

She and Ben bent simultaneously to correct the paper jam and came close to bumping heads. Laughing, Ben reached out to catch her shoulders, steadying them both.

"Careful there."

They continued to squat beside the printer, his hands warm and intimate on her shoulders, their faces only inches apart. Their mouths very close.

"Back up," Tessa demanded.

Ben displayed his even white teeth. "You back up."

Tessa shifted her shoulders, trying to dislodge his hands. "Why are you doing this?"

"Why am I doing what?" He removed his hands, but his gaze continued to caress her.

Tessa scrambled to her feet. Panic caught at her heart with fiery little barbs, because it seemed as if he might kiss her and if he had, she might've just wrestled him to the floor and had her way with him right there on the carpet.

Then how would she live with herself?

In her haste, she stumbled over her heels, and Ben jackknifed to a standing position, his hands coming out to grab her waist as he helped her catch her balance. Delight shivered through her as his fingertips pressed warmly against her hips.

Against her will, she remembered the taste and shape of his mouth, the excitement of his hands on her bare skin—the tender way he held her after they made love—and blood flooded hot to her cheeks. With the memory came anger at her inability to restrain this unruly streak of sensuality Ben had awakened in her.

She raised her hands in an attempt to push him away, but they betrayed her, sliding around his neck, tangling in his hair, and she clung to him, trying not to tremble with the pleasure of having his body against hers. A part of her had been waiting for this moment— longing for it—ever since he'd strolled back into her life.

"You're playing with fire, Tessa. One huge, hot, raging-out-of-control inferno."

Tessa didn't care. With purpose and careless determination, she pressed her lips against his. He gave a quick intake of breath, and for a moment, she worried he might pull away, then he yanked her closer and crushed her mouth with his, his hands moving possessively across her back.

His tongue danced and curled around hers, his lips claiming hers in slow, drugging kisses that left her head swimming and her senses reeling. Never in her life had she been kissed the way this man kissed her.

A sliver of rationality gradually wormed its way through her cocoon of desire, and she shoved him away. Hard. The instant her mouth was free of his, she turned her back on him, struggling not to gulp in air. She moved on shaking legs to put as much distance between them as possible. What was she thinking, letting Ben work his spellbinding ways on her like that?

Her lips were still warm and moist from his kisses, and she drew the back of her hand across her mouth, trying, but not succeeding, to erase the taste of him.

"What was that?" he asked, sounding as breathless as she felt.

"That was a bad impulse," she told him, too horrified to look him in the eye. This wasn't who she was. Tessa Caldwell never acted on impulse, good or bad. Her emotions did not rule her. "It shouldn't have happened."

"You were just messing with me? Paying me back?"

His tone of voice drew her attention. She could hear him grapple to remain calm, working to erase the emotion from his voice, his body rigid, his jaw muscles working. Even though he obviously didn't want to show it, he was undeniably and justifiably angry. *She* was angry—make that furious—with her lack of self-control. Control was the one principle by which she ran her life, the one constant she could count on to get her through anything.

"Maybe I was," she lied, relieved he'd offered her a plausible excuse for her temporary lapse in sanity.

Better to let him think she was playing games, than for him to know how badly she wanted that kiss, how much she ached to put her arms back around him and feel the heat and strength of his body against hers. She had no idea why her usual caution and inhibitions didn't work around this man. Did his bad-boy appeal call to the good girl inside her longing to break free? For whatever reason, she was letting him mess with her values, toy with her mind—to say nothing about what he did to her body—and this put her life goals in serious jeopardy.

She slowly released a pent-up breath and tried to calm her pounding heart. "I have to get the printer unjammed and get those proofs out. We're dangerously close to being late for the creative session."

Ben glanced at his watch. "You go ahead to the boardroom. I'll get the proofs printed and will be right behind you."

Thank goodness Ben was a professional, Tessa thought, as she collected the material she needed for the meeting. At the mere mention of their responsibilities, he'd dropped the entire kissing incident. When she left the room, he was down on his knees in front of the blasted printer, totally absorbed with getting it to work again.

If only she could put that kiss out of her mind as easily. Problem was, any kiss that affected her the way Ben's had was going to take some concentrated forgetting.

****

"Did you find an apartment yet, Ben?" Janey tucked her pen into the funny bun-thing she wore at the back of her head.

At first, it seemed strange how she always had a pen, or two, sticking out of that bird's nest in her hair, but he'd come to accept this as part of who Janey was.

A quirky, bright and genuine individual, who'd gone out of her way to be friendly with him. And he didn't mean friendly the way Dallas was friendly. Janey was simply a nice human being.

"I sure did," he replied. They stepped out of the boardroom together and paused in the corridor to continue their conversation. "In that building you suggested. Thank you for that. I move in next weekend, and it can't come soon enough."

"So Tessa was a help after all."

Ben glanced through the open door of the boardroom where he could see Tessa speaking with Travis Spellicy. "Grudging, but yes, she was." Ben smiled as he recalled her cranky demeanor that afternoon. His thoughts swung abruptly to the sizzling kiss she'd planted on him back in their office, and his smile cranked it up a notch.

His plan to lower her resistance must be working because she'd kissed him with enough steam to wilt his spine and stiffen another body part. It had taken every ounce of his control not to press her for more when she'd unexpectedly pulled away. His overwhelming sense of disappointment and frustration, along with scorching hot desire, had almost got the best of him and ruined everything. The idea was to let her make the moves. All he had to do was continue to subtly convince her she wanted him.

Morris came blustering down the corridor toward them, arms and jowls flapping. He waved a file folder from one hand as he called Ben's name. "Where is Tessa?" he bellowed. "I must speak with the two of you immediately."

"She's still in the boardroom. Our creative session

just wrapped up."

"Fine, fine." Morris took him by the elbow and propelled him into the boardroom. Ben threw a look over his shoulder at Janey, exchanging mystified smiles with her before she disappeared from view.

"Excuse us there, Spellicy," Morris said to Travis. "I need to speak to Tessa and Benjamin alone."

"Sure thing." Travis tipped his head Tessa's way, then Ben's, and loped out of the room with his long-legged stride.

Morris motioned for them to take a seat at the conference table and lowered himself into the large chair at the head. "I just got off the phone with a potential client," he told them. "He is opening a high-end restaurant and needs a marketing strategy. His direction is youthful, innovative, dynamic, so because the two of you are the youngest executives in our stable and presumably the most well informed in that area, I am trusting you to handle the RFP. I want you to come up with a selection of preliminary ideas for this package today, even if it requires staying late to finish." He directed a finger at Ben, then Tessa. "I don't care if you work all night; I expect some solid proposals on my desk by tomorrow morning."

RFP, request for proposal. Ben had mocked up plenty of them over the past five years, although this would be his first collaboration with Tessa. He glanced over at her but couldn't read her thoughts. She wore her professional face, the one he'd noticed she reserved solely for him and Morris.

"I don't have a problem working late," he confirmed. "Tessa?"

"No, me either. We'll get right on it, Mr.

Montgomery."

Morris's finger wagged at them again, and he pushed the file folder over to Ben. "I will not accept inferior work. It is a rush job that damn well better not look rushed."

"Nothing personal," Tessa told Ben as they returned to their office with Ben carrying the folder under his arm. "But I'm a little leery about working with you on this. It's obviously important to Mr. Montgomery that we land this account."

"What's to be leery about? Believe me, we're going to be dynamite together."

"In your mind, maybe. What about in reality?" Her freckle-dusted nose wrinkled. "What if we can't get along? What if we can't agree on anything? Who gets final say?"

"I imagine Morris generally gets the final say around here." He opened their office door and stood aside to let Tessa enter.

They sat side by side at the computer table, their elbows almost, but not quite, touching. Ben had to force himself to concentrate on work instead of how close they sat and how great Tessa smelled. Soon the ideas began to flow exuberantly from one to the other, just as he'd predicted. A strong sense of camaraderie formed as they exchanged opinions, interrupting each other constantly, laughing and arguing, excited by the thrill and challenge of seeing their schemes turn into solid proposals.

Finally, Ben leaned back in his seat and stretched the tension out of his back. "I'm famished. How about you?"

Tessa straightened, hands pressed against the small

of her back. "I need a break, too." She slid a finger under the sleeve of her blouse to check her watch. "No wonder you're hungry. It's after seven. We've been going steady for over four hours. Do you want to order some take-out?"

"Huh?" Ben realized he'd been staring slack-jawed at Tessa as she moved about the office, stretching and twisting as she worked the kinks from her body, and he valiantly tried to get his salacious thoughts back in order.

"Take-out." Tessa paused and frowned at him. "Didn't you just say you were starving?"

"I think we've done enough work for one evening. We have plenty of ideas to present to Morris in the morning. How about going out to eat?"

She started toward her desk. "No, thanks. If you don't want to continue working, I'll head home."

"Tessa, wait."

She dragged herself around to face him, clearly not hiding her reluctance. "What?"

He smiled a little self-consciously. It wasn't easy to admit weakness, not even simple loneliness. "It's my birthday today, and I could use some company."

Tessa's eyes grew wide. "I don't believe you."

"Why would I lie?"

"Why wouldn't you? Let me see your driver's license." She held out her hand and waited while he dug his wallet from his pocket. He dropped the plastic card onto her hand, and she scanned it quickly. "It says here you're twenty-nine today."

"That's right." He took the card back and returned it to his wallet. "You sound surprised. How old did you think I was?"

"I don't know," she replied weakly. "Older, I guess."

"So, I'm not much older than you?"

Tessa shook her head, her mouth opened, her lips moved. But, curiously, not a sound came out.

Chapter Five

Not much older than her?

Nope. A little basic math revealed Ben wasn't older than Tessa, at all. More like three years younger.

It had never occurred to her that he might be younger. Probably because of the expensive custom-made suits he wore and his confident demeanor. And she didn't know why it should bother her as much as it did. It made no difference in any important way. It wasn't as though they were involved with each other.

Uh, hello? Not involved? Then what were those tonsil-scorching kisses all about, earlier today?

Ben said something, but the words didn't penetrate. "Pardon?"

"I asked how old you were. Twenty-five? Twenty-six?" He slouched against the front of her desk and crossed his arms, waiting for her answer. Tessa's gaze followed the line of his body, from the sandy hair, mussier and more appealing than usual, to the broad shoulders and flat belly, down his long legs stretched out in front of him.

For some ridiculous reason, it embarrassed her to admit her age, so she tried to be coy, a trait that didn't come easily to her. "Really, Ben. A gentleman never asks a lady her age."

His lips curved in the most tempting smile. "A gentleman wouldn't, but—"

"You're not a gentleman," she finished for him, trying not to smile back. "I remember."

"So, how old are you?" he repeated conversationally.

She smoothed back a strand of hair, her eyes darting nervously. "You already asked."

Ben uncrossed his arms and braced them on the desk. "And you didn't answer."

"Exactly." Tessa went around behind her desk and started to tidy it in preparation to leave. Desperate to steer the conversation into safer channels, she began to babble. "I hate coming to work in the morning to a messy desk. It's one of those compulsive things, I know, but I always have to tidy it at the end of the day."

Ben lifted one haunch, pivoting sideways on her desk to watch her. "Since I've proven it's my birthday, will you go out to dinner with me?"

Taking a deep, unsteady breath, Tessa stepped back. "It's not a good idea. Besides, it's getting late."

He blew out a soft curse. "Woman, you're one hard sell." A trace of vulnerability replaced the usual confident look in his eyes and it touched a deep, hidden place inside Tessa. "I'd like to spend time with you socially." His voice turned wistful. "I don't have many friends. Not here, anyway. I'm not asking for anything romantic," he rushed to clarify. "Just two pals getting together for a meal."

Tessa didn't trust herself to remain impassive when he put such appeal into his voice. Masterful persuasion was his strong suit, and she warned herself not to let this show of apparent defenselessness fool her. He wasn't lonely and in need of companionship, it was merely a ruse to convince her to change her mind. After that humiliating lack of control she displayed earlier, she needed to distance herself from him, not get closer—she'd be crazy to allow him a firmer foothold in her life.

But her attraction to him was so compelling and her reaction so natural, she was hard-pressed to deny it. The slump of his shoulders scraped at her heart a little, and the wistful appeal in his eyes softened her resolve. What would it hurt to have dinner with him? It was his birthday, for pity's sake, and he was all alone in the city. The least she could do was keep him company while he ate.

"Dinner to celebrate your birthday?"

"You don't have to consider it a date."

"Don't worry. That's the last thing I'd call it." She planted her hands on her hips. As reasonably as she could manage, she said, "That thing that happened here earlier"—she tilted her head toward the computer table—"was merely a moment of insanity. It was wrong, and it shouldn't have happened. I've worked too hard and sacrificed too long to let sex compromise my job."

He sighed loudly, his shoulders raising and lowering with the intake and exhale. "Have it your way." He crossed his heart theatrically. "I promise I won't try anything you don't want me to. I just don't feel like eating alone on my birthday. I'll even let you pick out the restaurant."

"Well, in that case, how can I say no? Meet me at my house as soon as you're ready." Until the words were out of her mouth, even she hadn't known whether she'd agree to go.

****

"I always get the same thing whenever I eat here," Tessa told Ben as they shrugged out of their jackets and settled into a booth at her favorite neighborhood restaurant.

Ben gave a knowing grin. "Let me guess—beef, right?"

"Nope," she said with a smile, remembering the silly verbal joust they'd had about beef versus seafood while on the cruise. "Tortellini. It's the best in town."

"If it comes so highly recommended, perhaps I should have it, too."

"It's a bit of a lightweight for a big guy like you. As I recall, you said you loved seafood. The steak and prawns are awesome."

"You sure you aren't trying to manipulate me into eating beef?"

Tessa winked and smiled. "You'll have to take that chance."

A middle-aged waitress approached their table, her gaze appraising Ben with pleasure as she placed menus in front of them. "Howdy, folks. What can I get you to drink this evening?"

"I'll have a glass of house white," Tessa decided and lifted her brow in question at Ben.

"Make mine a hot chocolate."

"White wine and hot chocolate." The waitress scribbled on her pad. "Okay, I'll be back in a few minutes to take your order."

"I think we're ready, thanks." Ben handed her back the menu. "Tessa?"

Tessa gave the waitress her menu, too. "I'll have the cheese tortellini, please, with a green salad on the side."

"Gotcha. And you, sir?" the waitress asked, tucking the menus under her arm.

"I'll have the steak and prawns, steak medium rare, please."

When the waitress finished taking down their order and left, Tessa turned to Ben in surprise. "Hot chocolate? What kind of celebratory drink is that?"

"The kind you have after walking a gazillion long blocks in the freezing cold."

"It was barely four blocks, and it's much easier to walk than to find a parking space. That short walk was invigorating, and you can't possibly be cold."

"I agree, the walk was invigorating, and I'm frozen half to death. Look—" He clicked his teeth rapidly together several times. "My teeth are chattering."

Tessa giggled at his antics. "Poor baby. If you don't toughen up, you'll never survive a Calgary winter."

The waitress returned with their drinks, and Tessa lifted her glass in Ben's direction. "Happy Birthday."

He clinked his mug against her goblet. "Thank you."

As they sipped from their respective beverages, Tessa's mind swung back to the meals they'd shared on the cruise. Not once could she recall Ben having an alcoholic drink, not even a beer.

"Don't you ever drink liquor, Ben?"

He shook his head and rubbed the bridge of his nose. "No, I don't. My father was an alcoholic." He answered smoothly enough, but something—a dark shadow—hovered in his eyes.

"Oh, your father, not you?"

"Definitely not me. Alcoholism can be hereditary,

and I never wanted to chance that, so I decided at a young age booze was a poison I could live without."

"Good for you." She reached across the table to touch his arm. "It must've been tough as a child, to have an alcoholic parent."

His face went expressionless, and his gaze dropped to the table. He made a gesture of dismissal. "You could say that." He took another sip from his mug. "You were on fire today. It sure impressed me how you effortlessly came up with idea after idea for the new campaign."

Although Tessa wondered about Ben's reticence, she didn't feel she had the right to question him about his father, so she went along with the change of subject. "Thanks. It was a real rush, and you're no slouch, yourself, by the way. We work well together."

Ben grinned. "We're even better together in other ways."

She shot him a withering look to hide her true feelings. Feelings she didn't want to think about, much less have.

"Okay." He held up his hands in surrender. "I'm just saying we make a good team, in more ways than one."

The waitress arrived with their meals, and they fell silent while she put their plates down in front of them.

"Looks great, thanks a lot," Ben told the waitress, displaying one of his winning smiles. The woman practically melted into a puddle right there on the floor.

"You're shameless," Tessa said once the waitress was out of earshot.

"What did I do?"

She leaned in, ignoring her reaction to his

innocent-me expression. "As if you don't know." She gave his arm a light smack. "That poor woman practically swooned." Not that she could blame her. She thought she'd prepared herself to enjoy this evening, yet remain safe from his charms, but looking at him now, she had to wonder how any woman could possibly feel safe with a man as dynamic as the one sitting across from her.

They lingered long over the meal, talking non-stop, laughing together, arguing good-naturedly, then laughing again. The evening reaffirmed her first impression of him, from their time together on the cruise. Ben was an entertaining conversationalist with a wacky sense of humor that kept Tessa constantly amused. Their talk ranged over many topics, and the similarity of their tastes continued to amaze her. They enjoyed many of the same movies, read the same books, followed the same TV shows.

"Share a piece of cake?" Ben asked right about the same time Tessa decided she was too stuffed to possibly eat another bite.

"Cake?"

"You can choose what kind."

"Okay, for your birthday," she agreed and reached for the dessert menu, confident he would eat the majority of it, anyway.

"I have a question for you," Ben said, after the waitress had delivered two forks and the single plate containing strawberry shortcake, which Tessa had remembered was his favorite. He stabbed his fork into the cake and took a large chunk from his side.

"What is it?" Tessa sampled a much smaller piece from her side.

Ben swallowed his cake and reached for another forkful. "I've already asked and you didn't give a straight answer, but I'd like to know why you're afraid of thunderstorms."

He sounded genuinely interested, as though it mattered to him, and she found herself reluctantly deciding to tell him the truth, at least some of it.

"It's irrational and rather stupid, but I honestly can't help myself." Tessa set her fork down. Nothing would be able to get past the sudden tightness in her throat.

"You said you had a bad experience?"

She took a slow sip of ice water, aware of Ben scrutinizing her every move. "When I was a child, I stayed with some family friends at their vacation home at Sylvan Lake—that's a resort area just north of here. My friend Celeste and I thought it'd be fun to sleep in the boathouse, right on the lake. We had no clue a terrible storm would strike that night."

She crumpled her napkin in her hand, staring at nothing as she relived her childhood nightmare. "The thunder was so loud, it literally shook the boathouse, and the wind screamed and crashed waves up against the wall next to where I lay. I could almost feel the electricity crackling in the air, and I was positive I'd be fried to death at any moment. Celeste apparently slept through the entire episode, but it scared me beyond reason. It was the longest, coldest, most traumatic night of my life, and I've never been comfortable in storms since."

What she found too personal, too unbearable, to explain was how badly she'd wanted her mother that night. Yet somewhere in the back of her terrified nine-year-old mind, she understood her mom couldn't come to comfort her. That her mother could never hold her in her arms and chase her fears away again. Death meant gone forever, and her dad had told her, right before he'd sent her off with Celeste's family, that her mom had died.

From that night on, her newly developed terror of thunderstorms became intertwined with an excruciating ache of longing for her mom. An ache that broke her heart all over again every time it stormed and the torment hadn't eased in the slightest as the years went by.

She peeked up at Ben, expecting to see amusement or derision on his face and not finding it. "Silly, I know, right?"

He reached across the table and covered her hand with his, gentle and comforting. "It's not silly. You feel the way you feel. I'm sorry you experienced that." He lifted his hand and touched the slight bend in the bridge of his nose. "Sometimes things that happen as a kid have a way of sticking with a person for the rest of their life."

It sounded as if he spoke from personal experience, but she didn't get the chance to ask because the waitress chose that moment to present them with their bill, which set off a lively debate over who should pay. Ben thought he should because he invited her. Tessa insisted she should because it was his birthday. Tessa won, only because she talked the waitress into taking her side—as well as her credit card.

As they left the restaurant, Ben pulled Tessa in close, using the excuse that they needed to huddle together to conserve body heat. Whatever the reason, she couldn't find it in her to object, and they walked home briskly, arm in arm in the crisp darkness. Reluctantly, against her will, she had to admit he was a lot of fun to talk with, to be around. He laughed easily and often. Against all likelihood, she had enjoyed herself. In fact, she couldn't remember when she'd last relaxed and had such a good time with a man. She smiled with the thought—probably while on the cruise, with Ben.

She realized she actually liked him, as a person. She'd already acknowledged her attraction to him, but that was simply a physical phenomenon. This new feeling had more layers, more texture. It was admiration and affection woven through with passion and an undefined yearning for something more.

She turned to look up at Ben, his handsome face moving in profile beside her. "Looks like I didn't have to worry about having dinner with you tonight, after all. It ended up being fun. Maybe we can be friends."

"I'm glad you enjoyed yourself. I did, too." He tucked her arm more snugly into the crook of his elbow. "I knew we'd become friends, if you gave us half a chance."

At her front door, she lingered for a moment, wanting to invite him in, yet hesitating to say the words out loud. That look of longing had returned to his eyes. She tried to ignore it because it posed a danger to her already shaky equilibrium, but found she couldn't. Breaking eye contact before things got too heavy between them, she opened her purse and dug around for her house key. She unlocked the door, then turned back and smiled, hoping to recapture the ease that had existed between them only moments earlier.

"Do you want to come in to warm up? I make a mean hot chocolate."

He gave a dramatic shiver. "You don't have to ask twice."

Her smile faltered as her heart took up an uneven beat. With the words *frying pan* and *fire* reverberating through her mind, she fumbled with the doorknob.

****

Ben waited and watched in anticipation as Tessa opened the door, then motioned for him to enter. As she turned on the entrance light, an animated ball of long, silky fur appeared out of nowhere and circled his boots, fussing at him with a squeaky, high-pitched bark, charging at his ankles, yipping and yapping.

"Milo, be quiet." Tessa affectionately nudged the creature with her toe. "Don't pay any attention to my dog. He's the jealous type."

"*That's* a dog?" Ben asked, afraid to move his feet in case he accidentally squashed it.

"Funny. Of course he's a dog."

"A boy dog?"

"Yes, a boy dog."

"It has a ponytail," Ben pointed out in case she hadn't noticed the small blue bow holding up a tuft of hair on the top of its puny head.

"To keep his hair out of his eyes."

"Wouldn't it be less humiliating if you just gave it a buzz cut?"

Tessa took off her jacket and hung it in the closet, then held out her hand to take Ben's. "Ben has no fashion sense, does he, Milo?"

As if it understood her words, the dog began to dance around at Tessa's feet, whimpering and whining.

"Does the little hairball need to go out?"

"His name is Milo, not hairball," she corrected and closed the closet door. "He wants me to pick him up." Which she did. And she let the silly little thing lick the tip of her nose, before positioning it in the crook of her arm, where it stared suspiciously at Ben. "Make yourself comfortable in the living room while I get the hot chocolate."

Left alone in Tessa's living room, Ben did a slow circuit, taking in the ambience. The room was a quirky, eclectic combination of old and new, classic and whimsical, expensive and practical. Several framed landscape photos graced the walls and he vaguely remembered Tessa saying her sister was a photographer. He moved in closer to examine them. The woman had talent to go with her beauty.

Ben moved on to a photo Tessa's sister obviously hadn't taken. A family portrait, husband, wife and two small daughters. One blonde-haired angel sat on her mother's knee, while the other—a little scrap of a thing with skinny knob-kneed legs, who Ben surmised was Tessa at about six years old—stood in front of her father. Tessa's father was a tall, distinguished-looking man with thick brown hair and a bristly moustache. The girls appeared to take after their mother, who shared their delicate features and fair coloring.

"*Aarff.*"

Ben turned to see the little hairball standing in the entranceway, its stubby tail waving uncertainly as it yapped another warning.

"If you're trying to scare me off, you've failed miserably."

For several seconds, Ben and the dog stared each

other down. Deciding it was more pathetic than homely, Ben knelt and casually offered the back of his hand. Cautiously, the dog eased closer and sniffed his fingers with its cold, wet nose. Ben scratched it behind the ears, and the dog practically writhed with pleasure.

"Ah, you've discovered his weakness." Ben glanced up to find Tessa standing there with a steaming mug in each hand. "If you're going to scratch him that way, he'll be your friend forever."

"Lucky me." Ben got to his feet and brushed his fingers against his pants before taking a mug from Tessa. "Thanks."

"Why do I get the impression you don't like dogs?"

"That's not true. I just haven't known many."

"You didn't have a dog when you were a kid?"

"Nope. No dog, no cat, not even a fish or a turtle."

His father had no patience for animals, and although Ben resented it at the time, his mother had wisely decided it'd be best not to have a pet. There was no way of knowing what his old man might've done to the animal in one of his drunken rages.

Ben made a slight circular motion with his mug to indicate the living room, determined to take the focus off him. "I've been admiring your home. It has a quaint personality."

Tessa gave a smile like sunshine that had Ben's breath catching in his chest.

"How charmingly put. This is the result of two people with vastly different tastes taking a furnished home and trying to put their own personal stamp on it."

"Works for me. Very homey, very welcoming."

"Please, sit." She motioned for him to have a seat on the couch, and she sat at the opposite end. She shifted to face him, then tucked her legs under her. When she patted her knee, the dog jumped up, twisting itself into a little ball on her lap before turning its intense focus back on Ben.

"You said two people. Does that mean you live with someone?"

"Uh-huh. My sister, Lauren." She absently stroked the dog's back. "This is our family home. Dad moved into a condo several years ago, and Lauren and I stayed on here. I love this old house."

"It shows." Ben tasted his hot chocolate. "This is great. What about your mom, if you don't mind me asking?"

"My mom passed away when I was nine."

Her mouth turned down at the corners, and Ben felt a rush of sympathy. "I'm sorry. She must've been quite young."

"Yes, she was. She developed a mysterious virus that weakened her heart, and before the doctors could figure out what to do for her, she died." Tessa let out a long, sad sigh. "I never knew all the details, since it's not something Dad likes to talk about. I don't doubt he carries some guilt because his profession let her down." Her lips trembled, and she took a sip of her hot chocolate, holding the mug with both hands.

"Your dad's a doctor?"

"A very dedicated surgeon. You know how some people display books of animals or famous paintings on their coffee tables? We had medical books. I learned what a naked male looked like from *Grey's Anatomy*. The book, not the TV show."

Tempted to tease her into a happier mood, Ben almost made a crack about there being more interesting ways to explore the male body. Deciding it wasn't appropriate under the circumstances, he let Tessa continue uninterrupted, curious to hear more about her background.

"My father's been an inspirational role model. He's very focused on his career and has shown me the benefits of hard work." She glanced down at the small dog, then back at Ben. "He would've given anything if one of his daughters had followed in his footsteps, and it really disappointed him when neither Lauren nor I were interested. I actually did begin medical training just to make him happy. It didn't even take a year to realize I was trying to be what I thought I should be, instead of what I wanted to be. So I dropped out of university and enrolled in college, taking the marketing courses I should've taken in the first place."

"Smart move. It never pays to try to be someone you aren't." He squinted, as something suddenly occurred to him. "You went to university for a year and then to college for a marketing diploma?"

"Yes." She looked puzzled, clearly not following him.

"And you've been at Montgomery Group for how long?"

Now she looked wary. She patted the dog's back with brisk strokes. "Eight years."

"Tessa! That would make you older than me." Mortification was how he'd describe her swift change of expression, and without thinking, he hooted with laughter. "You are! You're older than me." The little mutt lifted its head and growled at him, showing plenty of tiny white teeth. Only then did Ben realize what the dog had already sensed. Tessa was genuinely upset.

"I'm sorry. I didn't mean to laugh. Come to think of it, it's kinda exciting. I've never been with an older woman."

His apology would've sounded more sincere if he'd managed to say it with a straight face, but he couldn't help himself. No wonder Tessa had refused to tell him her age when he'd asked earlier at the office. He threw his head back, laughing with glee as he remembered the stunned look on her face when she'd looked at his driver's license.

The tiny dog leapt to its feet, growling ferociously, ready to defend its mistress. The ridiculousness of that possibility made Ben laugh even harder.

"If I had known how amusing you'd find this, I surely would've told you earlier," Tessa said stiffly.

"I'm sorry." He swallowed, trying hard to stifle his mirth. "I mean it. That was rude." He leaned toward her, and the hairball bared its teeth again, warning him to back off. Ben slipped a hand under the dog's belly and unceremoniously set it on the floor. The dog gave a disgruntled yip, then settled at Tessa's feet, watching Ben intently. "If you wanted a guard dog, you shoulda got one that doesn't shiver when it growls."

Tessa's lips quivered, then she laughed. "Milo is very brave. Very gallant. Right, baby?" she cooed at the dog, who instantly stood up and wagged its stump of a tail.

"Are we all right, then? You accept my apology?" Ben linked his fingers through Tessa's, giving her hand a little tug. "I wasn't making fun of you."

Tessa sniffed. "Didn't sound that way from this end of the couch."

"Honey, you barely look twenty. I find it hard to

believe you're over thirty." She yanked her hand from his grasp and crossed her arms, shrinking as far away from him as she could. "What? What did I say? You act as if I insulted you again."

"It's not a compliment to be told I barely look twenty. I'm not some ditsy little girl, Ben. I'm an adult with a brain in my head, and I want to be treated as such. I wish you and everyone else would take me seriously for a change."

Although Ben wanted to slide in close and kiss away that scowl, he intuitively gave her the room she needed.

"Okay, for the record—I think you're the brightest, sharpest, most creative person I've ever had the pleasure of working with, regardless of age or gender. I don't care how old you are. And I don't care what you look like. At least, I don't as long as I'm not looking at you. Because when I'm looking at you, all I can think about is kissing your luscious lips and getting my hands on your cute little tush."

"Ben!"

"I'm joking. Okay, we both know I'm not joking, but as far as work goes, I completely respect those attributes, too."

Tessa rolled her eyes, but at least she wore a grin. "You never stop, do you?"

"Not when I'm going after something I want."

Just for a second, the possibility of tears glittered in her eyes, then she blinked a couple of times and plastered a phony smile on her face.

"Tell me how you broke your nose."

Ben stiffened. It didn't matter how many times he heard it, the question always put him on guard.

"You did break it, didn't you? Because your features are well balanced, darn near perfect, except that tiny bend in your nose. What happened?"

He fingered his nose ruefully as his father's image formed in his mind's eye. He saw the terrifying blaze of anger on his old man's face as he bunched his fist and drove it into a younger version of his own face. Ben could still hear his mother's screams echo in the recesses of his brain. She had put up with her husband's abuse for far too many years, yet all it took was for him to break her son's nose for her to finally find the strength to leave him. If Ben had only known all he had to do was get his father to turn his anger on him, he would've provoked him years earlier.

Not for the first time, he pushed aside the confusing memories of that night. When he spoke, he kept his voice tightly controlled. "It's personal, and I don't generally talk about it." Tessa had asked the question to change the topic, which was his fault for teasing her, but he refused to delve into this.

"Fair enough," she said, to his relief. "We won't talk about it. I've babbled on and on about myself all evening, so how about you share something about your childhood? I know so little about you. Did you grow up in Vancouver?"

She couldn't know, and he wasn't about to tell her, they hadn't changed the subject. He found it difficult to reveal much about his childhood or his parents, partly because his utter helplessness during those years embarrassed him, and partly because the memories were too painful. When he spoke about growing up, it was more travelogue than revelation. He lived here, he went to school there, he played that sport and liked those TV shows.

As briefly and lightly as possible, he gave Tessa his practiced spiel, carefully staying away from any ugly details. Afraid his expression might reveal too much, he lowered his eyelids, preventing her from meeting his gaze.

"This has been fun," he said when he finished the short dissertation. "But it's time for me to head out." He set his empty mug on a coaster on the side table. "Thanks for everything, for buying dinner and celebrating my birthday with me. I really do appreciate it."

"You're welcome. I enjoyed myself, too."

He began to stand, then found himself turning back to Tessa, a part of him reluctant to leave. "I believe it's tradition to offer the birthday person a birthday kiss."

"You already got a birthday kiss today." He could hear in her voice a wanting that matched his own.

"But"—he leaned into her—"you didn't know it was my birthday, so it doesn't count." He rubbed his cheek against hers, barely touching her, yet the sensation felt as intimate as if he was caressing every inch of her body. He thought she might be trembling as badly as he suddenly was.

She whimpered low in her throat, and he knew he had her.

"Go ahead," he whispered against her ear. "Tell me you don't want this. Ask me to stop and I will."

Chapter Six

How could Tessa tell Ben to stop when this was exactly what she wanted? What she'd been craving. Nothing she'd previously experienced with other men had prepared her for how it felt to be with this man. Maybe she was reacting in a way foreign to her nature, and maybe this reaction was wrong, but at this moment, she'd never wanted anyone half as much as she wanted Ben.

He stroked her skin, from cheek to collarbone, enflaming her senses, until she forgot everything except the exquisite way he made her feel.

"Don't stop," she managed to murmur before his mouth claimed hers. She gave an involuntary moan as he traced an erratic pattern of kisses down her throat and over to cover her pulse, beating feverishly in betrayal.

When his nimble fingers began working on the buttons of her blouse, she caught his hand and brought it to her lips, taking pleasure in kissing each finger. Her conduct shocked her, but she couldn't even blame Ben. He hadn't acted against her will. He had done nothing except incite a response he knew would be there. Waiting for him.

Ben looped his fingers through hers. "I can't stop thinking about making love to you all those months ago. How your touch drove me crazy, how your moans sent me over the moon. I loved making love to you, and I swear you felt the same." His voice was husky and unashamedly hungry. "You want this as much as I do, don't you?"

She bowed her head and nodded ever so slightly, finding it difficult to admit to something she'd been vehemently denying for so long.

He squeezed her fingers. "Say it with words. Say you want to make love with me."

She glanced at him and wished she hadn't, because the desire smoldering in his eyes dissolved what little resolve she had left. It felt as if he was stroking her entire body with that consuming gaze.

"I want—" Her voice cracked, and she had to stop and try again. "I want you. I want to make love with you." Her second effort hadn't been much of an improvement, but at least she got the words out. She'd never told a man she wanted him.

Ben nodded. His smile flashed on, then off, and he released an audible breath, as though he might be feeling the same tension as she was, and her words had come as a relief.

His grip on her fingers tightened again. "I've a proposition for you, and I'd like you to seriously think about it before you slap my face."

"Okay," she whispered, wishing he'd just shut up and kiss her again. She had such a burning need to feel his mouth back on hers.

"I want you to consider the idea of a purely physical relationship."

"Wh-What?"

He gave her hand a little shake. "A sexual relationship, totally enjoyable and satisfying, without any unnecessary emotional entanglements to drag us down. Just think of all the advantages."

A wave of shock and disappointment washed over her as his words sank in. He wanted her to be his *sex partner*. He called it a relationship, although he really meant an arrangement, a *physical* arrangement to have no-strings sex together.

She shook her head and pulled her hand from his grip. "I'm not interested." The tone she intended to be firm and assertive came out as a half-strangled croak, and she cleared her throat. "I don't need a physical relationship. I've always managed just fine without one."

That still might not sound as forceful as it should, but it was the truth. Rather, it *had been* the truth. She'd only had a small number of sexual liaisons, besides Colin Barry. A few other men had come and gone, although satisfying sexual needs had never been the driving force in any of her relationships. At least not on her part.

"I don't believe you. You struggle hard to conceal your passionate side, but you're too hot-blooded to ignore your desires." His brows arched mischievously. "I know. Remember?"

How could she not remember? Prior to Ben arriving to rock her rational world, she'd never done anything on impulse. He had awakened her passions, freed her of her inhibitions and allowed her to put aside her cautious nature. A part of her resented returning to that other life where she had to be practical and careful. Where everything had to make sense.

She linked her fingers together in her lap and looked down at them. "There might be an attraction playing between us, but we need to proceed carefully."

"Because we work together?"

"That's part of it." She grasped at the plausible excuse, refusing to admit to him or herself that she was afraid she might lose her heart in the bargain. "We've both been given a huge promotion; we need to stay focused on our work."

"I agree it's important to concentrate on our careers. That doesn't mean we should ignore our desires." She could practically hear his creative mind ticking off their options. "Making love doesn't constitute a lifelong commitment to the other person, and there'll be no danger of a problem developing if we don't allow it to interfere with our jobs. We could keep it a secret, if that makes you more comfortable."

"You want to have an affair?"

"An affair? No, I don't like what that word implies, as though we'd be doing something wrong. How about two good friends getting together for some mind-blowing sex without any messy expectations?"

She tried to calm herself and focus on his logic. Could it be enough just to be intimate friends with Ben? "A mutual convenience sort of thing, is what you're saying? Where we satisfy our sexual urges, while keeping our emotions out of it."

"Exactly. Do you know how hard it is to find a compatible person to be sexually involved with and not have to worry about it going beyond that?"

Why was she fighting this, when it'd be so easy to say yes? She wanted to say yes. She already had firsthand proof of his exceptional prowess in bed. And since that first delicious taste, she'd continuously craved more. Ben hadn't pretended his desire for her to be anything other than what it was—a physical yen for her body. He'd never offered insincere words of love or commitment; he simply said he wanted her.

She wished he didn't make so much sense because she didn't like the solution. It fell substantially short of her standard of behavior, but she was going to agree to it anyway. She just had to be smart enough to keep her heart carefully out of reach. They could come together as consenting adults, satisfy a biological function, and nothing else about their relationship had to change. If they could keep things at that level, it wouldn't get complicated.

Life had a way of complicating things whether it was wanted or not, a small voice of reason in her head pointed out. She quickly turned off the volume on that pesky inner voice. She didn't want any doubts clouding her decision.

"You've gotten awful quiet, Tessa. What're you thinking?"

"I'm thinking about it."

"Why think about *it*, when you could be doing *it*?"

Ben lowered his head and kissed her mouth, at first softly, then with certainty, sustaining it until it was impossible to keep from kissing back. The sweet pressure of his mouth, the heat of his body pressed against hers, stifled any thoughts of rejecting him.

Ben broke the kiss first. "Before this gets out of hand, I'd prefer not to use the couch. Especially if your sister is due home. And I'm not real big on audiences." He pointed at Milo, who lay at Tessa's feet with his chin on his front paws. Milo's eyes rolled in their sockets, and his ears twitched as he followed their conversation.

"All right."

"That means you're okay with this? You sure?"

His extraordinary eyes blazed with a sensuous flame that ignited the desire smoldering inside her. Her mind told her to resist; her body refused to listen. She nodded, not wanting to think too hard about what she'd consented to.

"Just let me shut the house up." She turned off the lights in the living room, leaving a single lamp on to light Lauren's way. Ben waited in the hallway while she checked the lock on the front door, then she led him up the stairs.

Milo followed behind them. When he tried to enter her bedroom, Ben nudged him back into the hall, closing the door on his maligned expression. Tessa drew on Ben's arm, leading him further into the room. They knelt face-to-face on the bed and undressed each other with aching deliberation, drawing out the pleasure, exploring, experimenting, caressing with fingers and lips. Their naked bodies came together tightly and Ben's hands went down to the swell of her buttocks.

"You feel so good."

"Do you have, uh, did you bring something?" Tessa asked, only now remembering they needed protection and not willing to take any unnecessary chances despite feeling awkward about asking.

"Yes." Ben got off the bed and reached for his pants on the floor.

"Turn off the lamp," Tessa said as he placed a condom on the nightstand. Suddenly self-conscious of her scrawny body, stripped bare and on display before him, she pulled a corner of the duvet over her.

Magnificently naked, and not in the least inhibited by it, Ben swept the covers off the bed and settled in next to her. "No way. I want to see you. I want to watch us make love."

"I don't," she started and then stopped, blushing furiously.

"Don't you have any clue how incredible you look?"

She closed her eyes. "Guys don't usually say things like that to me."

"Then you've been hanging out with the wrong guys." He drew a hand down the concave curve of her belly, leaving a sensual trail of sparks in his wake. "I don't want to hurry. I want to touch you, taste you, everywhere."

With tantalizing slowness, they toyed with each other's bodies. Ben kissed her lips, her neck, moving lower to capture her breast. Tessa's breath rushed in and out in little gasps. She tangled her fingers in his hair, needing something to hold on to as her whimpers turned to moans. She'd never experienced anything like this, never known such incredible sensations existed.

"Please, oh please," she begged, without knowing what exactly she wanted. For him to stop? For more? Desire threatened to consume her and her senses clamored for that final fulfillment. "Oh, please, please, puhleazzze..."

Ben eased down beside her and reached for the condom. As soon as it was in place, he pulled Tessa to him, and with a quick, shallow breath, she rocked her hips against him. He moaned, deep and low in his throat. "Easy, baby. We aren't in any hurry."

He slowly trailed hot, wet kisses along her jaw and

down her neck before reclaiming her lips, as their bodies began moving together in a sensual rhythm. Wound closely around one another, they whispered mindless, incoherent sounds of desire and need. As their pleasure intensified, so did their pace. Timelessly, being totally one, they climbed to sweet new heights.

It seemed like hours before their shuddering breath slowly returned to normal. Tessa snuggled against Ben's chest, their legs intertwined. His hand covered her breast and even though her body was sated, his touch caused a delicious ache. Tessa couldn't stop herself from wondering what he thought of her less than abundant endowment.

Interpreting her thoughts with uncanny accuracy, Ben pressed his lips to her brow. "You're exquisite, Tess. Don't ever hide your body from me." His hand slid to her hip, turning her so they lay face-to-face. Holding her snugly against him, he plied her lips with kisses, sweet, poignant kisses that ended far too soon and left her wanting more.

"I'll be right back." The mattress tipped under her as he stood. She enjoyed the view of his delectable butt as he snagged his boxers off the floor and left the room.

"What are you doing?" she asked moments later, levering up on an elbow to watch as he returned, wearing his boxers, and started collecting his scattered clothes.

"It's late. I have to get going." He glanced around, then headed toward his socks halfway across the room.

Tessa sat up, dismayed beyond belief that he wanted to leave after the intimacy they'd just shared. "You don't have to go."

He went back to the bed and stooped over to kiss

her. "Yeah, I do."

Her hand came around his waist, gently stroking the flat plane of his belly, teasing its way lower, hoping to change his mind. He removed her fingers from his boxer's waistband and pinched at his eyes with the fingers of his other hand.

"We better lay down some ground rules."

"Ground rules?" Her euphoria rapidly evaporated, leaving her not the least bit happy.

"This"—he pointed back and forth between them—"is strictly a sexual thing, right? That's what we agreed to. No emotional involvement, nothing serious, just a mutually satisfying physical relationship."

"I'm not asking for more. Still, it'd be nice to spend the night together. We did just make love, after all." Being naked in front of him while he did the remote act began to feel unbearable, and she used her arms to cover herself the best she could.

Ben lifted the covers from the floor and settled them around her. "Believe me, it's best not to spend the entire night together. It's easier to keep an emotional detachment that way."

Easier for her to stay detached, he must mean. He obviously didn't have a problem with that regard. He'd gotten what he wanted, so now he could leave and sleep in the comfort of his own bed. Tessa swallowed down her bitterness along with her angry words. She had known what he wanted from the start and had only herself to blame if she didn't like the boundaries he'd set.

"Stay in bed," he told her, as he tucked his shirttails into his pants and did up the zipper. "I'll let myself out." He returned to her one last time. "Sweet dreams." He pressed a kiss to her lips and backed away quickly as though afraid she might wrestle him down on the bed otherwise. "I'll see you at work in the morning."

Tears burned readily in her eyes as Ben left the room. Feeling angry and heartsick, she got off the bed and pulled on her nightgown. She'd give Ben a few moments to leave, then she'd call Milo up. Although she might want a big warm male body to cuddle, she'd have to settle for a small hairy one.

Ben had said no emotions allowed, and she had willingly agreed to his terms. If she wanted to make this incredible sexual dalliance work, she'd have to figure out a way to harden her heart and play by his rules.

****

Ben made his way quietly down the stairs, not wanting to run into Tessa's sister while sneaking out of the house. He hadn't heard Lauren Caldwell come home, although he reckoned a train could've driven through the place while he made love to Tessa and he wouldn't have noticed.

As he passed the living room, the small dog rose from the couch and gave itself a shake. "Hey, pup," Ben said, taking a detour into the room. "Milo, right?" He knelt and gazed into its wide-eyed, innocent stare. "Sorry for booting you out of the bedroom earlier, but I'm not real keen on sharing Tessa with another male."

The dog lunged forward and licked his cheek. Ben groaned in protest and collapsed onto his butt against the couch. The little bugger barked and tried for a second lick, this time Ben stopped it with a hand in front of his face. "I'm not into doggie kisses, thanks. Tessa, on the other hand, is by herself upstairs. I bet she'd appreciate a few of those."

Thinking of Tessa had him feeling simultaneously aggravated and guilty. He also felt more exhilarated than he could ever remember feeling after making love to a woman. Not a healthy combination of emotions, and his instincts screamed for him to get the hell out of this situation. He'd crossed his own private line and ventured into an area he'd sworn he'd never go. Tessa was a forever type of girl, and he should've known to keep his distance. Instead, he'd been a fool and if he didn't watch it, he was going to end up caring too much about her.

He gave the dog a pat on the head and grabbed his jacket from the closet, then left the house, taking care to set the latch on the old-fashioned door lock, ensuring he'd secured the door. An icy breeze touched his cheek as he stepped off the porch, and he shivered as he hurried to do up his zipper.

Talking to Tessa the way he had, the necessity of acting cool and detached, had proved exceedingly difficult. Leaving the warmth of her bed had been even harder. The devastated look that flashed across her face when she realized he wasn't staying had almost sent him climbing back into bed with her. But it'd be stupid to stay with her while having all those warm and fuzzy feelings. He couldn't allow emotions to infringe on this relationship. What they had—all they had—was friendship mingled with gratifying sex. He had to be careful not to confuse that with anything else.

Especially not something as stupid as love.

That thought gave him an unexpected tug of yearning, and surprised at himself, he quickly shut the feeling down. It was desire, nothing more, and he refused to be a slave to his hormones. Passion, like anger, was a weakness to be controlled. He could handle this—as long as he didn't let it make him want things impossible to have.

****

After a long, restless night, Tessa woke in a less than pleasant state of mind. In the cold light of day, all the difficulties that would arise from attempting Ben's type of relationship began filling her head with doubts, and she found herself questioning the sort of arrangement he had proposed—no commitment, no expectations, no hurt feelings when it ended.

Although she understood how some people might find such a proposal attractive, she had strong doubts whether she could do it. No matter how fantastic the sex was—and it certainly went beyond fantastic—she could never be physically close without getting emotionally close. How could she believe, for even one irrational moment, she might be capable of engaging in such an arrangement with Ben? She was the practical one, she reminded herself. A person who set goals and worked hard to achieve them, then checked them off and moved on to the next ones. She didn't contemplate sleeping with someone she didn't love—and who definitely didn't pretend to love her. If a relationship, no matter how intense the chemistry, didn't have the potential to amount to more than sex, she wanted no part of it.

She had to tell Ben they couldn't continue with the liaison they'd agreed to last night. It was important for her to be completely honest about this. Being honest with herself, she knew breaking it off would be difficult to manage. Something about Ben made her behave in a manner totally foreign to the person she believed herself to be. Mesmerized by his persuasive skills, the seductive pull of his compelling attraction, she had abandoned her own principles, and somehow, someway, she had to find the strength to break the mystical hold he had over her.

As she entered the building that housed the agency, still lost in her troubled thoughts, she didn't notice Janey standing in front of the elevator until she nearly stumbled into her.

Janey, her astute friend, who read her like a beloved book. She could've done without running into her just yet.

"Morning, Tess." Janey reached to push the elevator button. "I called you last night. Didn't you get my message? You know, if you ever remembered to turn on your cell phone, this wouldn't be a problem, right?"

"I'm sorry, Janey. I was out and then I forgot to check for messages when I got home."

They entered the elevator and Janey knuckled the button for their floor. "Out as in running errands or out as in on a date?"

Very subtle. As usual.

"Out with Ben. Not a date," she volunteered to save Janey the trouble of worming the information out of her.

Just as the elevator doors were about to slide closed, two women squeezed their way in, and while Tessa seized the short reprieve with gratitude, she could almost see the impatience steaming from Janey's ears. The moment the other women left the elevator on the fourth floor, Janey whirled and gripped Tessa's arm in excitement.

"Out with Ben? How could that not be a date?"

She had to say something, so she opted for the oblique. "We had to work late, and when we were ready to leave he told me it was his birthday. I couldn't let the guy eat alone, so we had dinner together. It wasn't a date."

"It wasn't? Why not?"

"Really? You have to sound so disappointed? I've already told you; I can't get involved with him. Besides the fact that we work together, he's just a kid."

The elevator doors slid open, and they stepped into the hallway. "All men are *just kids*."

Tessa glanced at Dallas's vacant desk as she loosened the scarf from around her neck. "He's, uh, he's only twenty-nine. That makes him a little more than three years younger than me."

Janey stopped in her tracks and threw her hands up in amused horror. "Three years! My heavens, that's a lifetime. Come on, chickie, get real. The man is interested in you, and you'd be crazy to turn him down. I sure wouldn't be booting him out of my bed if I ever had the opportunity to entice him into it, three years younger or not. Or in my case, it's more like seven."

"I mean it. He's an overgrown kid. All he wants to do is play without any responsibility or commitment. It's best if Ben and I remain business colleagues. And friends, of course, but that's all." Yeah, friends. Only, instead of friends-with-benefits they were about to become friends-with-complications.

Janey pushed open the door to the break room. She let out a small gasp and backed up so quickly she practically careened over Tessa.

"What's wrong?" Tessa tried to peer around her friend into the break room.

Horror streaked across Janey's face, and she pulled the door closed, effectively barring Tessa from getting by her. "You don't want to go in there."

"Of course I do. I have to hang up my coat and stick my lunch in the fridge." When she reached for the door handle, Janey grabbed her arm and dragged her away so forcefully, she almost lost her balance.

"Janey! Why are you acting like a crazy person?"

"Ben's in there. With Dallas."

Shock flew through Tessa, rendering her motionless for a long painful moment.

"So?" she said finally, impressed with her fake level of nonchalance.

"They're in there together. And I do mean *together*. I'm sorry, honey." Janey's voice revealed her pain on Tessa's behalf.

Tessa looked away from Janey's sympathetic eyes. Her throat closed, as though a hand had tightened around it, cutting off her breath. With her heart pounding in her ears so loudly, she couldn't hear her own voice, she said, "What Ben and Dallas are doing, or not doing, is none of my concern. Get out of my way, Janey."

Janey refused to budge, and the door suddenly opened behind them. Ben appeared in the doorway, and he smiled widely when he saw them.

"Hey, Janey. Morning, Tessa." He laid his hand on her shoulder in a possessive gesture, and she instantly shrugged off his touch, turning away, her hands clenched stiffly at her sides.

Somehow, she maintained her fragile control and

suppressed her hurt under a show of indifference. "Could you excuse me? It's getting warm standing here with my coat on."

She skirted around Ben and Janey, only to have Dallas block her path, as the redhead stepped into the hallway. Dallas wore a smile like the cat who had eaten the cream as she smoothed her hands down her way-too-tight sweater. Not caring if she came off as rude, Tessa pushed past her into the break room. Janey entered behind her, but Tessa kept her back to her friend as she shrugged out of her jacket.

"Oh, Tessa. That must've been awful."

She felt sick...bruised. Terribly humiliated. But she'd die before she admitted it. "Can we not talk about this? It's not as big a deal as you're making it out to be. I'd just finished telling you I'm not interested in Ben." She shoved her lunch bag into the fridge, picked up her purse, and stalked out of the room.

Her brain churned, trying to rearrange her thoughts into some semblance of order. She didn't know why it should surprise her to find Ben with Dallas. It's not as if she hadn't seen them together before. Besides, Tessa had no exclusive claims on him. There was only sex between them, not a commitment, not a chance at a future together. Merely an appeasement of their physical needs. Ben made that clear from the start. So why did she feel as though her heart had been ripped from her chest?

Her face burned as she remembered the things they had done last night. Incredibly intimate things she'd never done with another man—because she had trusted Ben to see her at her most vulnerable. A sense of inadequacy swept over her, and she couldn't help wondering if she didn't measure up in comparison to his other conquests, and so he had turned to the more voluptuous and experienced Dallas. What a humiliating, deflating thought that was.

Raising her chin, she assumed all the dignity she could muster and entered their office. Ben stood over by the window, and he turned as she came in.

"Hi," he said, smiling that warm smile again. "Hope you're not too tired this morning. I left awfully late last night."

She raked him with a look of complete disillusionment, and he met her gaze with not a hint of shame, only friendly affection and a touch of perplexity. His ability to put on such an innocent front, after what he'd just pulled with Dallas, shocked and disgusted her.

"Don't even talk to me." Her voice was raw, but she kept it steady. Ben hurried away from the window, stopping when she warned him off with a raised hand. "Don't you even look at me, and don't come near me."

Ben's eyes bugged. "Maybe you should tell me what the hell's going on."

"How could you? How could you go from my bed to Dallas's arms?"

The confirmation showed on his face as he looked away.

"There's nothing between me and Dallas."

"Don't lie. Janey saw you in the break room. And the least you could do is wipe the lipstick off your face before you deny it again."

Ben rubbed the tips of his fingers over his mouth, then looked at his hand. "There's nothing on my mouth."

"No? Then why wipe it?" She glared, daring him to have the nerve to defend his shabby conduct.

"To check what you thought you saw. I haven't kissed anyone today, so I knew I didn't have lipstick on my mouth."

Tessa threw up her hands in disbelief and plopped herself into the chair behind her desk.

Ben followed her over. "I'm serious, Tess. Dallas and I weren't kissing. I admit anyone who saw us might've gotten the wrong idea. Dallas can be relentless, and she came on a little strong this morning, but nothing happened because I refused to let it."

Tessa wavered, trying to comprehend his words. She wouldn't put it past Dallas to do exactly what Ben had said. That woman totally put the *B* in witch. On the other hand, how did she know if she could trust Ben?

"Honest?"

He reached out and hauled her from the chair, bringing her up onto her tiptoes, chest to chest. "Honest." He touched a fingertip to her trembling lips. "Dallas means less than nothing to me. She never has. And I wouldn't do that to you, anyway. I'd never intentionally hurt you." His tone was apologetic, and the absolute tenderness in his expression reassured her.

She let out her breath slowly and gulped with relief. "I believe you."

"So, can we call a truce?"

Tessa extricated herself from his arms. "I'm sorry I jumped to conclusions, but we have to talk," she said stiffly as she moved a few feet away from him. "About last night."

"What about last night? Besides saying it was beyond incredible. Hands down, best birthday, ever."

"I need this out in the open, to avoid any misunderstandings." Her reasonable tone hid a pounding heart and weak, trembling knees. Her stomach began to clench and roll. She hated this. She hated confrontation, and that's right where they were heading because Ben wasn't about to agree to end their arrangement without a fight. But their affair would eventually run its course, and she couldn't imagine working amicably together once it did. She had to end this before there was any permanent damage done.

"I admit my hormones start dancing all over the place whenever you come near me. If that flatters you, fine, feel flattered. The thing is, I can't have the type of relationship you're asking for. Last night shouldn't have happened."

The smile left his face, leaving his eyes greeny-gray, like a cold sea. "I don't want you. I want you. I don't want you, but I don't want anyone else to have you." He closed his eyes, as though praying for strength. "You're driving me blinking, bloody crazy."

Tessa didn't pause to consider whether his complaint was justified. "I'm sorry. I feel strongly about this. I've admitted I find you appealing—but it's not going any further than that. Last night was a mistake, a delicious mistake, and though I don't regret it, we have to go back to how it used to be."

His snort of indignation interrupted her. "Are you kidding me? Is this because I didn't stay last night?"

"No. Not really."

"Not really? But possibly? You're letting your emotions rule your head."

She folded her arms across her chest defensively. Even if what he said happened to be true, that didn't make it wrong. "And you let your head rule your emotions. In my book, that's much worse. I'm trying to be honest here. I'm not cut out to be a sex partner."

"And I'm not cut out for commitments and relationships," he replied tightly.

Aha. "Why is that, exactly?"

"Because"—he slashed a hand through the air, showing his frustration—"I have more important things to concentrate on, like my job. And why should I have to settle down? What the hell's wrong with just living in the moment?"

She'd heard those words so many times before. Live for the moment, and let the future take care of itself—her sister's motto, not hers.

"There's nothing wrong with it, I guess. If it's what makes you happy. It's not what I want, though, and I can't change who I am. Do you remember what you said last night? How it doesn't pay to try to be someone you're not? I've realized I'm not the type of woman who can have a casual affair. If you're willing to explore something further, I'd be there in a heartbeat."

He looked angry. He looked furious. Yet, he just stood there, holding everything inside. She was beginning to understand that he preferred to contain his anger rather than act on it, and it made her wonder why, but the jangle of the phone prevented her from voicing those thoughts.

With swift steps, Ben reached his desk and scooped up the receiver. He regained most of his calm as he spoke into the phone. "That was Morris," he told Tessa when he hung up. "He wants us and our campaign ideas in his office, ASAP."

When they arrived at Morris's office, their boss

signaled for them to have a seat, then took his time thoroughly perusing each of the mockups they had brought with them. Occasionally he broke the tense silence to ask a question. Finally, he took three of the mockups and set the rest aside.

"I want to run with this one, with these two as backups. Polish them up and, Ben, you will be on point for the pitch at the meeting I have set up with the client for a week from Monday."

Tessa tensed in her chair, then forced herself to relax, breathing slowly out of her nose. She might not like this, but it didn't surprise her. She'd known all along that while Morris willingly utilized her creative talent, he had hired Ben to interact with the clients, because he believed clients wouldn't take her seriously.

"You know, Morris," Ben said, reaching for the mockups. "Two of these ideas you've chosen were Tessa's, and she should pitch them."

Although Ben's unexpected show of support came as a complete surprise, she kept her expression neutral and said nothing.

"Naturally, Tessa will sit in on the meeting and be available to answer any questions; however, you will do the pitch. You are my closer." Morris's tone left no room for argument.

Ben glanced at Tessa, and his look suggested his willingness to pursue the matter further if she wanted. She shook her head, frustrated by the futility of the situation, and rose to her feet. Without another word, Ben collected the material from Morris's desk and followed her out of the room.

"Why didn't you stand up for yourself in there? I would've backed you," Ben said as they walked back to their office.

"There's no point. Defiance only makes him more determined to do it his way. But thanks for trying. You didn't have to, and I appreciate the effort."

"That man's a fool, and someday he'll pay a premium for his foolishness."

Tessa immediately squashed the flash of affection and admiration. It was gratitude, that's all. Although, their personal situation would be a lot easier to handle if he didn't have to go and act so darn sweet.

Chapter Seven

Ben paid the furniture delivery guy and braced himself to face the chaotic scene behind him. Furniture and boxes sat helter-skelter all over the room with barely a path to walk through to the hallway and kitchen area. The apartment wasn't anything to brag about, and the second-story view of the houses across the street sure couldn't compare to the million-dollar view he'd had at his Yaletown apartment in Vancouver. But it was all his and a huge improvement over that sardine can he'd just spent the better part of a month in.

He actually liked the apartment's old-fashioned layout, with the kitchen separated from the living room by a half wall, instead of being all one large living area the way most modern apartments were. There wasn't a formal dining area, which suited his lifestyle just fine. Breakfast could be eaten at the table in the kitchen, and any other meals at home he preferred eating in front of the TV anyway. Considering his lack of cooking skills, entertaining dinner guests was best done in a restaurant.

Mentally rolling up his sleeves, Ben started sorting through the stacks of boxes. His mother had helped him pack up his apartment in Vancouver, and now that he could finally unpack everything, he appreciated how she'd meticulously labeled the contents of each box.

He systematically moved the boxes into whichever room they belonged in, setting the ones he wasn't sure about off to one side to deal with later. As the room began to empty out, he pushed and shoved his furniture around until he had it arranged in the most logical positions. To make up for his sadly deficient decorating skills, over the years he'd methodically purchased good quality furniture, and he took pride in his possessions. He leaned his few pieces of artwork carefully against the wall, figuring they could wait to be hung until after the boxes were all unpacked.

It took an embarrassingly long time to hook up his TV and various other entertainment paraphernalia, and more than once he almost gave up in frustration. He'd always had a techie friend do this stuff for him in Vancouver. Getting the job done right had been worth all the good-natured ribbing about his inability to do this common 'guy thing'. He hadn't formed any support networks here in Calgary yet, so the onerous chore was all his to deal with. Only the knowledge that he couldn't survive long without TV and music kept him motivated.

Once the living room was semi-habitable, he turned his attention to the kitchen. He'd be the first to admit he didn't know a pot from a pan, and he had no interest in learning. He did know, however, how to make a mean cup of coffee. Well, he didn't, but his state-of-the-art coffee machine did, and his first priority was locating it and insuring it was operational for when he needed his next caffeine fix. No more inferior take-out coffee in paper cups for him, thank you very much.

He offered up another token of appreciation for his mother when, after a brief scan of the kitchen boxes, he located the one labeled 'Ben's caffeine addiction essentials'. He set the high-end coffee machine on the counter near the sink and placed the carousel of coffee capsules on the counter next to it, all ready for the morning.

The kitchen took far longer to organize than the living room, not counting the frustrating couple of hours spent on his entertainment center. Long before he'd finished, his growling stomach interrupted to tell him that the skimpy breakfast he had that morning had become a distant memory, and the lunch hour had come and gone as well. He'd maintained a meager supply of food at the travel apartment, so if he intended to eat any time soon, a trip to the grocery store needed to be the next item on his agenda.

As he pulled out of the apartment's parking lot, Ben turned right, even though he suspected he'd have better success finding a grocery store if he'd turned in the opposite direction and headed into the business section of the neighborhood. He drove slowly, admiring the old Victorian homes lining the quiet residential street. In no time, he arrived on Tessa's block. He'd seen the Honda parked in front of her place before and assumed it belonged to her. That likely meant she was at home.

He wondered, for the briefest moment, what she'd do if he knocked on her door and asked to borrow a cup of sugar. Although they'd seemed to set aside the disagreement about having a physical relationship, her attitude toward him was still decidedly cool, and she'd likely not find it amusing if he showed up uninvited. He continued a little farther down the block, then pulled a U-turn and headed back in the direction he should've gone in the first place.

No more driving past Tessa's house, he sternly told

himself. No more fantasizing about knocking on her door. No more fantasizing about her, period. She wasn't interested in him, and that was the best thing for both of them.

That didn't prevent him from slowing to a crawl as he passed her house for the second time. Or stop the sense of disappointment that washed over him at not catching a glimpse of her in the front window as he drove by.

****

Ben's legs barely carried him to his desk after lunch on Monday, and he sat heavily into his swivel chair, shaking with chills and nausea. He hunched over the desk, cradling his head in his hands. He felt miserably ill and needed to lie down, but the couch was too far away. His desktop would have to do.

"Ben?" Tessa's voice seemed to come from a great distance, even though she stood right next to his desk. "Are you okay? You look awful."

Resting his cheek on his hand, he gingerly turned his head to look at her. "I think I have food poisoning."

"Food poisoning? Really?"

"All I know is I felt perfectly fine this morning, then on my way back from lunch, I suddenly got sick."

She took a step closer. "You aren't trying to milk this for the sympathy vote, are you?"

He couldn't even find the oomph to come up with a witty response. Her hand reached out to brush his hair back from his brow. Cool fingers trailed down his cheek, across the back of his neck and then squeezed his shoulder briefly with compassion, before drawing away.

"I don't think it's food poisoning. You're running a

fever, and you probably have the flu. You should trudge off home."

"No way. It wouldn't look good to go home sick." Cold sweat broke out on his forehead, and he forced himself to breathe past the nausea and pain.

Tessa leaned in to wrap an arm around his shoulders and give him a shake. "But you *are* sick! Everyone gets sick sometimes."

"Not me. Besides, I don't have time to slack off. Not until this new campaign is up and firing on all cylinders." He popped some pain tablets from the plastic and foil blister he kept in his desk drawer. "A couple of these and I'll be good to go." His stomach protested when he tried to swallow them dry, and he wondered if he could hold off the nausea long enough to reach the bathroom. "Excuse me," he croaked as he lurched from the desk and out of the room with his hand clamped firmly over his mouth.

The ten feet of hallway to the bathroom seemed more like ten miles, and Ben barely made it into a stall before his stomach emptied itself. Feeling shaky and weak, he splashed water on his face and rinsed the sour taste out of his mouth at the sink. Talk about embarrassing. Bloody good thing no one was around to witness his humiliation.

Tessa wasn't in the office when he got back, and he sank gratefully onto the couch, closing his eyes against the burn in his belly. He'd told Tessa the truth. He never got sick, nothing more than the occasional tension headache, but something nasty sure had hold of him now.

A damp cloth placed lightly on his forehead announced Tessa's return. "Here, keep this there for a few minutes." He blearily cracked one eye open. Her concerned face came into focus as she bent closer to peer at him. "Are you all right? You look as if you might pass out."

The coolness of the cloth helped, and he tried to smile. "I'll be fine. Thank you." An inferno went off inside his belly, and he closed his eyes again, gritting his teeth to fight back the moan threatening to escape.

"I can drive you home, if you want."

"I'm not going home." That'd take too much effort. He'd rather just curl up and die right there on the couch.

****

Tessa scooped a couple of spoonfuls of dog food into Milo's bowl, then set it on the floor. "Here you are, sweetie. I'm afraid I can't stay long. I have to check on Ben. You remember the man from last week?" Despite the way Milo ignored her while he concentrated on chowing down his dinner, Tessa continued to speak out loud. "Ben's sick, and I'm worried about him, poor guy. He moved in down the block yesterday, so I'm going to pop over to see how he is."

Milo's stubby tail wagged, whether he was acknowledging her or simply enjoying his meal, Tessa couldn't tell. She rushed through her own meal, then hurried to change from her office clothes and pull on her warm parka for the walk to Ben's.

She pressed Ben's intercom button on the door entry and waited with burning impatience until he buzzed her up. It took awhile for him to open the door to her knock and, when he did, his appearance worried her. He looked uncharacteristically disheveled, with his shirttails hanging out and his hair sticking up in tufts. His face was pale and white-lipped, his eyes bruised with pain.

"Hi," she said. "I told you I'd check up on you, so here I am. I'm glad you made it home from work in one piece."

"I'm home. You've checked. Now you can go."

He remained holding the door and didn't invite her in, so Tessa squeezed past him into the room. There was furniture in place—good quality stuff, lots of leather, comfortable and masculine. Boxes were stacked here and there, and she guessed they'd be there for a while because Ben didn't seem in any shape to unpack. His ugly mood only confirmed how sick he must be.

"Have you had anything to eat?" She took off her parka and set it on top of a box. "I can fix you something."

Ben closed the door with a resigned sigh. "Hell, no. To answer your next question, yes, I've taken some pain meds." He sank stiff-backed onto the couch, one hand pressed to his midsection.

Tessa touched his forehead and let her fingers linger in a fleeting caress. "Did you? Because your face is really hot. You've still got quite a fever."

He brushed her hand away, a spark of anger flaring in his eyes, an instinctive denial of any weakness. "Stop fussing."

"I'm not fussing."

"What do you call it, then?"

Tessa almost giggled at his scowl, except being this cranky was so unlike him, worry tempered her humor. "Trying to take care of you. Do you really not want me here?"

He shrugged irritably. "Stay or go. It's up to you."

"Look, it's not as if you'll lose your lifetime supply

of testosterone if you admit to needing a little help."
She paused to gauge his reaction. He simply glared off
into space, refusing to look at her. "All right, then. If
you don't want me around, I'll leave. I'm checking
back in the morning, though, and don't you even think
about going to work." She picked up her parka and
started for the door.

"Tessa, wait."

She turned back. "Yes?"

"I'm not feeling so hot."

Tessa nodded, suppressing a trace of amusement at
his plaintive tone. "I know."

"Will you stay?"

He looked so sweetly vulnerable that her heart
went out to him before she could stop it.

"Of course, I'll stay." She felt an inexplicable urge
to wrap him in her arms and soothe his hurts away. "We
should get you into bed."

He managed something close to a laugh. "Do you
have any idea how I've longed to hear you say those
words? And just my luck, I'm not up for anything more
strenuous than watching TV."

Ignoring his silly innuendo, Tessa frowned,
thinking he'd be better off asleep. But when he refused
to budge from the couch, she agreed to watch TV.
Several times over the next hour, she caught him
grimacing and pressing a hand against his belly. When
she questioned him, he insisted he felt better. Although
the nausea had subsided, in her estimation, the pain in
his abdomen grew increasingly worse.

"How about I run you over to Emerg and have that
pain checked out?" she asked when the TV show ended.

"Not a hope." He rose carefully to his feet,

hunched forward slightly as if guarding the pain. "I gotta get horizontal, though. Sitting's gotten damn uncomfortable."

Tessa stood too. "Do you have any juice in this place? With a fever like yours, you need to take plenty of fluids." She mentally kicked herself for not thinking of that sooner. He most likely bordered on dehydration.

"I stocked the fridge yesterday," Ben said as he headed toward the hall at a cautious pace. "A glass of juice sounds good, if you wouldn't mind."

"Okay, get into bed, and I'll bring you something in a moment."

The kitchen appeared to be in a little better shape than the living room. Miscellaneous kitchenware Ben evidently hadn't found a home for yet cluttered the surface of a small bistro-style table, and only a few boxes remained stacked neatly against one wall. The countertop held a toaster, coffee maker and blender, all elaborate and expensive-looking.

Tessa opened the cupboard closest to the sink to find plates, cups and glasses. At least she wouldn't have to dig through boxes to locate what she needed. She randomly chose from a selection of juices in the well-stocked fridge and filled a small glass for Ben.

When she entered Ben's bedroom he was under the covers, still awake. Like the rest of his apartment, there was furniture in place, with several boxes lining the available wall space.

"Here you go." She handed him the juice and he drank thirstily, then set the empty glass on the night stand.

"I have another favor to ask," he said as he settled back against the pillow.

She sat on the edge of the bed and brushed her hand over his forehead. If possible, he felt warmer than he had when she arrived. "What do you need? A painkiller? Something for the nausea?"

"You."

Her hand fell away. "Excuse me?"

"Spend the night. Just to sleep, just to lie next to me," he hurried to add when she began to protest. His hair was in a tangle and his eyes burned brilliantly out of his pale face, yet he'd never looked so adorable, nor more vulnerable.

"You'd sleep better by yourself."

His hand came up to grip her arm, the heat from his fingers penetrating the fabric of her shirt. "I'll sleep better with you beside me. Please."

She suddenly wanted to cry and didn't know why.

"You can wear one of my T-shirts, and there are new toothbrushes in the bathroom cabinet. Help yourself." His words ended on a groan, and he closed his eyes with a grimace.

That settled it. No way could she leave him in this condition, she wouldn't sleep a wink worrying about him. She located a clean T-shirt in the drawer Ben indicated and took it with her to the bathroom. The shirt hung almost to her knees and it gave her a cheap thrill to wear an article of Ben's clothing next to her naked body.

Knock it off, she told herself as she locked up the apartment and turned off the lights, leaving on just the hallway one. She was playing Florence Nightingale, not a lusty femme fatale. Ben was seriously ill and needed care and compassion, not some woman obsessing over how sexy his T-shirt felt against her bare skin and wondering what, if anything, he had on under those covers.

Ben appeared to be sleeping, so she quietly crawled in on the other side of the bed, hoping not to disturb him. He rolled toward her, and feverish lips pressed against the side of her chin, his arm creeping around her waist to snuggle her closer.

"This is how it should always be, Tessa Leigh. You, sleeping in my arms." He tucked his head against her neck and began to breathe heavily as he drifted back to sleep.

When his hold loosened, Tessa extricated herself carefully. That was just fever talk. He must be delirious, because what he said contained so much emotion it had her throat burning with unshed tears. The Ben she knew didn't do emotion. He had told her there were no feelings involved, other than the purely sexual ones he openly admitted to.

He had insisted they couldn't spend the entire night together after they made love, yet just now he said sleeping in each other's arms was how it should be. How it *always* should be. Could he possibly mean it? No, it had to be the fever, nothing more. Merely the fever and his need for comfort while feeling ill.

Tessa didn't sleep for the longest time, she watched Ben instead. Occasionally, he shifted and groaned in his sleep, would thrash around a bit, then settle back down. Mostly, he slept soundly with a sweetness and innocence he rarely showed while awake.

Being light-hearted about love wasn't in her nature and to fall for Ben would be disastrous, but as the long hours of the night slowly passed, a stirring began growing inside her. A stirring that told her she was headed for complete disaster. She could fight it all she wanted; it didn't change the fact that this was more than lust, much more than affection or friendship. She loved this man lying asleep beside her. She loved him with every fiber of her heart and soul.

Now, what exactly did she propose to do about it?

She couldn't just blurt it out to him. Because Ben had never led her on with words of love. From the day he arrived in Calgary, he'd pursued her openly, being completely honest about what he wanted. And all he wanted was an uncomplicated physical relationship, leaving him free to aggressively pursue his career. Telling him, oops, somewhere along the way she had fallen in love with him, would definitely complicate matters.

She curled up against the fiery heat of Ben's body and kissed his cheek. He rolled to his side, his arm coming out to encircle her. She placed a light kiss on his lips and wrapped her arms around him, pressing close. The taste and feel of him had become blissfully familiar and she reveled in it.

She had no idea what she should do, didn't know what might come next. But the truth of her feelings was abundantly clear. She was completely, irrefutably, wondrously, frighteningly, in love with Ben Dunham.

****

Tessa sleepily blinked her eyes a couple of times, then glanced over at the bedside clock, relieved to see it was still early. She rose carefully to not rock the mattress and wake Ben. After tucking the blankets around him, she dressed, then stopped in the kitchen to make coffee and phone Janey.

"Hi," she said softly into her cell phone when

Janey answered.

"Why are we whispering?"

"I'm at Ben's and he's asleep."

"Ah, do tell."

Tessa approached the coffeemaker on the counter with trepidation. Trust Ben to have a complicated machine. It was one of those individual cup dealies that made fancy cappuccinos and lattes. She'd seen various versions of them and knew they were supposed to be easy to operate, but this one had two reservoirs and about a million buttons. With her brain suffering from serious sleep deprivation, she had no clue how to turn the darn thing on, never mind make coffee with it.

"He's sick. Real sick," she told Janey, abandoning the intricacies of the coffeemaker to concentrate on their conversation. "And I'm going to try to convince him to go to the hospital when he wakes up."

"What's wrong?" Janey's voice rose in concern.

"At first I thought it was the flu, but the pain is getting worse. I think it might be appendicitis. Please tell Mr. Montgomery I'll be in as soon as I know what's up with Ben."

A stand, similar to a spice rack, stood on the counter next to the coffeemaker; it held a large variety of little coffee pods. After ending her call with Janey, she opened the compartment on the top of the machine and fit a coffee pod into the slot, then dug around for a mug in the cupboard by the sink and placed it carefully under the nozzle. So far, so good.

Water had to go into the thing if she wanted coffee to come out. But how? She inched the machine away from the wall to get a closer look. *Aha.* The back reservoir contained remnants of water drops. She poured a cup of water into it and pushed the button whose icon looked the most like a regular cup of coffee, then crossed her fingers. To her immense relief, aromatic coffee soon began to fill her cup.

She sat at the cluttered little table and drank what could only be described as a most exceptional cup of coffee. Hoping to clear the remnants of fog from her brain, she fixed herself a refill and returned to Ben's room. She drew a chair up beside the bed and sat down, drinking the coffee as she watched over Ben. He still slept, but not soundly. He moaned often and turned his head back and forth on the pillow. An enormous swell of affection and concern enveloped her as she sat vigil. She set her empty mug down and reached over to check his temperature. As she suspected, he burned with fever.

"Hey," Ben said, his voice rough with pain. "Good morning."

"Or not so good, if you feel as bad as you look."

"It's just a bellyache."

"I have a notion it's a lot more than that. Will you show me where it hurts?"

He dropped the covers from his bare chest. Desire, laced with tenderness, streamed through Tessa, and she swallowed hard at the sight of his gorgeously muscled chest and flat belly. She sternly jerked her gaze away from the area covered by gray jersey boxers.

Florence Nightingale, remember?

Ben shifted his hand across his upper abdomen and downward to his lower right side. "Through here."

"I'm going to check something, and I apologize if it hurts." She pressed her palm firmly into his abdomen on the right side. "Does that feel worse?" He shook his head. "How about now?" She quickly released the pressure.

Pain yanked him back against the pillow. "Yeow. What the hell was that?"

"I'm pretty sure you have appendicitis, and you have to see a doctor right away."

He studied her through fever-bright eyes. "You think it's serious enough to get checked out?"

"It's serious enough that I need to take you to the ER immediately. Get dressed, then lie back down. I'm going home to freshen up and change my clothes, and I'll be right back with my car."

The fact that he didn't try to argue revealed the extent of his illness.

****

"Hey," Tessa said softly, pulling a chair closer to the hospital bed, while not taking her eyes off Ben's starkly pale face. "How you doing?"

She had barely been able to concentrate at work, for worrying about him. Even though every phone call she made to the hospital told her the same thing—he'd weathered the surgery just fine and was resting comfortably—she couldn't wait for the workday to end, to see for herself.

"I'm about ready to split this lemonade stand. Will you help me make a run for it?" Ben's killer grin was weak and wan, but still in perfect shape. Only his sea-green eyes revealed the pain he did his best to conceal.

The tug on her heart had her blinking with astonishment at the sheer strength of her feelings. How had she come to love him this deeply so quickly?

"You won't be running, or in your case, tottering, anywhere for a day or two. You had a close call, you know. Your appendix was pretty wild, and there's lots of infection. It was so close to rupturing, they had to take it out the old fashioned way, which is why you have such a big owie on your tummy."

"Who's been telling tales about me?"

"My dad's a bigwig surgeon at this hospital, so I have my sources." She smiled and tucked the blanket snugly around him, then smoothed her hand over his shoulder. "Besides, you look awful cute in that green hospital gown. Brings out the color of your eyes." And did ghastly things to his ashen complexion. That last little tidbit she'd keep to herself.

He captured her hand and brought it up to his mouth to kiss. Although his lips were dry, his fever seemed under control. When he lowered his hand to the bed, he kept her fingers entwined in his.

"Thanks for dragging my sorry ass down here. You saved my life, which makes me your responsibility for the rest of our lives."

Tessa's heart did a slow, painful flip. It might've been said as a joke, but it sounded awfully good to her.

"So, what's happening at the office? I bet Morris is pissed as hell because I'm stuck in here when I should be concentrating on the new campaign."

"You had major surgery this morning; I refuse to talk shop with you. And if Mr. Montgomery is angry, he'll have to deal, because the only thing you need to concern yourself with is taking your medicine and getting some rest."

"Yes, Mommy."

Tessa grinned at his petulant tone. "Speaking of mommies, do you want me to phone yours and let her know you're in here?"

Ben rolled his head from side to side on the pillow. "She'll just worry over nothing. I'll call her tomorrow when my brain function returns. I wouldn't even bother, except she knew I was moving into my new apartment over the weekend, and if she doesn't hear from me, she'll get concerned."

He closed his eyes and turned his head away. She wondered if he was just tired or if he wanted to conceal his emotions. It dawned on her that she'd discovered another tender side of Ben. Whenever he mentioned his mother, his affection for her sounded in his voice, and Tessa found it touching he was such a caring son. It didn't go with the image he tried to portray of an emotionless womanizer. It spoke of another Ben, a sweeter, caring, Ben.

"Are you tired? Of course you are," she added, preempting his denial. "I'll be on my way."

As she went to stand, he tightened his grip on her hand. His eyes grew ingenuous.

"Kiss me goodbye."

"Ben!"

"Kiss me goodbye."

What could she do? She was responsible for him, and if he needed a kiss, her only choice was to give him one.

His chin and cheeks were raspy with stubble, but he kissed pretty darn well for a guy recuperating from surgery.

****

"Hey, Tessa! I'm glad you stopped by," Ben said as he opened his apartment door to her on Thursday evening. Dressed in sweats and a shapeless T-shirt, he still looked drawn and pale, but his expression was cheerful. "Come in and meet my mom."

"Your mother's here? I won't intrude, then. I just wanted to see how you were doing since getting out of the hospital."

When Tessa started to back out, Ben gripped her arm with surprising strength and tugged her into the apartment.

"Nonsense. Mom wants to meet the woman who took such good care of her boy. Hey, Mom," he called over his shoulder. "Come out here for a sec." Ben turned back to Tessa and winked. "She's in her glory, unpacking and reorganizing my apartment."

A quick glance confirmed that the majority of the boxes that had been stacked in the living room were gone. A petite woman entered the room, and Ben rested an arm across Tessa's shoulders, his movements stiff and careful as he led her over to his mother.

"Mom, this is the friend I told you about, Tessa Caldwell. Tessa, meet my mother, Grace Dunham."

Tessa tucked her gloves into a pocket and extended a hand to Ben's mom. "Pleased to meet you, Mrs. Dunham." Tessa recognized Ben's good looks in the face smiling back at her. The green eyes were an older version of Ben's eyes, the hair was sandy-colored much like Ben's, only heavily threaded with gray.

"Oh, please, call me Gracie." Grace glanced from Ben to Tessa, curious speculation showing in her expression. "Ben has told me so much about you, I feel like I know you, Tessa. Such a nice girl. Come in, come in. Here, let me take that." She reached for Tessa's parka. "Can I offer you a refreshment?"

Tessa caught Ben's eye and bit her lip to stifle a grin. He looked distinctly uncomfortable, as though he

146

couldn't be sure what might come out of his mother's mouth next.

"Thanks, but I can't stay long," she told Grace, more as a way to reassure Ben. "I just wanted to check up on Ben."

"How nice of you." Grace beamed over at Ben. "Isn't that nice of her, honey?"

"That's Tessa. Very nice."

He lifted his eyebrows suggestively, and his mouth curved in a smile that made her blush in response. Thankfully, Grace was busy hanging up Tessa's parka in the hall closet and missed the interaction.

"Behave yourself," Tessa whispered. He lowered himself into the easy chair, the movement clearly causing him considerable pain. She sat on the side of the couch closest to him. "I hope you're not overdoing it."

He pressed a hand to his side and laughed with real amusement. "Are you kidding?" He gestured in Grace's direction. "With the queen of all mother bears here to guard over me? I'm lucky if I get to go to the bathroom by myself. Just joking, Mom," he told Grace as she came further into the room. "You know that, right?" He shook his head at Tessa and mouthed, *I'm not joking*.

Grace placed a hand on Ben's shoulder and smiled at him with doting affection, her indulgent expression telling Tessa she'd long grown accustomed to his quips. "I'll leave you kids to your visit and get back to my unpacking."

Ben's features softened and green lights sparkled in his eyes. "Not for much longer, okay? Those boxes aren't going anywhere, and I won't have you wearing yourself out on my account."

Grace bent to kiss her son's cheek, then smiled at Tessa and left the room. Tessa was glad Grace had come to take care of Ben. It was one less thing for her to worry about while she concentrated on the challenging task of finishing her first big campaign without Ben's valuable input.

As he often did, Ben seemed to read her mind. "Tell me what's going on at the office. How's the campaign going?"

"I've been meeting every day with the creative team, and things are proceeding smoothly. The meeting with the client is set for Monday, although Mr. Montgomery said he's considering bumping it back, or bringing in one of the more experienced senior execs to take over the pitch."

"That's crazy," he protested, jerking forward in his chair. The grimace of pain that flashed across his face didn't deter him. "You know this campaign better than anyone. You should be giving the pitch, not me, and not someone Morris hauls in at the last moment. That's it, I'm calling the office tomorrow to set the stupid bugger straight."

Her face grew hot. She didn't like anyone coming to her defense, while at the same time, the idea of Ben wanting to defend her touched a tender spot deep inside her.

"Leave it alone, Ben. I can handle it."

He leaned back with a scowl. "See that you do, damn it. Because if I have to go in there and kick some oversized Montgomery ass, I will."

"Yeah, right."

Ben's chin came up. "Yeah. Right."

"How long is your mom here for?" Tessa asked to

diffuse the tension and change the subject.

His hand restlessly stroked the arm of the chair. "Until I can convince her I'll survive on my own. And definitely until there's not a single box left to unpack." He shrugged. "Next week, I guess."

"I'm glad she's here."

A reluctant, rather bashful grin tugged at his mouth. "Me, too. She has a very caring nature, my mom. I love her to bits, and I've missed her."

So her instincts had been correct. Ben was a momma's boy at heart. And the thought made him even dearer to her. She sprang to her feet to avoid inadvertently revealing her feelings.

"I should go. I don't want to tire you out."

"You don't have to hurry." He put both hands on the arms of the chair to hoist himself out, then sank back into it, obviously hurting.

Tessa had to stop herself from going over to help him, knowing he'd hate any acknowledgement of his frailty.

"You might as well stay sitting. I do need to leave right away." He ignored her suggestion and slowly stood. "I've another male waiting for me who's feeling mighty ignored with all the attention I've been giving you."

"You do?"

His strangled tone had her heart singing. She shouldn't be so pleased that he sounded just the tiniest bit jealous, but she couldn't help herself.

"Milo."

"Oh, the mutt."

Definitely shades of relief in his voice now, and Tessa ducked her head to hide her smile. "He's a purebred Yorkshire terrier, not a mutt." She retrieved her parka from the closet and called down the hall. "Goodbye, Mrs. Dunham, I mean, Gracie. It was nice meeting you."

Grace appeared in one of the doorways, and she hurried toward Tessa, taking her by surprise with a heartfelt hug. "It was a pleasure to meet you too, Tessa. And thanks so much for getting my boy to the hospital when he needed it. And for visiting him while he was in there. That was very considerate."

"I'm glad I could be of help."

Ben walked Tessa to the door. "Call me tomorrow after the meeting, and let me know what's been decided, okay?" His usually lively eyes were dim with weariness, a sure indication of his low stamina.

"We'll see. You're supposed to be taking it easy, not worrying about office politics." She impulsively rose on her tiptoes and pressed a kiss to his pale cheek. "Feel better fast." Turning quickly, she left before she gave in to the urge to throw her arms around him and hug him tightly.

Ben stood in the doorway between Tessa and his mother. The notion that Grace hadn't witnessed their goodbyes got blown to hell when he turned around and saw the large, pleased smile wreathing her face.

"You care about that girl, don't you?"

"I don't know what you're talking about."

He shuffled over to the couch and slowly lowered himself, holding a hand against the pain in his side. His elation over seeing Tessa was rapidly evaporating, leaving him exhausted. His eyes burned with fatigue, and tension tightened the back of his neck and shoulders. He reached for the TV remote. Before he could switch the set on, his mom sat next to him and removed the remote from his hand.

Her smile faded without quite disappearing. "You don't have to put on an act for me, son. I'm aware of your behavior pattern, how you go from relationship to relationship, always backing out before your heart becomes caught up. This time, you did get caught, didn't you?"

He rubbed his knuckles tiredly along the crease between his eyes, then dropped his hand and tried to smile. "Do you have a point? If so, please get to it. I want to catch the sportscast."

He wasn't up to coping with this conversation tonight. He craved Tessa's company almost constantly, couldn't get enough of her. Not nearly enough. And it wasn't just a sexual thing anymore. He simply wanted to be near her. This was a novel experience for him, not one he necessarily liked, and no way was he explaining that private and confusing revelation to his mother.

"From the moment I got here this morning, I've heard nothing but glowing reports about how great this girl is, how nice she's been to you, how smart and talented she is."

A muscle clenched along his jaw. "Tessa is someone special," he admitted somewhat grudgingly. "But what I feel for her accounts for nothing."

"Why? I've always been inclined to think you're someone special, too." She made a clucking sound of exasperation. "Let her see who you really are. Show her what's behind the face you put on for the rest of the world."

"What's the point? We both know I'm not exactly marriage material. After all, I am my father's son." His fingers strayed to the bridge of his nose, and when he realized what he was doing, he irritably dropped his hand to his lap.

Grace stiffened. "What do you mean by that?"

He closed his eyes, willing himself not to get angry. When he opened his eyes, he was calm and his voice was level. "I mean, my father was an ugly drunk, and he treated you like garbage. Some role model I had."

His mother's eyes clouded with visions of the past. "Your father loved me. He was always sorry afterward."

Ben swallowed a curse. "Don't you dare defend him. Don't you *dare*. You didn't deserve the treatment you got from him, and if I had been bigger or older, he'd never have raised a hand to you. I would've protected you." When he realized he was close to ranting, the fury drained from his body. He felt confused, embarrassed. He shook his head in an attempt to clear it, to repress his anger. "I-I'm sorry. I didn't mean to get angry."

A look of tired sadness passed over his mother's features, and the shadows deepened under her eyes. "You really hated him, didn't you?"

He worked to keep his voice controlled, annoyed with himself for revealing his anger a moment ago. "I didn't want to hate him, but what option did I have? The father I was supposed to look up to beat on my mother when I wasn't around. You know how fast that makes a kid grow up? What kind of things I carried around with me every damn day?"

"You're wrong, Benjie," she said softly. His mom only called him by that childhood name if she was concerned or exasperated. At the moment, Ben guessed, she was probably a little of both.

"About what?"

"About what you're thinking. I see that look in your eyes, wondering, not sure if you're like your father. Afraid you might be."

He didn't speak. He was too busy reassembling his emotions, because her remarks cut way too close to the truth. It wasn't until after his old man had left that Ben's frustration levels began to drop and he'd started to get a handle on his anger. With the memories of those uncontrollable rages never far from the surface, he had good cause to wonder if he could be an abuser like his father. And that was an excellent reason for never getting too close to a woman. He'd rather live out his life alone than risk repeating his father's mistakes.

Warm, gentle fingers closed over his arm. "Kids look for themselves in their parents. And when they see their father being mean and nasty, they don't understand. It's confusing for them. It's only natural for a young man to see himself in his father's image, but you've made a conscious effort not to be like him. And you won't, because there's too much goodness inside you. You're a much better person than you give yourself credit for."

"Can you honestly say you've never been afraid that he lives inside of me, waiting to escape?"

The tense lines of her face relaxed, her eyes grew tender with understanding. "No, never. Never, ever."

That was because she'd never witnessed his ugly side. He, however, was extremely aware of it. And he refused to let himself forget.

An ache started behind his eyes, and he swallowed

hard. "Well, I am afraid, really afraid. There might be a monster hiding inside me, and I can't ever risk letting it out."

Chapter Eight

Tessa turned off the overhead projector and exited the computer program, then glanced swiftly around the conference table, her gaze landing on Morris's stern face, before skittering away to the more friendly features of Janey and Travis. Travis had no place at this meeting, he'd attended to show support for Tessa, and she greatly appreciated his calming presence.

"And that concludes the slide view portion of our presentation," she told the people seated around the table. "As you saw, it covers the four main advertising media: digital, television, radio, and print. The package's design allows the client the choice of going in any single direction or with several. Naturally, we'll highlight the benefits of him choosing all four." She lowered herself straight-backed into the empty chair next to Janey, keeping her demeanor professional. "Does anyone have any questions or concerns?"

This was where, most certainly, Morris would try to take control of the campaign away from her. Why else would he have asked a couple of the highest-ranking executives to sit in on the meeting?

Morris ahemmed importantly and leaned back, folding his hands across his pudgy middle. "Thank you, Tessa. Well done, my dear." His voice dripped with condescension, making Tessa's neck hair stand on end. "Lloyd, Jonathan, do either of you want to contribute?"

Lloyd Greene glanced at Jon Barton, then over at Tessa, and she braced herself for their reaction. If either of them wanted to eliminate her as their competition, this would be the time to make their move. If they chose to cut her presentation to pieces, Morris would undoubtedly ban her from any significant involvement in future campaigns.

"It appears Tessa has thoroughly covered every relevant aspect," Lloyd said, looking thoughtful. "Her pitch was both professional and intriguing. Very cutting edge. I, for one, think she has a winner on her hands."

Jon nodded his head. "I agree. This may be Tessa's first presentation, but I don't see anything Lloyd or I could add to it." He grinned at Tessa. "Great job."

Tessa released the breath she'd sucked in long moments ago and returned Jon's smile, because unlike Morris's empty words of praise, he meant what he said. Both Lloyd and Jon were highly competitive, and they didn't dole out unwarranted compliments.

"Thank you. I appreciate that."

Before she could bask in the congratulations of her colleagues, Morris spoke the words she'd both dreaded and prepared herself to hear. "It is not feasible at this late date to cancel the meeting due to Benjamin's illness, so we will have to carry forward without him. How do your schedules look for Monday morning, gentlemen? Which one of you would care to make the presentation? I need a strong closer."

Ben's face scowled with disapproval in the back of Tessa's mind, reminding her of her promise to stand up for herself. She took a deep breath and held it while she searched for her courage.

Hoping she looked more determined than she felt,

she steadied her voice to say, "Excuse me, sir, but I believe I should be the one to make the pitch. I've worked hard on this campaign. I designed it from the start and know it inside and out. Lloyd and Jon have confirmed I handled the presentation well. Before you consider replacing me, I'd appreciate an explanation of why you don't want me on point."

Morris didn't welcome having his decisions challenged, and his lips compressed with anger at her. He didn't have an acceptable reason for taking the presentation away from her, and this must have irked him even more. He probably hadn't expected her challenge because she'd rarely questioned his directives in the past.

She couldn't back down now. Today was a pivotal point in her career, and the way she handled this situation would impact future outcomes. She deserved to make the pitch, she had the qualifications, and no way would she let Morris dictate otherwise.

Travis lifted his chin, and his eyes disappeared behind his glasses as light flashed off the lenses. "I have to agree with Tessa, Morris. She gave a polished and impressive first-time performance and personally, I found it inspiring. Why promote her to senior executive if it's nothing more than an empty title? She deserves the same rights as the others at her level."

Murmurs of agreement went up around the table, and Tessa's stomach twisted nervously as Morris glared in her direction.

"Fine, if the general consensus is that Tessa should give the presentation, I will concur." Morris rose to his feet. "This meeting is over," he announced in his deliberate manner.

Tessa could scarcely believe he'd agreed so quickly. With a heady sense of unreality, she accepted her colleagues' handshakes. She hurried to gather her supplies together, anxious to return to her office and call Ben with the fantastic news.

"One moment, Tessa," Morris said, effectively puncturing her euphoria. "I would appreciate speaking with you alone." He smiled broadly as he ushered the others from the room. She caught a quick glimpse of Janey's double thumbs-up before he closed the door.

"Yes, Mr. Montgomery. Was there something else you wanted to go over?" Tessa kept her voice calm and her smile pleasant, even though her stomach did a frantic version of the funky chicken.

"Just one thing." His expansive smile disappeared, and he puckered his lips in a distasteful way that made him look like an owl contemplating a plump mouse. "Signing this account is of utmost importance to me. This client has the potential to bring the firm a great deal of future business, and I do not appreciate the way you maneuvered me into allowing you to run the show."

"I'm sorry you feel that way, but—"

"Do not interrupt me, young lady." The cold note of warning in his voice gave Tessa a sinking sense of foreboding. "I want to make something abundantly clear to you. If your lack of competency loses this account for the firm, I will readily, and with great pleasure, return you to your lowly cubicle. Do not doubt for one single moment that if you fail to deliver big on Monday, you will lose the word *senior* from your title. Do we have an understanding?"

Catching herself up, Tessa struggled to stifle her

anger. The unfair conditions were humiliating, and she wished she could tell him exactly where to go and what he could do when he got there. But any attempt to argue would only give him the excuse he wanted to reverse his decision and remove her from Monday's meeting. Summoning all the dignity she could muster under the circumstances, she agreed to his terms.

Janey had waited for her in the hallway, and she fell in step beside Tessa. "You did an incredible job in there. I'm so proud of you, my little chickie. What did Morris want?"

Tessa heaved a sigh. "To go over some conditions for the presentation."

Janey made a small gesture of incomprehension. "Conditions? What do you mean conditions?"

Tessa moved her shoulders in a shrug of anger. "Oh, nothing much. Just that if I don't land this account, I'm busted back to junior executive."

Janey stopped in midstride and turned, surprised disbelief spreading its way across her face. "He can't do that!"

"He just did." Resentment boiled up inside as she recalled Morris's smug tone. "You can be sure he wouldn't have put the same conditions on Ben. And I'm damn sure none of the other seniors had this type of thing happen to them when they first started out." Frustration made her eyes sting, and she blinked hard against it. "You're so darn lucky you don't interact directly with the clients and have that insufferable man breathing down your neck all the time."

Janey followed her into her office and closed the door. "This isn't fair. What're you going to do?"

Tessa dropped her supplies on her desk and rotated

her shoulders, tipping her head back and forth to ease the tension in her neck. Her anger slowly gave way to determination. "The only thing I can do. I'm going to land this account and then enjoy watching every mouthful of crow Mr. Montgomery has to choke down. I don't intend to let him win this one."

Her mind was already busy, going over the minute details of the presentation. What she would wear, how she would stand, the tone of voice she would use. She'd prove her worth to this firm the only way she knew how, the way she'd always had to. By working hard, and being creative and intelligent. She'd prove to everyone that she deserved equal treatment.

Despite her convictions, her victory tasted stale, and she was no longer in any hurry to share the news with Ben.

****

When Tessa answered the knock at her door late Saturday morning, it surprised her to find Ben standing there, dressed in a navy blue ski jacket and a pair of faded jeans. He showed vast improvement over Thursday evening. The color in his cheeks was only partially due to the chilly air, and his casual poise revealed the return of his natural vitality.

"My goodness, Ben. What are you doing here?"

"That's exactly the sort of nice, warm welcome I was hoping for when I walked over to see you."

"I'm sorry. Come on in." She opened the door wider to let him enter. "You walked all the way over?"

He scratched his head and grinned. "If one and a half city blocks—level blocks, mind you—can be considered *all the way over*, then yes, I indeed walked all the way over here." He unzipped his jacket and handed it to her. "Truthfully, I needed to get out of the apartment before I went stir-crazy."

The soft cashmere pullover he wore hugged the contours of his torso, emphasizing the hardness of the body underneath. Tessa had never seen him in jeans, and he looked oh-so-good in them. The well-worn material stretched tautly over powerful thighs and a tight butt, and Ben seemed as at home in them as he did in the expensive tailored suits he wore to the office.

When he caught her staring, she pointed to the crease in his jeans, using that as an excuse for gawking. "You press your jeans?"

Ben's grin turned sheepish. "It's my mom. She irons everything. If I'm not careful to check, she'd even starch my underwear."

"You look good. I mean, ah, you know"—green eyes watched merrily as she floundered with her words—"for someone who just had surgery."

"Are you going to offer me a cup of that excellent coffee I can smell?"

Tessa hesitated. Lauren was home, and Tessa expected her to make an appearance downstairs at any moment. She had a strong reluctance to introduce Ben to her sister. "I suppose so."

"Do try to curb your enthusiasm."

"I'm sorry," she repeated, sounding as stupid as she felt. She was thrilled to see him, or would've been if her sister weren't right upstairs. Her beautiful sister, the one who made men pant with little more than a sultry smile. After witnessing Ben's reaction to Dallas's blatant and sleazy sex appeal, she didn't look forward to his reaction to Lauren's dazzling beauty and alluring sensuality. Especially because Lauren wouldn't be able to resist him. And Tessa couldn't bear to watch Ben become her sister's latest conquest.

She led him down the hall to the kitchen and motioned for him to sit at the table. "How do you take your coffee?"

"Black's good."

Tessa poured two cups and brought them over to the table. "Here you go. Is your mother still in town?"

"She sure is." He shook his head and laughed. "Apparently everything had to come out of the kitchen cupboards, so they could be properly washed out first. I finally managed to talk her into taking a break. She's borrowed my car to shop at some outlet mall."

Milo came in from the backyard through his doggie door. Claws tapped across the kitchen tiles as he rushed at Ben's feet, yipping excitedly.

"Milo!" Tessa admonished, snapping her fingers at him.

"It's okay. I was wondering where the little hairba—, er, fella was." Ben leaned down to scratch Milo underneath his hairy little chin. He glanced back over his shoulder toward the door. "Did it just come in from outside all by itself?"

"Milo's a boy, not an it, Ben. It's okay if you refer to him as such. To answer your question, I had a doggie door installed a few years ago. It took awhile for him to get the hang of it, but now he can come and go as he pleases."

Milo gave Ben's hand a quick swipe with his tongue, then pranced over to greet Tessa, his little body gyrating with pleasure when she reached down to pat him.

Ben straightened in his chair and took a couple

quick gulps of coffee. "You didn't call me yesterday."

"I was supposed to?" Feigning innocence, she gave Milo a few more pats, then told him to lie down.

"I asked if you'd call after the meeting with Morris, remember? How'd it go?"

"Mr. Montgomery decided it was too late to cancel the meeting with the client, and he asked Lloyd and Jon if one of them would handle the pitch. I suggested I should do it, and the others backed me. In the end he agreed." Tessa didn't see the point of telling Ben the part where if she screwed up and lost the account, she'd be busted back to junior ranking.

"I'm glad he came to his senses." Ben drained his mug and lifted it in her direction. "Mind if I have another? Those blasted painkillers make me groggy."

"No problem." Tessa started to rise from her chair to get the coffee pot, but Ben beat her up, surprisingly agile for someone less than a week post-op.

"I'll get it." He set the mug on the counter while he poured coffee into it. "Are you pumped about giving the presentation? You've never done one, have you?" He lifted the mug with one hand, put his other hand in his pocket and leaned back against the counter. His posture emphasized the force of his thighs and the slimness of his hips.

Tessa had to tear her gaze away from his impressive physique and focus on his face. "You know I haven't. I'm nervous, that's for sure, but I'll do okay."

I have to.

Ben took a long swallow of his coffee, watching her over the rim. He set the mug back on the counter and crouched in front of her. "You'll do way better than okay, so have a little faith in yourself, all right?" He took both her hands in his. She was electrically aware of the contact, and it took all her concentration to pay attention to his words instead of the feel of his fingers, strong yet gentle, cradling hers. "You have the brains and guts to accomplish anything you put your mind to."

A pulse began to pound in Tessa's temple, and her mouth went dry. She dipped her tongue out to moisten her lips, and Ben's gaze followed the movement. He took a quick breath in, and it gave her a sudden, burning urge to kiss him. It seemed, as her head slowly lowered in his direction, that he leaned infinitesimally forward to meet her, his fingers tightening on hers, encouraging her.

"Morning," Lauren sang as she entered the room in a cloud of expensive perfume. Milo and Ben both jumped to their feet at the sight of her. Ben remained stationary, while Milo pitter-pattered over to Lauren. "Stay down, Milo. If you run my hose, I swear I won't be held responsible."

Lauren's stern words had Milo doing an abrupt about-face, and he skedaddled over to hide under Tessa's chair. Lauren's eyes developed a distinctly predatory gleam as they lit on Ben. She gave him a once-over, then a twice-over, and softly smacked her lips.

"Hello, there," she drawled when her examination was finally complete.

"Lauren, this is Ben Dunham. Ben, my sister, Lauren." Tessa did the introductions as calmly as she could, despite having knots in her stomach. She clenched her hands until her nails dug into her palms.

Awareness glinted in Ben's eyes as he dropped a subtle glance down Lauren's body, then came back to her face. "Hi." He offered Lauren his hand.

Lauren made no effort to retrieve her hand after they shook. "You're seriously cute, you know that, Ben? And I happen to be a big fan of cute." Her voice contained a provocative note that Tessa couldn't help resenting.

Ben winced, and Tessa wanted to cheer, then he gave an adorable half-smile that confirmed Lauren's 'seriously cute' opinion, and Tessa's heart sank to new depths.

"Thanks...I think." He jiggled his hand free of her grip and glanced over at Tessa. "Mind if I use your bathroom, Tessa?"

"Go ahead," Tessa told him, relieved to get him out of the room, even if only momentarily. "It's down the hall, by the stairs. You can't miss it."

"Yeowza, the boy's a hottie," Lauren said once he'd left. She poured a cup of coffee and added a generous dollop of cream to it. "So, is this Mr. Right or Mr. Right-now?"

"Neither. He's just a friend."

Tessa had little choice but to lie. Lauren wasn't the type of person who inspired confidences, and besides, Tessa didn't know how to classify her relationship with Ben. What could she say? They were former sex partners? That Ben was the man Tessa loved? Her feelings for him were so intimate, so private, she couldn't tell another soul before she admitted them to Ben. And since that day would likely never come, referring to him as a friend became a necessary lie.

"He's the coworker I told you about, the one who had the appendectomy."

Lauren took a sip of her coffee, leaving a smear of

scarlet on the rim. Her smile was appreciative, and she gave a small, sensual shiver of delight. "You forgot to mention he was gorgeous. He has terrific bone structure, doesn't he? With all those interesting planes to his face, I bet he's highly photogenic. Not to mention that fabulous bod. I wonder if he'd let me shoot him?"

Tessa closed her eyes against the sick feeling in her stomach. "You won't know unless you ask." She opened her eyes in time to see Ben return to the room.

"And here he is, right on cue." Lauren fluttered over to him like a delicate butterfly. "I was just telling Tessa I'd love to photograph you, Ben. No charge, of course." She reached up and took his jaw, turning it this way and that, scrutinizing him, then ran a finger along his jawline, flicking it playfully off the tip of his chin. "It'd be my pleasure."

"No, thanks." He backed away, tempering the firm refusal with an amiable smile.

"Oh, please. I do fantastic work, if I say so myself." She batted her eyelashes. "If you don't believe me, ask Tessa."

"I believe you." He retrieved his coffee mug from the counter and plunked himself down at the table next to Tessa. "I just don't see myself as the male model type. Sorry."

Lauren pouted dramatically and looked at her watch. "Oh, pooh, I have to go, or I'll be late again. Anthony hates when I'm late for a shoot. We could make beautiful pictures together, Ben. Let me know if you change your mind." The smiling glance she gave him from over her shoulder was blatantly flirtatious, and she left the room slowly, hips swaying, trailing the heavy scent of perfume in her wake.

Tessa noticed the way Ben stared, almost transfixed, as he watched after her.

"She's quite something, your sister," he said at last, still staring at the doorway she'd just exited.

Tessa dropped her lashes to hide the hurt his words evoked. "Lauren's the complete opposite of me. She's very outgoing and flamboyant. Men really go for her. Appears you're no more immune than the rest of them."

Ben turned to her, surprise clear in his expression. "You think I'm interested in your sister?" he asked, his tone more affirmation than question.

"Aren't you?"

For a terrible moment, he didn't answer, then he hunched forward in the chair. His large hand came up to cup her cheek, and his gaze wandered over her face with a possessiveness she found highly satisfactory under the circumstances.

"Your sister is totally beautiful, I just happen to find you considerably more attractive and infinitely more interesting."

His words vibrated through her, and she had difficulty comprehending what they meant. "Wh-what?"

Ben took his hand back and rested his forearms on the table, his fingers beating a little tattoo on its wooden surface. "Why are you so insecure when you've got so much going for yourself?"

She reached for her cooling coffee and spent an unnecessarily long time taking a sip from it. When she spoke, she formed the words precisely, anxious to give them no special emphasis. "It wouldn't be the first time a man chose Lauren over me. And why not? I can't compare to her." She raised her gaze to find him still watching her, and his squint showed his perplexity.

"A man you cared about dumped you for your sister?"

She suddenly couldn't admit the humiliation of finding out the man she thought she loved hadn't even bothered to tell her he'd moved on with her own sister. There was no need for Ben to learn about her sorry history with men. "I didn't say that. I said men prefer Lauren's looks and personality to mine. Be honest, Ben. She's beautiful and sexy—and I'm, well, I'm not."

"I already admitted she was beautiful. But her beauty is the kind that's polished and primped and perfumed. Yours is all-natural, which makes it far more attractive. Damn it, Tess, after all we've done together—and I'd kill to do again *and* again—how can you possibly think I don't find you sexy?"

This side of Ben's personality was so appealing, and when he looked at her with those sea-green eyes darkened with desire, she could almost believe she might be just the teensiest bit sexy. A wave of emotion swept over her, and her heart nearly burst with the effort it took not to reveal how much she loved him.

She knew, by the depth of her feelings for Ben, that what she'd felt for Colin had been little more than infatuation. That didn't mean her pain at his betrayal was any less real and it had left her with such feelings of inadequacy she'd never fully recovered what little confidence she'd had with men.

"Maybe there was a guy once," she admitted hesitantly, not certain why she'd decided to tell him. "At the time I thought we were in love, then he took one look at Lauren, and it was all over between us." Lifting a shoulder, she shrugged with fake nonchalance.

"It was a long time ago."

Ben scowled. "Not long enough, obviously. The jerk. And that wasn't terribly considerate of your sister, was it? You forgave her?"

Tessa gave another half-shrug, feeling the need to defend her sister despite the pain she'd caused. "Lauren was just being Lauren. I may've been a little bitter at first, but we're sisters. I love her and she loves me, despite our faults." She cast around for something else to talk about. Her gaze settled on the kitchen window. Earlier that morning, there had just been scraps of clouds dotting the sky. Now they were filling in, becoming seamless, and snow had begun to fall. "Look, it's snowing again."

The expression on Ben's face told her that although he'd recognized her evasive tactic, he was sensitive enough to her feelings to go along with the change of subject. "That's what it's doing, all right."

Tessa went to the window, going up on tiptoe and leaning forward to look into the backyard. "It's so pretty."

Ben brought their coffee mugs over and set them by the sink next to Lauren's half-full, lipstick-stained cup. He reached over Tessa's shoulder to shift the curtain away from the window. "I can't freakin' believe this. Isn't it supposed to be March?"

Tessa glanced back at him and couldn't help laughing at his dour expression. "And your point would be?"

He bent closer as he scowled out the window. "My point would be—spring. It should've sprung already."

His breath, scented with coffee and mint toothpaste, drifted warmly across her cheek, and her own breath became tangled in her throat. Leaning back a mere fraction of an inch would place her squarely against his chest. Instead, she pressed into the counter and sidled away sideways. She reached for the mugs and dumped the contents of Lauren's down the drain, then put all three in the dishwasher.

"Technically it is spring. That's why the snow's so soft and pretty. It's spring snow. In the winter, the snow is all crisp and crunchy." She closed the dishwasher door and braced a hip against it. "Say, are you up for taking a walk? Just a little one?"

"Sure. After being stuck indoors for almost a week, some exercise and fresh air will do me good."

Tessa led the way back into the hall and retrieved their jackets from the closet. "You really should wear a toque," she told Ben as she handed him his jacket.

"I don't own a toque. I've never had a need for a toque."

She pulled a knit cap on and tucked her hair under it. "You better get one before next winter or your ears will freeze off. Here"—she reached to the top shelf and took down a blue and green plaid scarf—"put this on. It'll help keep the chill out."

"It isn't necessary," Ben started, then gave in with a tolerant smile when Tessa went up on tiptoe to wrap the scarf around his neck.

Her fingers lingered with pleasure, adjusting the folds of the scarf against the warm skin of his neck, pulling his zipper up another inch. When it became apparent she was touching him just for the sake of touching him, Tessa hastily retreated. She scooped Milo up for a goodbye hug, snuggling his little body close while she explained to him why he wouldn't enjoy walking in the wet snow with her and Ben.

Enormous designer snowflakes floated down around them as they left the house, rapidly covering the sidewalk and everything else in sight with pristine whiteness.

"Isn't this beautiful?" Tessa cried, breathing the bitingly clear crispness deeply into her lungs. She loved walking on snowy days like this, when the temperature was moderate and the wind was negligible. The added bonus of sharing it with Ben only served to make the day all the more perfect.

Ben scooped a handful of snow off a parked car and packed it into a ball. "If you happen to like messy snow."

Tessa made herself a snowball, shaping it easily in her gloved hands. "It's not messy, it's perfect snowball-making snow." She threw the snowball at a tree trunk and missed by a foot.

"You throw like a girl," Ben crowed and, with a casual overhand toss, hit the tree dead center with his snowball.

"And you're a showoff." Tessa quickly formed another ball. She took careful aim, and her snowball exploded against Ben's chest. She half-heartedly attempted to suppress her giggles at his squawk of surprise. "How's that for a girl?"

Before she could back away, he wrapped an arm around her waist and hauled her up against him.

"An unprovoked attack like that calls for a face washing."

"No, Ben," Tessa begged breathlessly. Even through all their layers of clothing, she found herself reacting to the strength of his body against hers. "You might hurt yourself."

Ben scraped a few flakes of snow from his jacket and rubbed them into Tessa's nose. The icy coldness did nothing to cool the heat caused by his touch. "Do you honestly think a little pain would stop me? I'll wrestle you any time, anywhere."

Tessa backed out of his arms before she ended up kissing him right there on the street. It was those ever-changing eyes of his. They made her want things she shouldn't. "Come on, we're supposed to be walking."

They passed Ben's apartment building on the other side of the street and continued on. When they reached the busy intersection at Tenth Street, where traffic crunched slowly along the snow-packed road, they turned and headed back. As they approached the far end of the street, a couple of blocks down, the For Sale sign in Doris Pidlasky's front yard caught Tessa's eye.

"Cross the street. Quick, quick." She tugged on Ben's arm to turn him in that direction. "Look. There's a *sold* sticker on the sign."

"And why would that get you all excited?"

"That house means a lot to me, and it's been sitting empty and forlorn for too many months. Look at it. All it needs is for someone to love it."

On this snow-covered, Christmas-card perfect day, the house didn't look quite as lonely. The branches of the large evergreen in the front yard bent under the snow's weight, and the surroundings were pristine white and sparkling.

"I hope a family bought it. With loads of kids. That'd make Mrs. P happy." She struggled to control her voice, feeling silly that something as inconsequential as a *sold* sign would get her all emotional.

Ben's arm came up to circle her shoulders, and she leaned into him a little as she continued to stare at the old house through misty eyes.

"Care to clue me in to what this is all about?"

She glanced up at him, then back at the house. "This is where I spent most of my time when I was a child, after my mother died. Mrs. P, that's Doris Pidlasky, was more than simply a babysitter. She was a surrogate mom, best friend, and confidante. Oh gosh, I have such great memories of that wonderful lady."

She sniffed and blinked her eyes a couple of times to clear them. "And some recent not-so-pleasant ones too. Mrs. P has been diagnosed with Alzheimer's, and she's in a nursing home now, down at the coast. I miss her a great deal." Her sentence ended on a sob, and Ben's arm tightened, his fingers giving her shoulder a gentle squeeze filled with compassion.

"I'm sorry," he said, his breath warm and reassuring against her brow. "Try to hang on to those good times, okay? And if you ever feel like sharing your memories, I'm here to listen."

Tessa took comfort in the gentleness of his tone, the protective warmth of his arm around her. Talking to him about Doris made her feel better, and holding her the way he was helped more than he could imagine.

She turned in the warm circle of his arm. His creased forehead and the concerned expression in his eyes revealed just how much he cared. She reached up to touch his cheek with a gloved hand. "You've let your secret slip. You really are a gentleman."

He rolled his eyes and laughed, and again, she fought the urge to kiss him. Instead, she did the sensible thing—she took in a deep breath and started for home. By the time they neared her house, the sun had found its way through the clouds, and the snow was already disintegrating into piles of slush, leaving the street a sloppy mess.

"This"—Tessa stepped off the curb and sank ankle deep in slush—"is starting to look more like summer snow. Be careful not to slip."

"*Summer* snow?"

"Uh-huh. We sometimes get snow in the summer. It's as if the skies opened to dump a slushie all over us. Real sloppy. The good thing is, it melts fast."

"Summer snow," Ben muttered darkly, much to her amusement, as he followed her across the street. "Give me a break."

Chapter Nine

"I'm starving, how about you?" Ben asked when they arrived back at Tessa's place. "Wanna get something to eat?"

Tessa took off her parka and gave it a shake before hanging it up. "Won't your mom be expecting you home?" She hung her cap on the closet door handle to dry and ran quick fingers through her hair.

Ben unwrapped the scarf from around his neck and looped it over Tessa's shoulders. He blew on his hands and then rubbed them together. Little droplets of melted snow fell from his hair with the movement. "I'll give her a quick call to check in. Feel like pizza? I've got the pizza delivery guy's number in my contacts. Along with the Chinese food place and just about every other restaurant around here that delivers."

Tessa scooped Milo into her arms to stop his whimpering and let Ben hang his own jacket. She laughed. "Not so big on doing your own cooking, huh? I could throw something edible together, but pizza sounds good. Would you like something hot or cold to drink?"

Ben consulted his watch. "It's time for my medication, so I'll settle for a glass of water."

In the kitchen, Tessa got Ben the water and watched as he removed two different pills from his jeans' pocket and swallowed them down.

Slush had found its way into Tessa's boots, leaving her socks sodden, and the kitchen tile felt cold beneath her damp feet, making her toes curl uncomfortably. "My socks are wet from the walk," she told Ben. "I'm going to run upstairs to change. Are yours okay?"

They both looked down at his feet. Ben wiggled his toes in their thick cotton socks. "Nice and toasty. I'll make those calls while you're busy."

Tessa left Ben to his calls and went upstairs, with Milo following at her heels. She peeled off her damp socks and hung them over the hamper, then dug out a warm pair from a drawer and tugged them on. She made a quick stop in the bathroom to run a comb through her hair. Glancing in the mirror, she paused to examine her face more carefully. Her cheeks were pink from the fresh air, and her eyes shone vibrant blue. Definitely nothing fancy or exotic about her.

Ben had told her she had all-natural beauty. Natural beauty, really? She scrunched up her freckled nose and stuck her tongue out at the reflection in the mirror. Nope, no beauty there. Healthy, maybe, and wholesome in a diminutive sort of way, but still just plain-vanilla.

When she returned to the living room, she found Ben sprawled in the corner of the couch, sound asleep. Milo jumped up beside him to sniff his leg.

"No, Milo, don't," she whispered urgently and picked the little dog up. "Don't wake Ben up. He's all tuckered out."

Tessa curled into the armchair, with Milo on her lap, and watched Ben sleep. Long legs were stretched out in front of him, one hand lay open on his lap, the other rested on the arm of the couch. His head tilted back and slightly to the side, his face peaceful, his full lower lip curved as though he enjoyed his dream.

To be able to drink in the sight of him without his awareness gave Tessa such pleasure, it amazed her. *I truly love this man*, she acknowledged with quiet desperation. Nothing had changed since she first discovered the strength of her feelings. Nothing, including what to do about those feelings—because she couldn't possibly admit anything to Ben.

She didn't even know what he was doing here, and the way he said one thing, while doing another, left her confused. He insisted he didn't want to get emotionally involved, yet he seemed to enjoy spending his free time with her. He told her he didn't believe in romance, and he wanted a physical-only type of relationship, so why was he hanging out at her place on a Saturday, going for a walk with her and ordering in pizza?

None of that meant he had feelings for her, and she wasn't about to confess to anything based on what might be nothing more substantial than a need for companionship.

She had never been comfortable with impulsive decisions. It was necessary to plan things out and proceed carefully with all aspects of her life. And falling in love with Ben was not a part of her plans. It could ruin everything she hoped to accomplish. Telling Ben, putting it all on the line and opening herself up to the risk of rejection? No way. She couldn't do it. It could destroy everything. Their budding friendship. Their professional relationship. Her position at work. All of it could go up in smoke with three little words.

I-love-you.

The doorbell rang, and Milo leapt off her lap, yapping frantically.

"Milo, shush," Tessa hissed and even though he quieted immediately, it was too late. With a bewildered moan, Ben sat up, gazing around as if he had no idea where he was. "Sorry, Ben. I didn't mean to wake you so abruptly. The pizza's here."

"I fell asleep?" Ben asked, jerking to his feet. He rubbed a hand over his face and headed for the hallway, his sleepiness giving him an unsteady gait.

"I'll get some plates and napkins," Tessa said, after they'd paid the delivery boy and sent him on his way. She set the pizza box on a magazine on the coffee table. "Be right back."

Ben stood, staring out the living room window when Tessa returned. His hands were in his front pockets, pulling his jeans tightly across his backside. The shiver that passed through Tessa almost made her drop the tray of plates and soft drinks she carried.

"Here we go," she said, her voice coming out unnaturally high and loud. She placed the tray on the table next to the pizza and told herself to smarten up. "Come and dig in while it's hot."

Ben turned from the window, stifling a yawn. "I can't believe I fell asleep."

"You were tired from our walk."

"That's not it. It's the pills. And I'm not taking them any more. I can't stand the way they mess with my head."

"It's important for your recovery that you take all your medication." She sat on the couch and opened the pizza box, shooing Milo and his inquisitive nose away from it. "The doctor prescribed them for a reason."

"Oh, I'll finish the antibiotics. Just no more painkillers. I don't need them."

Tessa recognized his need to deny anything signifying weakness, and knew it'd be a waste of time to disagree. Besides, a strong, fit guy like Ben probably could manage fine without pain medication. She reached for a slice of pizza, curious about which toppings Ben had chosen. A cursory exam had her dropping it back in the box.

"Eww, yuck!"

Ben joined her on the couch, laughing as he leaned over the pizza box. "What?"

"Anchovies."

He pointed. "They're only on my side."

"Yeah, but they're going to swim right over to my side, you watch."

Ben lifted the slice she had abandoned and bit into it. "Umm, how can you not like anchovies?" he asked around the food in his mouth.

Tessa carefully inspected another slice to confirm it anchovy-free. "They're too...fishy."

"Exactly why I like 'em." Ben polished off the pizza slice with a minimum number of bites and reached for another one. "Got any good movies to watch?"

Tessa set her plate down and went over to the TV stand to rifle through the stack of DVDs. Knowing Ben was a Star Wars fan, she chose a likely candidate from the pile. "How about *Attack of the Clones*? Or have you already watched it too many times?"

"Is there such a thing as watching Star Wars too many times?"

"A man after my own heart."

The words were out before Tessa realized how they might sound. Why did she have to choose those actual words? She didn't mean it literally—even if it happened to be true. She simply meant they both loved Star Wars. And why had Ben suddenly become quiet? What could he possibly be thinking?

With her pulse hammering off the charts, she snuck a nervous glance over her shoulder and almost laughed her relief out loud, her momentary panic now seeming ridiculous. His concentration was focused solely on enjoying his second, or possibly third, piece of pizza, completely oblivious to the implications of what she'd said.

She opened a can of soda and poured it into a glass of ice cubes for Ben, then poured one for herself and settled back against the couch with her feet on the coffee table. Ben lifted his feet up beside hers, only a few inches separating their toes. Tessa stared at their feet, resting intimately next to each other, and she took a long swallow of her soda, trying not to recall the incredible sensuality of having her limbs entwined with his. Barely more than a week ago, right upstairs in her bedroom.

Suppressing yet another shiver, she motioned for Milo to jump onto the couch with them, needing a buffer between Ben's big body and her highly susceptible one. Milo watched Ben as he ate, waiting, ever hopeful, for a morsel to drop so he could pounce on it. When Ben noticed his attention, he picked off an anchovy and offered it to the dog. Milo sat up on his hind legs and begged prettily.

"Good boy," Ben told him as the anchovy disappeared into the little whiskered mouth. "Tell Tessa how tasty that was."

Milo wagged his tail, then comically turned to

Tessa and tilted his head, as though to confirm Ben's opinion.

Tessa couldn't help but laugh. "You're bribing him. Of course he's going to take your side."

"Try a bite," he cajoled, offering her his pizza. "You'll never know whether you like it, if you don't try."

Ben had introduced her to a number of things she'd never tried, and she'd liked them all—was crazy about a few of them—but that wasn't the case this time. "I've tasted anchovies, and I don't like them. And for the record, I always try something before I decide I don't like it."

"Fair enough." He placed his plate on the coffee table and leaned on his elbow toward her. For a long moment, his gaze searched hers, then his head came down to rest on her shoulder. "Do ya want to give necking a try? We haven't just cuddled up and necked." He waggled an eyebrow. "I bet you'd like it."

Tessa swallowed, trying to ease the sudden tension in her throat. Decision time. Did she follow her cravings, her instincts, and kiss this man the way she'd been longing to ever since he'd shown up at her door? Or did she follow her principles—that annoyingly rational part of her mind she'd begun to hate—and put a stop to this before it got out of hand?

Principles won the short battle with desire once Tessa reminded herself that she was the kind of woman who had to give her heart along with her body. She had been such an emotional mess after her experience with Colin, and Ben could shatter her heart a million times worse. Unlike with Colin where her self-esteem, more than her heart, had taken a battering, this pain would be real and long-lasting.

She slid her shoulder out from under Ben's head, moving away to put some much-needed distance between them. "You're in no condition for hanky-panky, even if I were inclined to go along with you. Which I'm not. So behave and watch the movie."

Relief felt an awful lot like disappointment when Ben sat back up without arguing. They remained sitting close together, side by side on the couch, watching the movie. Milo lay with his head worshipfully on Ben's leg, soaking up the attention Ben absentmindedly gave him.

Tessa watched from the corner of her eye as Ben picked off small pieces of cheese to feed to the eager dog. When the pizza was gone and Ben set his plate to the side, Milo returned his head to Ben's leg with a little groan of contentment. Ben reached down, his large hand entirely covering the small head. His fingers lazily caressed a silky ear, and if Milo had been a cat, he'd be purring like a blender.

If those talented fingers were doing the same thing to her, she'd purr too, she didn't doubt, and she wondered if she should feel jealous. The real question was, jealous because Milo had shifted his allegiance over to Ben or because Milo was receiving the attention and caresses she craved for herself? If only she could snuggle up against that strong chest and have his arm around her, his hand gentle in her hair.

Ben dropped back onto his elbow, shifting even closer to Tessa, near enough for the evocative tang of his cologne to tantalize her senses. She caught herself squirming and tried to drag her wanton thoughts off the white-hot thrills coursing through her body by concentrating on the movie. It was at a favorite part, where Obi-Wan and Anakin chase the assassin into the space nightclub. Besides being an amusing scene, it showcased Ewan McGregor, wearing those yummy white pants and high boots. Beard or not, the man was one heck of a hottie.

Problem was, the flesh-and-blood male sitting next to her was also one heck of a hottie.

"Did you catch that?" Ben asked with a laugh, referring to a play-on-words that only a true Star Wars aficionado would get.

"I did." She also caught the way Ben's laugh had her overly-receptive nerve endings tingling with awareness. It suddenly seemed excessively warm in the room. Would it be too obvious if she up and moved to the armchair?

Some of those Jedi hypnotizing tricks would come in handy right now. Imagine if she had the ability to convince Ben to rethink his life, ultimately concluding that he was tired of empty relationships and ready to explore a deep, meaningful commitment with the woman who was perfect for him. And that woman just happened to be Tessa, of course.

Now, she really was losing her marbles, and she'd be better off using those mind tricks on herself. A very powerful one that would brainwash her into believing Ben held no appeal to her. He'd simply become a coworker and friend, nothing more—definitely not the sexiest man alive, who had taken control of her heart, not to mention her treacherous libido.

She glanced down at Ben's hand resting inches away from her thigh. She could almost feel the electricity flowing from his fingers, those long, sensual fingers that were capable of creating absolute magic when they touched her. *Not what you're supposed to be thinking about, Tessa. Watch the movie. Look at Ewan. Forget about Ben sitting next to you. Right next to you.*

Oh, lordy.

Somehow, she made it through to the end of the movie without surrendering to the palpable sexual tension radiating between her and Ben. When the credits rolled onto the screen, she reached for the remote with a sigh of relief.

"Well, that was nice."

Nice? Not bloody likely. She'd not only found no enjoyment from one of her favorite films, she could barely recall watching it.

Ben lifted her hand off her lap and raised it to his lips, his touch sending shockwaves of delight reverberating along every nerve. He kissed each finger, her palm, then pressed his mouth to the tender skin of her inner wrist.

"What should we do now?" His voice dropped an octave, taking on a disturbingly husky note. "Wanna get naked?"

At times, he seemed capable of reading her thoughts, her emotions, practically before she knew them herself. It came as no surprise that he recognized her mood. When she opened her mouth to reprimand him, he leaned in, then stopped inches away from her lips. Just when she thought he wouldn't do it, he captured her lips in a kiss that sent her heart soaring and her body aching.

His mouth was firm and moist, and it demanded a response. His tongue, insistent and probing, was an exquisite invasion she eagerly welcomed. For a long, glorious moment, she gave in to her need for him, greedily drinking in the sweetness of his kisses, the intimately wondrous touch of his hands on her body. Then, with desperation, she pushed him away.

"I told you I wouldn't do this and I meant it. I don't want this type of relationship."

Ben threw his head against the back of the couch with a loud sigh of frustration. "What do you want? Romance and flowers? Because if you're looking for romantic love, the place to find it is in a bookstore, in the poetry section. Only a fool thinks it can be found in the real world."

This sounded like a man forcing himself to believe his own words. "You're wrong. True love really exists."

"Yeah, and I believed in the tooth fairy once too. Then I grew up."

Time for a little prying. "I don't believe you. I think you won't allow yourself to love and be loved back. Why? Why won't you?"

Ben's gaze darted away, something darkening those wary green eyes. "You don't know what you're talking about."

"Don't I? The night I stayed with you at your place, you told me that you and I sleeping in each other's arms felt right. That it was the way it always should be."

Ben's head jerked sideways, and he spat out a heated curse. "I don't remember saying that. I obviously wasn't in my right mind, because of the fever."

Tessa wondered if he really didn't remember, because although he seemed annoyed by her revelation, he didn't appear surprised.

"That was my reasoning at the time, too. Then I got to thinking. You never say you don't want a commitment. You say you don't do them, or it's not your style. That's completely different. So tell me why you think you can't have a relationship. The truth."

He made an impatient gesture, then dropped his hand. "Okay, I admit what I want and what I can have are sometimes two different things." His voice developed an unsure quality not typical of him. "Sometimes a person can't have something, no matter how much they want it." The hesitation in his words was slight, only the tightening of the muscles in his throat betrayed strong emotion. "That's the way it is with me."

Tessa hadn't expected him to admit anything, and as much as she appreciated his acknowledgement, she didn't understand what he meant. "You'll have to explain that one. Please."

He slumped back against the couch, and Tessa could feel him drawing into himself, putting up protective barriers against her probing. He sat there unmoving, totally unapproachable. She'd never seen him like this, and it worried her.

She laid a hand on his arm. "Ben? Hey, come on. Let's talk about this." He didn't answer, and as the silence began to stretch, she wondered if he'd even heard her. "Why do you think you can't have what you want? What happened to make you feel that way?"

He shivered and fixed his gaze on a point above their heads as though looking at her disturbed his thought process.

"Ben?" She shifted to face him, her back against

the arm of the couch, her leg tucked underneath her. Growing more worried by this uncharacteristic demeanor, she took his chin in her hand, tilting his head in her direction. "Look at me. Talk to me. Tell me what's made you so commitment-shy."

He pushed her hand away, but kept his gaze locked on hers. His shoulders hunched forward, and his eyes, dark brooding green, held traces of guilt and confusion. "Maybe there are a few things about my past that prevents me from moving forward. My old man wasn't much of a role model, after all. But, look, I'd rather eat worms than psychoanalyze myself."

"I'm not asking you to analyze anything. I'd like to hear more about your relationship with your parents though, if you don't think I'm overstepping." She had always wondered about his background, but the few times she'd asked, he had put her off without outright refusing to answer. She'd come to the conclusion he didn't like personal questions. And he seemed reluctant to go into detail now. She touched his leg lightly. "Please."

"I try not to think about my childhood. I don't like to remember what my mom endured."

"You mean living with an alcoholic?"

"That, yes. And so much more. My father was a demanding and critical man. Mom has always been anxious to please, easily manipulated. Way too many times he used her as his personal punching bag, but if I confronted her about the bruises, she'd make excuses for him, say it was her fault."

"What a horrible man," Tessa exclaimed, forgetting for a moment he was Ben's father. She had no idea Grace Dunham's husband had abused her.

She'd seemed like a warm, caring person who'd be easy to love.

Ben looked away into an upper corner of the room, sitting very still and stiff. His eyes were the only part of his face that seemed alive, full of memories, brimming with emotion. His deep breath had a ragged edge and so did his voice when he spoke. "Horrible just about describes him, yet my mom was like a puppy, crawling and practically licking his feet. 'I'm sorry,' she'd say, 'I'll do better. I love you.' The dude had bloody well hit her, and she was the one begging his forgiveness. He'd tell her he loved her too and all was forgiven. Until the next time."

He paused, tilting his head slightly, his eyes still focused on the corner. "It made me sick to my stomach listening to them. Even though I felt sorry for her, she frustrated the hell out of me too. A part of her must've loved him to put up with all the abuse, although I can't fathom why, because he also frightened her. I certainly was scared of him. So scared of setting him off. And then, at some point, I simply grew angry."

It touched Tessa to see the confident man seated next to her grow hesitant and embarrassed by his own words. Her mouth softened as he fidgeted self-consciously with the tassel of a pillow near his elbow. He shook his head and closed his eyes, his face reflecting his disgust.

"Tell me about it," she urged softly.

"Forget it, Tessa." He rubbed a hand across his eyes. "It's the medicine talking."

"Oh no, I'm not letting you off that easily. If the medicine has started talking, let it finish."

"There are places in me, even I won't visit. I'm

sure as hell not going to take you there." His face was stiff, overly controlled. His expression didn't match his tone, and his tone didn't match his words. His hand strayed to his nose, where one finger touched his crooked bridge absentmindedly, and Tessa's stomach took a sudden sickening dive as an awful realization hit her.

"Oh my gosh, your dad hurt you too! Did he—" She had to stop and swallow down the urge to cry. "Was he the one who broke your nose? Is that why you won't talk about it?"

His hand jerked away from his face and disappeared into his jeans' pocket. For a long moment, he sat silent, frozen into position, his eyes a curious mixture of loathing and fright. Tessa ached to comfort him, to soothe the confused little boy hiding inside the shell of a handsome, self-assured man. She suspected there was a lot more to his story, all she could do was hope he trusted her enough to share it.

Images and words wove swiftly in and out of Ben's mind. They were ugly and painful, and he didn't want to think about them, much less talk about them.

He sighed and focused on nothing in particular. "You don't want to hear my sob story."

"Look at me," Tessa insisted, and with reluctance he gave her a sidelong glance. All her attention focused squarely and alertly on him. He couldn't recall anyone ever meeting his gaze as unwaveringly as she did, and her concern affected him deeply. He appreciated it even while it made him uncomfortable. She leaned closer and gave his knee a brief touch. "If you truly have a sob story to tell, let me be the one to hear it. Trust me enough to tell me the truth."

He wavered, doubts sweeping over him. If he admitted his dark past—the secrets, the helplessness, the shame—what would she think of him? How could he explain his childhood to her? She had never lived with a drunken father. She knew nothing about the violence, the rages, the blackouts and broken promises of an ugly alcoholic.

Ben shut his eyes, suddenly drained. What the hell, if she wanted to know, he'd tell her.

"Yes, my father broke my nose. He'd give me a good cuff every so often, but that was the first and last time he really clobbered me. I came home to find him slapping my mom around. She was crying, begging him not to hurt her, and he wouldn't let up. All my anger and frustration up to that point didn't come close to the rage that overtook me when I saw what he was doing to my mother," he told Tessa, putting into words the ugly images behind his closed eyes. "I pulled him away from her, swinging wildly, trying to connect a punch, trying to obliterate him. But what did a shrimpy fourteen-year-old know about fighting a full-sized, angry drunk of a man?"

A trembling started in his hands, a throbbing in his temples. Reliving that night made him physically ill. The impotent fury that seethed through the young man as he tried to attack his own father. The wrathful, remorseless expression the grown man wore as he ruthlessly plowed his huge fist into his own son's face. The pathetic screams of the hysterical mother as she forced her way between them, shielding her bleeding child with her own small, defenseless body.

"Ben? You're not breathing. Are you all right?"

The concern in Tessa's voice and the soft touch on

his arm somehow got through to him, and he released a long-pent breath. "Sure, yeah, I'm okay." *What a lie*.

Tessa stared, wide-eyed with shock. "What happened then?"

"My father knocked me on my pathetic butt with a single punch, and my mom threatened to call the cops unless he left and never came back. The woman had been a prisoner of fear for more years than I care to think about and couldn't stop the abuse for herself, yet she found the strength to do it that night to protect me." He shook his head, still unable to believe how easy it had been. "That's all it took. If only I had known."

Completely embarrassed by such personal revelations, he fell into an uneasy silence. He felt wary and exposed, wondering if Tessa thought less of him. Until now, he had kept his past a well-guarded secret, unable to speak of it to anyone. Women might say they liked men to drop their macho defenses and show their inner selves, but Ben didn't believe they would find the weakness he'd shown even slightly admirable.

Tessa reached out and squeezed his shoulder, rubbing it, offering comfort and compassion. He doubted she had any idea how much that simple gesture meant to him.

"How awful that must've been for you and your mother. You sure got a raw deal in the dad department. I'm sorry, but a man who can't control his anger around women and children is less than a man."

Agreed, Ben thought miserably. Not a man, but a beast. And that was why he never drank, afraid that liquor might release the rampant animal hiding inside, just as it did with his father, turning him into a violent monster who enjoyed beating on defenseless women.

"I never saw him again," he said, barely able to speak through the tightness in his throat. "He got drunk one night not long after and wrapped his car around a tree. If I was supposed to feel sorrow over his death, I didn't. I felt relief. Relief that it was over, finally and forever. My mom could forget about him and get on with her life."

"Ohhh..." Tessa sighed, her voice trailing off uncertainly.

Ben started guiltily, in his self-absorption he'd almost forgotten she was listening. He could see that tears were perilously close, and he didn't deserve to have Tessa cry over him. "I'm sorry, Tessa. I don't usually talk like this."

She squeezed his shoulder again, her hand coming up to touch his cheek. "No need to apologize. I know it wasn't easy for you to tell me. Every bit as much as your mother was a victim, you were too—a small defenseless victim, yet you seem to carry a burden of shame because you couldn't fix the problem. You have to let those feelings go. You did nothing wrong."

Ben listened, his gaze riveted on the coffee table, staring at nothing, but staring intently. He wanted with all his heart to believe her words were true. If only it was as uncomplicated as she made it sound.

"This doesn't explain why you think you can't have a relationship. If it's because your parents had a bad marriage, so you think you might too, things don't work that way."

His frustration surged. After everything he'd just revealed, Tessa still wanted to know why he couldn't commit. Why he avoided serious relationships. Telling her the truth should be enough to send her screaming into the street, wanting nothing more to do with him. He couldn't quite make that final admission—how when he looked in the mirror, he was terrified he might see his father's face looking back.

It had probably been a mistake coming here today. It definitely was a mistake to open up the way he had. He'd most likely lost a lot of ground with Tessa, respect he might never recover, but in order for them to work successfully together, he had to maintain some semblance of credibility. To tell her anything more would kill all hope of that.

"Look—" He fought to keep his voice level. "I gotta get home. My mom was taking a nap after lunch, tired from her shopping, and I'm sure she's awake by now. I don't want her worrying."

He rose abruptly to his feet, putting a stitch of pain through his side and startling Milo, so the dog jumped from the couch with a disgruntled yelp.

Tessa followed him from the room and down the hall. "I'm sorry if what I said upset you, but this conversation's not finished yet."

Although he struggled to keep his anger in check, he could feel control slipping away from him. "No, you know what? I'm sick of talking. There's nothing more to say." Ignoring the flash of hurt that crossed her face, Ben stuffed his feet into his boots without lacing them up and pulled his jacket on, zipping it as he left the house.

He was his father's son, he reminded himself, as he trudged through the melting slush, and somewhere inside of him, there was a bomb waiting to go off. The proof of this was in the mindlessly violent way he'd reacted the night he found his father hitting his mother.

He hadn't been physically capable of hurting his father that night, although if he had been, he willingly would have. And that destructive, despicable feeling was something he'd have to live with every day for the rest of his life.

****

Despite the fact her heels killed her feet, Tessa could barely restrain from skipping down the hall to her office after the presentation. Still high on the adrenaline rush of success, she mentally reviewed each step of her pitch, proudly reliving her performance. She couldn't wait to get to a phone and share the good news with Ben.

Unfortunately, it hadn't been all smooth sailing. Morris had shown up to sit in on the meeting, something he rarely did, leading Tessa to believe he only did it to remind her of their deal. Lloyd and Jon had attended, also. Morris must've asked them to be there in case she needed to be pulled from a hole she might dig herself into. But she'd been too focused and too determined to let her boss's petty little games undermine her confidence, and it had paid off in spades.

Pearce Jeffries, the restaurateur, had been a dream to work with. His vision for his restaurant meshed excellently with the campaign Tessa had designed for him, and it hadn't been difficult to get him completely onboard. It had taken exactly one half hour to sign her first major account.

As soon as the office door closed behind her, Tessa kicked off her pumps. "Ohh, thank goodness," she moaned with relief, walking with careful little crippled steps as the blood surged back into her cramped toes. She lived for the day when she could throw out every single pair of torture devices she owned and never again wear anything higher than one-inch flats. She had no one to blame for continuing to put up with the discomfort except her own foolishness and a lack of confidence in the power of her femininity.

"Why do you insist on wearing those stupid things if they hurt your feet?"

"Oh my gosh, Ben! Hi." She picked up the offending pumps and set them out of the way, beside the computer table. "What are you doing here?"

Ben rose from his chair and came around the desk. "I work here." A quick smile touched his lips, then just as quickly disappeared. "This is still my office, isn't it?"

"Of course it is. I just wasn't expecting you." She took in his casual attire, a gorgeous fisherman knit sweater matched with dark brown cords. A brown leather jacket lay on top of his desk. "You don't look dressed for work. Besides, it's way too soon for you to think about coming back."

"I dropped Mom off at the airport and had some time to kill before I'm due at the hospital to get the staples removed, so I thought I'd stop by to see how the presentation went. And?"

"Great," she bubbled. "Pearce Jeffries loved my ideas—our ideas, I mean. With only a few minor adjustments, he wants the whole enchilada. Can you believe it? Mr. Montgomery sat in on the meeting, as did Lloyd and Jon. But I didn't let it shake my composure. I took a few deep breaths and remembered all the good advice you'd given me and before I knew it, the presentation was over, and everyone was smiling and shaking my hand. It was the most incredible feeling in the world."

Somehow, she managed to get a small grip on her excitement. "Excuse me for babbling on. I think I'm drunk on my own success. There's no way Mr. Montgomery can carry out his threat to bust me back to junior level now that I delivered on this account."

Ben's eyes widened and his teeth dug into the fullness of his lower lip. An expression Tessa couldn't decipher came over his face. Anger? Shock? Disappointment? She couldn't be sure what, beyond recognizing it as a strong emotion, something brief and raw that flashed on for a second before being covered by one of his smooth salesman smiles. He stepped forward to clasp both her hands briefly in his.

"That's wonderful, Tess. Marvelous. But I can't take any of the credit. It was you in that room, all by yourself. This is your accomplishment."

"Are you okay?" Tessa asked, her exhilaration rapidly evaporating. Something was definitely bothering him, and she wondered if last Saturday's discussion at her place had made him feel awkward.

His smile slipped a notch. "Why wouldn't I be okay? You just gave me some fantastic news. I'm so happy for you," he said with a shade too much emphasis.

Tessa crossed her arms and cocked her head, eying him carefully. "You seem, I don't know—like something's off. Are you sure everything's all right since we talked last?"

"I haven't taken any pain medication since Saturday, and I feel like myself again." He blew out a quick breath. "Sorry I can't stay and celebrate your success. I have to get to my appointment now. We'll talk real soon, okay?"

Tessa had meant whether he felt comfortable with her after opening up about his past, but she got the impression he deliberately chose not to understand her.

Before she could find the words she wanted, he scooped his jacket off the desk and bounded out of the office. She stood in place, staring at the door for the longest time. Ben evidently wanted to act as if he hadn't revealed anything personal, and while she didn't like it, she could accept it. It didn't explain, however, the curious reaction he'd shown when she told him she'd landed the account. If she didn't know better, she'd have sworn he wasn't happy about it.

But why?

Chapter Ten

Tessa slipped her sketchbook into the top desk drawer. She stole a glance at her watch, then over at Ben, working at the computer table. She had a dinner engagement with her dad and Lauren shortly, but she was torn between leaving and staying with Ben. He had no business returning to work a mere week after his surgery, and it troubled her that he might be overdoing things.

Despite her protestations, he had immersed himself in the Jeffries account when he unexpectedly showed up at work bright and early Tuesday morning, and Tessa knew that even if she skipped her dinner, Ben wouldn't want or need her help making the final changes.

He must've sensed her scrutiny because he turned and glanced over his shoulder. "Shouldn't you be heading out?"

She rubbed the heel of her hand against her forehead, fighting the stress headache that had pulled at her the past few days. "I'm not happy about leaving you here to work late. You shouldn't even be back on the job yet."

Ben scowled and swiveled in his chair to face her. "We already discussed this. If I can get the last of the revs done tonight, we might be able to get Jeffries to sign off on this campaign tomorrow. Go enjoy your dinner with your dad, and stop worrying about me."

She *was* worried about him though, and it went far deeper than the fact he had returned to work too soon. The perpetually teasing light had disappeared from his eyes, and he hadn't once attempted to flirt with her. Since their brief meeting on Monday, he'd handled her with careful consideration, overly polite and professional, as though they were nothing more than business acquaintances. He gave her no option but to treat him the same way.

And all this forced composure drove her crazy. Instead of being properly grateful he'd finally ceased his constant come-ons, she couldn't stop obsessing over why he'd changed toward her. Was it regret over what he'd revealed about himself, or did it have to do with her signing Jeffries without him? Either way, something significant had shifted between them, and she mourned the loss of their friendship.

"Maybe I should stay until we've run over everything one more time," she suggested. "Just to make sure we haven't overlooked anything."

"That'll make you late. You don't think I'm capable of wrapping this up on my own because it was your presentation, is that it?"

"No—no, of course not. I just..." The determined set to his jaw told Tessa she'd get nowhere trying to voice her concerns. "I feel as if I'm deserting you. That's all."

"I told you I'd handle it. Now go, and let me get back at it." Without waiting for her reply, Ben turned back to the computer screen and immediately appeared engrossed in his work.

"Fine then," Tessa told the back of his head. She

only agreed because her father was a real stickler for punctuality. Even the chronically tardy Lauren rarely risked his ire by arriving late.

With her desktop cleared to her satisfaction, she fetched her heels out from under her desk and started from the office. She pulled the door closed behind her and as she turned, she spotted Dallas hovering in the hallway nearby. It was obvious the woman had been waiting for her to leave before approaching the office, and it made Tessa wonder what she was up to. When Dallas attempted to step past her to reach the door, Tessa held her ground in front of it.

"What do you want?" She didn't bother with pleasantries. They'd be wasted on Dallas anyway.

"I need to see Ben. It's important."

Important? Dallas was more transparent than the see-through blouse she wore, and Tessa could guess how important it was. "What about? He's busy."

"If it were any of your business, I guess I'd be here to see you, wouldn't I?"

"Eww, stinging comeback." Tessa waved a hand at the closed door. "He's in the office. Help yourself."

Dallas's smile oozed poison. "I plan to."

Tessa frowned and resisted the urge to follow her back into the office. Despite knowing it was none of her business, if time constraints weren't against her, she'd have made a point of finding out what Dallas wanted with Ben. But time was against her, and despite her misgivings about leaving Ben alone with that man-eater, she had to leave, now.

****

The office door opened and closed behind Ben, and the tension immediately cranked it up a notch in his already tight neck muscles. Why did Tessa have to come back? He could barely concentrate with her around, and the past three days since he'd returned to work had been hell on him. He'd been looking forward to a few hours of peace and quiet, to get some actual work done without the distraction of her worried blue eyes following his every move.

He had irrevocably changed the way she saw him since his insane confession last weekend, and he deeply regretted that fact. He wished he'd kept his big trap shut. He shouldn't have felt compelled to talk about a topic so personal, something he never discussed with anyone. Now he had to distance himself from her, and he'd had no idea it'd be this difficult.

It'd be much simpler if they didn't work in such close proximity, but they did, so he had to find a way to deal with it. Maybe, just maybe, he could arrange it so they didn't have to share an office, at least. That'd take a little pressure off him. Until the present situation improved, he had to keep his mind—and his hands—on work and off Tessa.

"Did you forget something?" He wheeled around to see Dallas, not Tessa, sashaying across the room toward him. "Oh hey, Dallas. I thought you were Tessa."

"That's not a mistake too many people make."

The intended slur against Tessa irritated him, and he didn't bother to hide it. "Is there something I can do for you? Because, to be honest, I'm swamped."

She favored him with the practiced, intimate smile he'd come to recognize as second nature to her when speaking to men. "I haven't had a chance to give you a proper welcome back." Her fingers smoothed over his sleeve, and she watched him through slanted tiger-eyes.

201

Joyce M. Holmes

"I heard you've been sick, yet here you are, looking all virile and handsome, like you'd be up for just about anything."

There was no doubting the innuendo behind Dallas's words, nor the caressing motion of her hand along his arm. Ben eased his arm away and rolled his chair back a few inches.

"The only thing I'm up for at the moment is working on this account. Thanks for checking on me."

She moved away like a restless panther on the prowl, and for a split second, Ben wondered if he was a fool for not wanting what she had to offer.

With a provocative twist of her body, Dallas eyed him from over her shoulder. "Phooey. You know what they say about all work and no play?" She glided back toward him. "How about it? You, me, and some mind-blowing sex. Right there on that couch."

Ben shook his head, gaping at her in disbelief. It didn't matter how many times he told her he wasn't interested, she kept coming back for more. Much the same way he used to be with Tessa. Only difference being, he *knew* Tessa cared about him, hell, maybe even wanted him, in a way he'd never want Dallas.

Dallas nudged her hip against his shoulder. "Close your mouth before flies get in. You know what I'm saying makes perfect sense. Neither of us wants a relationship, just some good old down and dirty. So what do you say?"

His jaw clinked shut, and he gave his head a mental shake. What was going on here? A gorgeous redhead was offering him exactly what he wanted, a strings-free liaison of fun and pleasure, and he had no inclination to take her up on it. How weird was that?

"Uh, Dallas..." He brought both hands to the sides of his head, rubbing his temples with his fingers. "I'm flattered, I am, but I've told you I'm not in the market for what you're offering. You're a beautiful, desirable woman; men must trip all over themselves to be with you." He rolled his head left and right, trying to work the knot of tension out of his neck.

"Look at you," she cooed. "You've been working too hard. Here, let me make it all better." She moved behind his chair, touching the back of his neck, massaging gently.

If he had a lick of sense, he'd tell her to stop. She didn't need any encouragement. He was so tired and, damn, whatever she was doing back there felt good. He relaxed into the padding of his chair, letting his head roll forward to facilitate her massage.

"You like that?"

"Ummm," he murmured. Hell, yeah, he liked it. The tension was melting away like an ice cube on a hot July afternoon.

She took his head in her hands, pulling him back against the softness of her breasts, her fingers working their magic on his temples. "I know something else that's guaranteed to relax you. All we have to do is lock the door." She brushed the top of his head with her lips and slid her fingers over his shoulders and down his chest.

Lock the door? What the hell was he thinking, letting things go this far? Dallas certainly didn't need any unintentional encouragement on his part. He jerked his shoulders, derailing her hands from their southern journey.

"Don't."

She gave him a smile of such calculated charm, he felt a sudden sharp yearning for Tessa's guileless sincerity. "Why not? Come on, Ben. We could have such fun, if you'd just go with it."

He was nuts, totally and officially nuts, because for some incredible reason, he found what Dallas was doing, what she was saying, a complete turn-off.

"The only thing I'm interested in at the moment is my work. So if you'll excuse me."

She knew how to use those full, overly-glossed lips to her best advantage, pouting prettily because she wasn't getting her way. "You're no fun. What's wrong?" Her eyes narrowed. "Don't tell me you're involved with someone?"

When had he changed his mind about what he wanted from a woman? When did the idea of casual, meaningless sex become so abhorrent? Had the confusing and unwanted emotions Tessa stirred up in him gone and ruined what had once been a perfectly satisfying sex life?

"There's no one else." He didn't allow himself to wonder if he'd lied. "And that's the way I want it. I have my career to focus on." At least that much was true. Doing his best to ignore the way Dallas hung over his shoulder, he refocused on the computer screen.

"Are you seriously going to sit there and work?" she whined from behind him.

He grunted an affirmative and continued to ignore her, figuring she'd eventually get the hint and leave.

"Little Tessa is quite the artist," Dallas said a few moments later, using her sugar and arsenic tone. "Have you seen her sketches? They're very enlightening."

Ben whirled around in his chair. He'd almost

forgotten Dallas was still there. She had wandered over to Tessa's desk and was flipping through her sketchpad.

"Get away from there. You have no business going through Tessa's stuff."

She closed the pad and dropped it on Tessa's desk. "Don't get defensive. It was sitting right here in plain sight."

Tessa never left any work material on her desktop when she left for the night. It was one of her little quirks. "Leave, okay, Dallas? You've made your pitch, and I explained my position. Again. There's no point sticking around."

Dallas sauntered back over to him. She propped her shapely rear against the computer table and leaned in to rest her hand on his thigh. Her lethally-tipped fingers tap-danced a little higher, those feline eyes of hers suddenly glittering and dangerous. She smiled a sly, spiteful smile. "I always get what I want, Ben. That's the kind of woman I am, and it's time you figured that out."

Before he could tell her it'd never happen, she pivoted and left, hips swaying provocatively with each step. Ben let loose a stress-releasing laugh and turned his attention back to the computer screen, but he couldn't help thinking there was something not quite right about that woman.

****

"I want to see you in my office immediately, Tessa."

"Of course, Mr. Montgomery. I'll be right there," Tessa replied and hung up the phone.

The overly stern tone of her boss's voice gave her an ominous sense of impending trouble, and she wondered what bee had got up his butt now. A quick glance at her watch revealed it wasn't even one o'clock. Morris was famous for his long Friday afternoon lunch hours, so to disrupt his routine must mean it was serious. The only reason she'd been at her desk to take the call was because she had worked through her lunch break to catch up on some matters that had been shuffled to the side while she focused on the Jeffries pitch.

Tessa fumbled for her shoes, which were lost under her desk as usual, and hurried to step into them. Morris's door stood open when she arrived at his office; however, he preferred his employees to knock and wait to be asked in.

"Enter, Tessa, and do close the door behind you." It was not so much an invitation as an order.

Tessa shut the office door and approached his desk. He peered owlishly up at her. A hand rubbed over the balding crown of his head, then he licked his lips quickly, a sure signal she was about to get a lecture. What it was about this time, she couldn't even hazard a guess.

"I had the most perturbing discussion this morning with one of your coworkers. It was such a disturbing conversation, in point of fact, it necessitated cutting my lunch short in order to deal with it promptly."

Still standing because he hadn't invited her to sit, Tessa studied Morris's face as she considered what this could be leading up to. His customary dour expression gave no hint of his thoughts, but she got the impression he might be enjoying this exchange, despite the severity of his words.

"It was a curious tale, a curious tale indeed. It

would seem as though some serious impropriety has been occurring within the company for some time, and it has elevated to such a level that it became necessary to have the situation brought to my attention. I immediately recognized that such a critical lack of decorum must be dealt with posthaste."

Morris Montgomery could never settle for using one simple sentence when half a dozen long-winded ones would do, and he spoke in the manner of a schoolteacher lecturing a class, even though Tessa was his sole audience. She bit back a sigh, wishing he'd get to the point, but experience told her it wasn't in her best interest to interrupt.

"We have rules for such behavior here, and all the employees are well aware of those rules. They are in place to prevent this exact type of incident from occurring. Would you care to make a venture as to what that impropriety might have been?"

This sounded serious, and Tessa leaned forward, clasping and unclasping her hands. She wished she could sit down, but refused to ask for permission. "I can't imagine, sir."

"A grievous accusation has been lodged against you, Tessa. From my understanding, it would appear you have been behaving in a sexually aggressive manner, and when your attentions were not reciprocated, you resorted to verbal abuse and threats. The acceleration of your repugnant behavior left this concerned employee with no recourse other than to report it before it escalated further."

For the space of several seconds, Tessa grappled to find something to say in her own defense. The accusation came so completely out of left field, it rendered her numb with shock. She'd wondered, at first, if perhaps someone had found out about her and Ben. But it was much worse than that. Much, much worse.

Feeling like a fly caught in a web, she blurted, "Mr. Montgomery, I swear, I would never do any such thing."

Morris sat back, his fingers steepled in front of his chin. He oozed self-importance, and he pompously replied, "I have it on good authority you have indeed done just such a thing."

Her stomach plunged, making her dizzy with a sick sense of unreality. It must be a mistake or some pathetic joke. The entire scenario was such a cliché, it couldn't possibly be real.

"I'd never do anything like that, Mr. Montgomery," she repeated. "Surely after all these years you know that about me."

"What I know for fact about you is that you have been behaving in a manner completely out of character as of late. You have even become unreasonably demanding with me. This promotion I was so generous in awarding to you has obviously swelled your head, and you have since developed the audacity to challenge my authority in front of the other employees. How am I to know you would not have executed this inexcusably reprehensible act as well?"

When she tried to get a word in, he paid no attention and continued with his condemnation, his body language denoting a sense of superiority she heartily resented. "The only feasible option is to demote you. You do understand that as a matter of course, I will also have to place you on probation. If there is even a hint of further impropriety, I will dismiss you outright. There are laws against harassment in the workplace. Consider yourself fortunate that I am not pressing charges."

This meant he didn't even consider the possibility of her being falsely accused. She was to be tarred and feathered and rolled out of town without a chance to defend herself.

"I didn't do it—whatever *it* is. There has to be some other explanation. Who is this person? Who said such horrible things about me? I have a right to know."

Morris looked away and began shuffling some papers together on his desk. "Please do not insult my intelligence by continuing to plead your innocence. You have no grounds to ask who justifiably reported this serious offense."

Tessa felt as if she'd been sucker-punched. "You aren't being fair. You have to check into this and find out why someone would say this about me."

His voice cut like acid across her protest. "I know why it was said. Because you did the deed."

"I didn't! You can't just demote me like this."

"I already have."

The contempt in his voice sparked her anger. "What if I refuse to accept this without some sort of investigation?"

He leaned back in his fancy leather swivel chair, elbows parked on the armrests, hands folded across his rounded paunch. "That would be extremely unfortunate for you." His tone made it clear the meeting was over, and with a dismissive gesture, he busied himself with his papers as though he were already alone in the room.

Tessa set her teeth against the arguments hovering

there, knowing they'd be useless at this point. Aching with defeat, she went to the door and was on the threshold when Morris spoke again.

"You have one half hour to remove your personal belongings from Benjamin's office. I believe your old cubicle is still vacant." He tugged his tie into place and smoothed his hair over his bald spot. "I will notify maintenance immediately regarding your desk."

Something snapped inside her. She simply couldn't do this anymore. She refused to let this obnoxious bully continue to undermine her dignity.

"No, you know what? I'll do you one better. I'll remove my personal belongings from this entire office building. I quit."

She didn't slam the door, but she found a measure of satisfaction in closing it firmly on his blustering response.

****

Operating on autopilot, Tessa arrived home with no clear awareness of making the trip. Although she vaguely heard Milo offering his usual exuberant greeting, she was far too distracted to acknowledge him. She dumped the box from the office onto the floor in the hallway and hung her jacket up. Hopping on one foot, she pulled off a pump and hurled it down the hall.

"Damn!"

Hauling off the other shoe, she sent it flying in the same direction as the first one.

"Damn. Damn. Damn."

Milo squeaked and scrambled toward the kitchen. Still moving like an automaton, Tessa lifted the box and put it on the coffee table in the living room, then went upstairs to change out of her dress into jeans and a pullover.

The phone began to ring as she headed back downstairs, sounding loud and intrusive to her overly sensitive nerves and nearly causing her to stumble on the steps. She had a lump the size of a grapefruit lodged in her throat, and it would've been impossible to talk around it, so she waited, huddled on the stairs, until voicemail picked up.

With faltering steps, she wandered aimlessly over to the living room window and stared blankly out into the front yard, blind to the view on the other side of the glass. Somehow, some way, she had to pull her scattered thoughts together and attempt to make some sense of the chaos in her mind—the chaos that had taken over her once-orderly life.

She turned away from the window. Milo sat in a puddle of sunshine on the floor, contemplating her with soulful eyes. Poor baby. He'd most likely been cowering under the kitchen table, afraid of the crazy shoe-throwing, swear-word-calling woman who looked like his sane and sensible Tessa, but was behaving nothing like her. She clicked her tongue, and he gave an eager whine, scampering toward her. When he sniffed cautiously at her feet, she bent down and scooped him up for a cuddle. The little dog nuzzled against her, licked her cheek and nestled in closer.

"I'm sorry, baby," she whispered hoarsely. "I didn't mean to scare you." Milo tried to console her with more doggy kisses, and she hugged him tightly until he squeaked in protest.

The telephone started ringing again, the sound making her jump. She put Milo back on the floor and turned the ringer off on the phone, to avoid having to deal with any calls until she felt more able to cope.

Tessa spent the rest of the day in a state of numb abstraction, wandering from one thing to another throughout the house, unable to settle anywhere. The events of that afternoon seemed at once unreal yet completely clear, down to the tiniest details. She could recall Morris's gloating expression; his crooked tie, the ugly green polyester one she'd always hated; the way the fluorescent office light flashed off the bald spots on his head. Mostly she remembered the crushing humiliation of being forced to leave her job after having done nothing wrong.

She turned the volume back up on the phone's ringer at dinnertime. Janey had left several messages and would likely show up at her door if she couldn't contact her soon. Tessa couldn't face anyone right then, and she was relieved Lauren was out of town. It gave Tessa some needed time alone to assimilate what had happened.

Barely five minutes later, the phone rang again, and Tessa had to take a couple deep, bracing breaths before she could answer.

"What's going on?" Janey demanded almost before Tessa had finished saying hello. "I've tried to reach you for hours. And I must have sent fifty texts. You've got me worried half to death."

"I'm sorry, Janey. I turned the house phone off for a while, and you know I'm not real good about checking my cell."

"Everyone's talking at the office, saying you cleared your stuff out and left. Is that true? Did you quit?"

It surprised Tessa to hear that Morris hadn't

broadcasted the way she'd had to quit in disgrace. "Yes, it's true I left, but I had no choice after Mr. Montgomery demoted me and put me on probation."

"*He what?*"

In as few words as possible Tessa described what transpired in Morris's office. "I have no idea who would've done this to me, or why. It was just the excuse Mr. Montgomery needed to get rid of me, especially after he felt forced into letting me make the Jeffries' presentation. He was as cold as a politician's heart when he told me I was demoted."

Even saying the words out loud didn't make it seem any more real. More like a colossal joke, and any minute now someone would 'fess up, releasing her life from this nightmare that gripped it.

"Oh, Tessa, sweetheart. How could Morris possibly believe that about you? It's preposterous. You're not capable of such monstrous behavior. Do you want me to come over? I can pick up ice cream."

Although her friend's obvious indignation on her behalf touched Tessa deeply, she couldn't face anyone yet. "Thanks for the offer. Not tonight, okay?"

"Fine. But I'm coming by to check on you tomorrow. No arguments. And if I hear anything, I'll let you know straight away."

"Thanks, Janey. Talk to you tomorrow then."

She had barely hung up from Janey when Travis called, and after her conversation with him, Tessa began to feel a little more grounded. Neither Janey nor Travis believed the lies about her, and while she still couldn't fathom this whole mess, the solid backing of her friends helped considerably.

Instead of supper, Tessa fixed herself a strong pot

of tea. Taking it with her into the living room, she sat quietly, sipping her tea and listening to the soothing tick of her mother's antique mantel clock. The tea's heat eased the dry ache in her throat, and she finally relaxed enough to begin thinking with some degree of rationality.

Time to end the pity party and figure this mess out. She deliberately let her mind race in search-and-retrieve mode, assessing potentials and assembling possibilities, clicking with mechanical precision, sorting out what she knew. A thought stirred once or twice at the bottom of her consciousness, not yet clear enough to interpret, and she sat as still as possible, concentrating on bringing it to focus.

In a sudden, almost painful flash, a brilliant light in her brain clarified that elusive thought, and her dazed feelings transformed into horrible suspicion. Why hadn't Ben checked in with her? Both Janey and Travis had. Surely, Ben must wonder what's going on. Or did he believe the worst of her? Or even more awful, did he know she wasn't guilty because he had set her up? Could he possibly have been the one to lodge the complaint?

Her heart immediately denied what her mind was contemplating. Not Ben—not *Ben*. The Ben she knew wouldn't possibly do this to her.

The nagging in the back of her mind refused to be still, and she had to wonder if the Ben she thought she knew was the real Ben, after all. Two plus two was beginning to add up to ten, and it all pointed toward Ben's guilt. She instantly erased that thought from the surface of her mind, but it continued to work busily below her consciousness until it refused to be denied.

The harder she tried to ignore the truth, the more it persisted, and the facts began to fall into place with such speed, she could practically feel the vibration. That same morning, she had seen Ben leaving Morris's office. When they came face-to-face in the hall, a look of guilt had crossed his features, briefly, just long enough for her to recognize the emotion.

She couldn't deny the evidence any longer. It had to be Ben. Nothing else made sense. Her mind grew wild with anger, and her eyes burned with tears of fury at his betrayal. She should've known he'd find a way to get his own back. He was aggressive about his career aspirations, and even though he said he didn't mind sharing the promotion, he must've resented it. He'd deviously cultivated her friendship and trust, just waiting for the opportunity to get rid of her.

She remembered his expression the day he'd unexpectedly showed up at the office after her presentation. At the time, she couldn't gauge what those emotions meant, but now they became all too clear. He was upset because he'd hoped she'd screw up the presentation and lose the account. For all she knew, he might've been the one who suggested the idea of the demotion to Morris if she wasn't able to sign Jeffries. He had certainly pushed her to insist on doing the presentation despite knowing Morris hadn't wanted her to.

Tessa had to swallow a sob of anguish at the thought of such treachery. She had loved Ben beyond comprehension, and now she struggled not to hate him. She didn't want to hate him, yet how could she not? He had destroyed her. He not only ruined her career and reputation, he'd toyed with her heart and then callously crushed it under his heel as though she meant nothing to him.

She reached for her sketchbook in the box in front of her and began flipping through its pages, searching for the sketch she'd made of him. She wanted to look at his face, study it. See if she could figure out what would make him do this to her.

When she reached the blank pages at the back without coming across it, she started from the beginning again, but it wasn't in there. She set the sketchbook on the coffee table and sat back to stare at it. Who would've removed the sketch? And why would someone take it and not say anything to her? It didn't make sense. Then again, nothing made sense anymore.

The doorbell chimed, and Milo leapt from the couch beside her, yipping loudly as he flew down the hall to the door. Tessa went to the window to see who it was. She was in no mood for visitors. Lauren's car, at home because Lauren refused to leave it at the airport, and her own were the only vehicles she could see parked out front. Whoever was at the door stood just beyond her line of vision.

"Go away," she muttered. "I don't want to see you."

The bell rang again, a long impatient peal, and Milo's barking became more frantic. The person obviously didn't intend to leave, so Tessa put on a brave face and crossed over to the entranceway. She swung open the door, prepared to send the intruder packing—and almost fell over in shock.

Ben.

No, please, not Ben.

Chapter Eleven

Milo surged forward, yelping with excitement as though greeting a much-missed friend. Using the momentary distraction to regain her equanimity, Tessa collected the dog from the porch and hugged his furry warmth close against her chest, then raised her chin with a cool stare in Ben's direction.

"What do you want?"

Both of Ben's eyebrows shot up, then he blinked twice. If the chill in her voice startled him, it was the least he deserved after what he'd put her through.

He shook his head as though genuinely puzzled. "What do you mean? What do I want? I want to know what the hell's going on. I get back from lunch to find you gone. All your stuff is gone, everything. I tried calling here every half hour all afternoon and kept getting your damn voicemail."

"Is that right?" He might have done so, her elderly home phone didn't have caller ID. "You could've left a message. Or texted my cell." Which was likely dead and buried in the bottom of her purse, but still.

"I wanted to talk to you, not some frickin' machine. My God, Tess, I've been out of my mind."

She choked, suffocated by how easily the lies came to him. "Yeah, I bet."

"What does that mean? And are you gonna let me in or what?"

"I'd rather be alone."

Milo wriggled furiously in her arms, and she let him jump to the floor. Ben took the opportunity to sidestep through the doorway, pulling the door closed behind him.

"What's going on?" He gave her arm a little squeeze. "Why did you leave without saying anything?"

She shoved his hand away and stepped back. "I don't have to explain my actions to you." Annoyance propelled her down the hall, not knowing or caring if Ben followed. When she got to the living room, her gaze landed on her sketchbook, lying on the coffee table. She glanced back and found Ben hovering in the entranceway, his hands shoved in his pockets and his shoulders hunched forward. Watching her with careful, measuring eyes.

Beautiful, fake, lying eyes.

"Did you touch my sketchbook?"

"What?"

"At work. Did you go through my sketchbook and remove one of the sketches?"

"No. Never. Is that what has you so pissed?"

"Seriously? You're going to play innocent with me?" she flung at him, using attack to disguise the aching vulnerability that clawed at her. "This is all your fault. Don't try to deny it," she snapped when he started to do just that.

He narrowed the space between them, one hand lifted in a gesture of defense, his face looking more confused than anything else. "You're starting to scare me."

"Don't. Don't. Don't you dare touch me."

The hand dropped. "Come on, Tess, please. What's

my fault? What did I do?"

Certain her heart was about to splinter into a million pieces, she turned her back on him, needing to remove him from her line of sight. "I quit my job. Mr. Montgomery accused me of doing something terrible that I didn't do, something I'd never do. And now I don't have a job, and there's no hope I'll be able to find anything decent in marketing after this."

"You're not making any sense. Why did you quit? And what does this have to do with a missing sketch? Sorry for sounding dense, but I'm not following you."

"This doesn't have anything to do with a missing sketch. That's a separate issue." Using much the same words, she explained to him what she had told Janey and then Travis. Tessa doubted if anything she said came as a surprise. She had to hand it to him, though. He put on a convincing show of looking outraged. Just not convincing enough.

"I always thought that old buzzard was on the wrong side of stupid, now he's proven it. As if you'd try anything so ridiculous. Any fool would know you're not the kind of person who'd make unwanted advances on someone else. You won't even make wanted advances."

A lame joke, but Tessa couldn't believe he'd tried to crack it under these circumstances. It wasn't funny. Nothing about this was funny. She made her way to the couch and sank down, convinced her knees were about to buckle from under her. Rocking slightly, she wrapped her arms around her middle, trying to hold on to her composure. She was strung so tight she might shatter at any moment.

"Someone had to have lied about it, to get me

demoted."

Ben looked blank for a moment, then understanding dawned on his features. "You think that someone was me?"

Her laughter was brief and edged. "In a word, yes. I-I saw you, remember? This morning, coming out of Mr. Montgomery's office. You brushed right by me with an expression that said you wished I hadn't seen you."

Ben tossed his head back and huffed out a loud sigh. "Oh shit." He pressed the palm of his hand to his mouth for a moment. "Tessa, that was about something else. Honest." That fleeting look of guilt crossed his face again, and it cut right through her heart.

"How could you be so cruel? How could you do this to me?" She recognized the rising hysteria in her voice and cut herself off. Even though she'd tried to prepare herself for the eventuality of this confrontation, she didn't know how she'd get through it without tears.

She tried again, her voice angry, but calmer. "You wanted to get rid of me, to have the position all to yourself, or for some other selfish reason I can't begin to fathom. You used me, and you used our friendship. I hope you're happy, because your plan was a great success."

Ben crossed his arms, his stance suddenly defensive and edgy. "I see. You've appointed yourself judge and jury and found me guilty without hope of an appeal."

For a brief moment, Tessa's assurance of his guilt was shaken. Hadn't she felt the same way when Morris refused to hear her side of the story? Her heart warred with her mind, making her physically ill. She had to give him a chance to tell his side.

"Explain then, why would Mr. Montgomery say someone had accused me of this? Who else besides you would have anything to gain from me being demoted?"

Ben tossed his hands up and dropped them, his face the perfect picture of sincere perplexity. "All I know is, I didn't do it. I have never acted with malicious intent toward you. I never would. You have to believe that."

He had no defense. He was guilty as hell and thought his unerring appeal could convince her otherwise, but his smooth act would never fool her again.

"It took me a while to connect all the dots; once I did, the picture became far too clear." Breaking off when the lump in her throat got too big to talk around, she swallowed hard, then coughed, choking on the words she was about to say. "I hate you for what you did to me. I think you're a despicable person, and I want you to leave. Now."

For the first time in their acquaintance, she saw Ben Dunham completely at a loss for words. Something flared briefly in his eyes, then he closed them, and a strange mixture of emotions crossed his face. The look passed so swiftly Tessa almost wondered if she imagined it. Except she'd seen that look before. The day she'd told him about her successful presentation to Pearce Jeffries. The day he stopped treating her as a friend, and lover, and became a polite stranger.

"Why do you look like that? As though you're angry. Or hurt. You've won, Ben. I'm out of your way. Why aren't you gloating? It was a brilliant plan and, sap that I am, I fell for the whole package." Her voice broke, but she went on, forcing herself to say everything that needed saying. "I can't believe how you suckered me in with your smooth lies and smoother smiles. And fool that I was, I believed every one of those glib lines. Tell me, now that we're finally getting the truth out in the open, were you sleeping with Dallas the whole time? Did you have a good laugh at my expense as you went from her bed to mine and back again? Did you, Ben, did you?"

"Don't do this. Don't get this all twisted around into something it's not. Why do you want to hurt yourself this way?"

The bewilderment in his voice compounded Tessa's few remaining doubts. Could he be telling the truth? Could anyone, even Ben, fake such an uncomprehending look? Could she believe him, or was he using his slick salesman's tactics to tell her what she wanted to hear?

He was just like Colin Barry, her whispering, punishing brain insisted. They'd both used her to get what they wanted. The only difference was, Colin had wanted her sister and Ben wanted her job. In the end it amounted to the same thing, she was the one left feeling humiliated, and it made her wonder if she'd been born with a stupid-about-men gene or if this was just something she had cultivated over the years. She might still bear a few scars, but she had eventually gotten over Colin. It'd take much longer for her heart to heal this time.

"Tessa, please."

Their gazes locked and held for five long seconds, and the guarded vulnerability in his expression squeezed her heart. She had to glance away, not wanting to see that tender, gentle side of Ben she loved.

"You need to leave."

And she prayed he'd go without further argument, because what she knew was rapidly becoming overruled by what she felt. She wanted to hug him one last time, to kiss his lips and hold him to her heart, and if she did, it'd be her undoing. He had betrayed her. He had lied to her and treated her in the most despicable manner. To let him convince her otherwise would only lead to worse heartbreak down the road.

Ben came down on his haunches beside where she sat. He reached out a hand, but didn't touch her. Tessa could see a faint tremble in his fingers, and her lips trembled in response.

"I can't leave you like this. I can't leave with you thinking this about me."

She glanced at the ceiling, willing her eyes to remain dry. "If you won't go, I will."

The faint thread of hysteria had returned to her voice, and Tessa made a dash for the hallway, not needing the final humiliation of disintegrating in front of him. He caught her from behind and held her, her back pressed tight to his chest. She squirmed madly, trying to escape, except he was much larger than her.

"Don't fight me. Oh God, Tessa, I won't hurt you. I promise, baby, I promise. I'd never hurt you."

The stark pain in his voice stifled her need to struggle, and his arms gentled as he turned her toward him. He didn't ask anything of her. He simply held her, offering comfort and compassion, and the need for understanding even after all the accusations and insults she had hurled his way.

He wasn't wearing an overcoat and his suit jacket, still holding remnants of cold air from his walk over, smelled reassuringly of the Ben she loved. His closeness was like a drug, a dangerous, addictive drug. She rolled her forehead on his shoulder, trying not to cry. She wanted him to protect her and tell her everything would be all right. She wanted to believe him. If only for this one moment.

But she couldn't. She couldn't risk repeating the biggest mistake of her life—loving and trusting this man had turned out to be the worst mistake she'd ever made.

And with that thought, she couldn't hold back the tears. They burned down her cheeks as she pushed away from him. He held her tighter, pressing her head against his shoulder. Her wracking sobs made it impossible to speak.

"It's okay, Tess. We'll get to the bottom of this. We'll find the person who did this, and he or she will pay. Believe me, please, believe me. I'm going to make sure whoever did this to you pays dearly."

When Ben tried to raise her head, she burrowed closer to him, ashamed of the tears she couldn't stop. They were tears of confusion and heartache, not self-pity. Ever since that incomprehensible meeting with Morris, it seemed as if her life had spun out of control and with it, her self-respect and already shaky confidence had taken a nosedive. She felt weak and useless and stupid and totally hopeless.

Ben soothed her, stroking her head, his fingers wandering down to rub the sensitive skin at the nape of her neck, and gradually her sobs turned to hiccups.

"I'm ruining your suit," she said inanely into his chest and tried to wipe the tears from the front of his jacket.

"Don't worry about my suit, it can be cleaned. All I care about is finding a way to convince you I didn't do this."

"I don't know what to believe anymore. I can't trust you." She sniffed a couple of times and dabbed the tip of her nose with her knuckle.

"Yes, you can. Think about this. Think about us. You have to realize after everything we've been through together, this past month…before that…I could never do what you accused me of doing." Although she couldn't see his face, she could hear the sadness in his voice and could feel the strain in his muscles, the trembling tension in his body as he spoke.

With an effort that left her aching, she fought down the tangle of emotions strangling her and spun away from his embrace. She crossed the room to pluck a tissue from the box on the end table. Shuddering from a combination of residual emotion and mounting mortification, she swabbed at her cheeks and nose with the tissue. "Who initiated the meeting this morning, you or Mr. Montgomery?"

Ben's shoulders sank. "I did." He'd answered readily enough, even though he looked as if he'd rather not have this conversation.

Tessa crumpled the tissue in her fist. Not the answer she'd hoped to hear. "Why?"

"I asked if there was any way you and I could have our own offices." He lifted his hand at her gasp of indignation. "Wait, wait, before you go getting all upset again, I only asked because I thought it was the best solution for both of us. I definitely didn't suggest there was any impropriety on your part. Not in the least. I didn't give him any reasons for my request. All I said was we deserved to not be cramped together in the same office. I tried playing the male diva, but I guess I wasn't convincing enough because he turned me down flat."

Tessa hadn't thought she could feel deeper pain, yet his words hurt. They really hurt. Despite the recent tension between them, she couldn't believe he'd go behind her back to talk to the boss about her. And if he'd been that determined to get her out of his office, what's to say he didn't include some lies in that conversation guaranteed to remove her from the entire company? She'd heard enough of his version of the truth and just wanted to be left alone, not torn between her love for him and this overwhelming fear that he had betrayed her.

Turning her back on him, she crossed her arms around her middle to hold herself together. "Leave me alone, Ben. Just leave. Go." She barely recognized her own voice, it sounded so cold and final, but it must've gotten through to him, because moments later his footsteps thundered down the hall and the front door slammed closed.

****

Ben woke up Saturday morning in no better frame of mind than he'd been in Friday night when he left Tessa's place. He'd spent the entire evening, and most of the night, mulling over the situation, trying to figure it out. No matter how he added events together in his head, they refused to make sense.

Tessa had lost her job and believed he was the cause. Hearing her say she hated him had put a burning agony in his guts that couldn't have hurt more if he'd been stuck with a knife. He could barely comprehend the accusations she'd flung at him—accusations made more painful because she believed they were true—but his mind kept going back to it, remembering her caustic words, her accusing expression, the anguish in the blue depths of her eyes.

He'd thought Tessa knew him better than anyone else, that she understood him far better than he wanted her to. How could she believe him capable of purposely hurting her in such a callous manner?

It didn't improve his disposition to know he might've had a hand in what happened to her, albeit in an inadvertent way, because of his talk with Morris yesterday morning. But he hadn't so much as hinted that she'd behaved inappropriately. How could he, when it was his own behavior that had been questionable, not hers. His inappropriate thoughts, his previous foolish actions and fears that he might head in that direction again, were the reasons why he'd asked for separate offices, not anything Tessa had done.

Poor Tessa.

The thought of what she had gone through had Ben's heart suddenly seeming too large for his chest. He'd easily read the pain and confusion on her face when she told him how Morris had drilled accusations at her without giving her a chance to prove her innocence. If only Ben had been there, he could've supported her. He would've protected her from that damn bully. Because there was no bloody way Morris would've gotten away with what he had if Ben had been around to stop him.

Come hell or high water, he was going to figure out who did this to Tessa and get payback. Then he'd insure Morris not only offered to reinstate Tessa, but that the old buzzard also included a healthy bonus as way of an apology.

While he ate breakfast and tidied the apartment, Ben's nagging thoughts continued to spin endlessly on a loop, his brain leapfrogging from one possibility to another, making him edgy and frustrated.

What in hell was it he knew?

Maybe if he didn't try so hard it would drop quietly into his mind. Thinking physical exercise might dispel his restlessness and let him reason more clearly, he left the apartment and headed down to the storage locker for his bike. With automatic, mechanical motions, he adjusted his helmet strap under his chin and wheeled his bike out into the sunshine.

It was a gorgeous blue-sky day, giving Ben hope that spring, and possibly even summer, might actually make an appearance before the next onset of snow. He crossed the Bow River on the bike path that ran beneath the C-train bridge and turned left on the other side, following the path along the river. Even though he couldn't maintain a vigorous pace without putting a stitch of pain in his side, his increasing stamina encouraged him. Under normal circumstances, he would've enjoyed the outing. Today he had trouble shaking that nightmarish scene with Tessa from his mind.

Two separate pieces of information continued to tease at him. Tessa had accused him of removing something from her sketchpad, and someone had spread a vicious rumor about her. Something about those two facts bothered him. Somehow, they seemed connected. What did he know that he couldn't put his finger on?

The path along the river flowed with pedestrians,

cyclists and bladers enjoying the warm sunshine. Despite needing to keep his wits about him as he negotiated through the throngs of humanity, Ben's attention wandered, nonetheless, as snatches of memory pulled at him, driving him crazy with their elusiveness.

He wove around two young women—one of them a statuesque redhead—leisurely pushing baby carriages. Suddenly his breath caught and his feet stilled on the pedals as everything jelled in his mind. With stunning swiftness, pieces began to fall into place. He veered off the path and came to a stop, giving his healing body a chance to rest while he concentrated.

Thursday evening, when he'd worked late, Dallas Christopher had been hovering around, making a general nuisance of herself. She'd done her usual vamp act, and he'd done his usual rejection. He remembered her making a comment about Tessa's sketches and how he'd turned around to find her flipping through Tessa's sketchpad. Which sketch had she been looking at, and why had it captured her attention? Could it be the one Tessa accused him of taking? Just because Dallas hadn't removed anything from the office at the time, didn't mean she hadn't returned later. Neither he nor Tessa ever bothered to lock the office door when they weren't there.

Ben pushed off and continued pedaling down the path, then made a left-hand turn onto Centre Street Bridge. Excitement built as details of that evening continued to come into focus. The one thing that stood out clearly was Dallas's spiteful smile and eyes that shone with a touch of mania when she told him she always got what she wanted.

Why would Dallas think she had to remove Tessa

to get him? He didn't understand where the perceived threat lay; her reasoning didn't make sense. Even though he couldn't comprehend her motives, Dallas definitely topped his suspect list.

Ben's mind had been bouncing around inside his head like a rubber ball for far too long, and he couldn't believe he hadn't clued into the facts right away. What an absolute idiot for not figuring it out immediately! Everything appeared blatantly obvious now.

He crossed Memorial Drive with the flow of traffic and turned back toward his apartment. Ways to finagle the truth out of Dallas began to form, coming together quickly in his mind. By the time he reached home, he felt positive he could vindicate Tessa, and he wished it was Monday instead of Saturday so he could put his plan into motion immediately.

He wanted to rush to Tessa's and explain his suspicions, but he couldn't do that until he had the proof to clear both her name and his own. And every moment that went by with Tessa thinking the worst of him was a moment longer than he could stand to wait.

****

"I come bearing gifts." Janey held out a bag from each hand. "We have ice cream, mint chocolate chip, of course. And we have wine. Chardonnay for you and a very fine Merlot for me."

Tessa accepted the bags from Janey, who promptly got down on her knees to greet Milo. "Hello, baby. And what a good boy you are for not barking." He nosed her hand, then the pocket of her cardigan, then her hand again. "Yes, *Aunty* Janey has a treat for you, too."

Milo sat prettily while he waited for Janey to dig a biscuit from her pocket. It was a ritual with them, started when he was just a pup. If Milo didn't bark when Janey came over, she rewarded him with a designer doggie cookie.

"Aunty Janey spoils you, Milo." Tessa hefted the two bags, one at a time, like a seesaw. "Aunty Janey spoils me too, but honestly, wine in the middle of the afternoon? Do we plan to drown my sorrows?"

Janey dropped her oversized purse to the floor, shrugged out of her cardigan and hung it on the closet door handle. "Perhaps we'll have a reason to celebrate."

Hope flared. "Did you hear something?"

Janey took one of the bags, then looped her other arm through Tessa's, and they started down the hall to the kitchen. "About your job? Sorry no, love. I did happen across a fine bit of serendipity, though."

"Serendipity, fate, that feeling in your bones. You must be confusing your beliefs with mine."

Disappointment had her sounding decidedly bitchy. Thankfully, Janey didn't seem to take it personally. She placidly opened the ice cream carton while Tessa got out bowls and spoons. When they each had a healthy portion dished out, they took their bowls into the living room.

Tessa curled her legs under her on the couch and made room for Milo on her lap. "So, tell me, what's all this foolishness about serendipity?"

Janey settled herself in the armchair, then stuck a loaded spoon into her mouth. "Answer me something first," she said after she'd savored her treat. She took another spoonful of the sweet green ice cream, making Tessa wait while she licked the spoon clean. "How badly do you want your job back?"

"You have to ask? Janey, all I have is my career.

That's been my sole focus for more years than I care to think about."

Janey pointed her spoon at her. "A career in marketing or a career at Montgomery Group? It's not the same thing."

Tessa began to lose her patience with this senseless conversation. "Unless I clear my name with Montgomery Group, my career in marketing is over. Who'll hire someone with a blemished record like mine?"

Janey grinned like a Cheshire cat, which did nothing to improve Tessa's cranky temperament. "We'll get back to that. First, answer my question. Were you honestly happy at Montgomery's?"

Tessa set her bowl to the side, practically untouched. "My nerves can't take much more. What are you driving at?"

"Does this ring a bell? 'I swear if I had anything better to do with my life, I'd be out of here so fast the door wouldn't have a chance of hitting me on the way out.'"

They were Tessa's own words, spoken during one of her more dire moments of frustration with her job. She'd wanted to quit more times than she could recall, when Morris had thwarted her efforts, belittled her talents, or promoted a male employee over her, even though she had seniority. She had often discussed with Janey the possibility of leaving, except she didn't know where she could go. The devil you knew and all that garbage.

"Okay, we both know I've had a challenging time at work, and sometimes I got frustrated and needed to blow off steam. Still, it was a good job. Until someone decided to set me up."

Janey inspected the inside of her empty bowl, no doubt contemplating licking it clean, then set it aside with a sigh. Her mouth scrunched to the side as she glanced over at Tessa. "Do you have any idea who would've done that?"

Tessa remembered with fresh agony the episode with Ben last night, but she closed her mind to the ache it caused. "Only one person and one reason."

"And?"

"Ben." Bitterness, she couldn't control, spilled over into her voice. "So he wouldn't have to share the promotion with me. Nothing else makes sense."

Janey frowned. "That doesn't sound like something Ben would do. He has more confidence in himself than that."

It didn't sound like Ben. It really didn't. And after the way he had been so gentle, so understanding and kind last night, even with all the harsh words she'd flung at him, Tessa wished she could reject her suspicions out-of-hand. Instead, her doubts continued to cling like tentacles, insidiously choking her belief in him.

"He's the only one with a motive."

"Not necessarily. It could've been any number of people. You never know what someone's motives might be."

Tessa raised an eyebrow. "Are you telling me it was you?"

Janey nodded like one of those head-bobbing toys. "Yeah, I wanted you out of the way, to have Ben all to myself."

"You didn't have to get me to quit for that. Ever

since he's returned to work, he's been acting as though I've come down with some contagious disease he doesn't want to get close enough to catch." Tessa's emotions regarding Ben were too raw, too excruciating, to discuss. Time to change the subject. "Enough joking. Spill whatever it is you're trying so hard to keep me in suspense about."

Janey picked up her bowl and got to her feet. "Let's get some wine first."

Tessa consulted the mantel clock. "It's only 2:30."

"That means it's past noon and is a perfectly acceptable time for a drink. Or two, or possibly three." She collected Tessa's bowl and started out of the room. "Coming?"

Tessa threw up her hands in exasperation. "Then will you tell me what's going on?"

"Promise."

Wine glasses in hand, they returned to the living room, and Janey joined Tessa on the couch. She took a swig of the dark red wine, smacking her lips with appreciation.

"Okay, grab something heavy, because you're about to be blown away." She paused dramatically, and her features grew animated. "I had a phone call from my cousin Braden this morning. We discussed that job proposition of his at great length. It sounds next to perfect."

"But he lives in Vancouver."

"Yes, he does. And his boutique agency is very successful and highly lucrative."

"Janey! I can't believe you'd consider moving to Vancouver. What about your parents? And Stevie?"

"Not me, silly. *You.* I told Braden about your

situation, and he jumped at the chance to work with you. If you don't believe in serendipity, call it synergy. The timing's ideal."

Tessa gave Janey a look, clearly suggesting her friend was crazy. The idea was so stupendous, so seemingly impossible, she couldn't quite comprehend it, yet at the same time she had to admit it also held some intriguing potential.

"I couldn't..."

"Of course you could. Think about it. It's exactly the type of job we've daydreamed about. No more high pressure kowtowing to the multimillion-dollar clients. You can take what you know and apply it to small businesses, help them to market themselves appropriately. Really do something good with your skills, instead of just making the rich richer."

Tessa sipped her wine, contemplating Janey's proposal. She saw immediate possibilities, and while her instincts clamored for her to go for it, she questioned whether she could. Could she leave Calgary? Leave her home. Her family and friends. Leave Ben?

Scratch that. Ben stopped being a factor in her life when he decided his job held more importance than she did.

Still, she found herself hedging. "It's a big decision. I'd have to think it over."

"Sometimes it's better to dive right in."

"I never dive right in. I like to wade. Slowly." Tessa chewed her lower lip. Mrs. P had often told her as a child she had an old head on her young shoulders, and that had never changed. There was nothing wrong with thinking things through and assessing them rationally. "All my life, I've been practical, organized, careful. I always plan ahead and consider my future, my goals."

For several moments they studied each other, Janey's gaze uncomfortably sharp and appraising.

"Maybe that's the problem. You're too...I don't know...steady, I guess. You think too much. Everything neatly ordered, including your love life."

"I don't have a love life at the moment." Her words were lighter than her heart.

"So what's keeping you from going?"

"Are you trying to get rid of me?"

Janey's faint smile held a trace of sadness. "Of course not. I'd miss you like crazy, but we'd still see each other all the time. Between company meetings and visiting family, I'm in Vancouver at least every other month. And you can always come back here for visits, too. It takes no time to fly."

It wouldn't be the same, though. Then again, nothing in her life would ever be the same whether she took the job or not. Maybe a fresh start was the best thing for her. Tessa took a deep breath and expelled it slowly. "Okay, go ahead and tell me more about this wonderful opportunity."

"Atta girl. Let me refill the wine."

Janey returned a moment later, each hand gripping a wine bottle by the neck. She refilled their glasses, then sat cross-legged on the couch, facing Tessa.

"This position has such great potential, I get shivers just thinking about it. Bray doesn't want an employee, he wants a partner, meaning you'd be your own boss."

While Tessa listened carefully, Janey raced on and

on, details tumbling out of her, immediately spawning new possibilities. Her enthusiasm was contagious, her logic persuasive. Tessa's arguments continually failed to stand up, and she slowly found herself beginning to take the idea seriously.

Chapter Twelve

At the first hint of Tessa wavering, Janey dove in for the kill. "I've got an idea. Why don't we call Braden, and you can talk with him personally?"

"No. We can't possibly bother him on a Saturday afternoon."

"Why not? He'd be thrilled to discuss the position with you. Come on, we'll put him on speakerphone." Janey jumped up and left the room. When she returned with her cell phone, she shot Tessa a triumphant look and began scrolling through her contacts. A second later, she turned on the speaker and set the phone on the couch between them.

"Hey, Bray," she sang out when he answered. "It's Janey. Guess who I'm with?"

"The Easter Bunny?" an echoing voice asked.

"Good guess, but no, I'm at Tessa's. I told her about our phone conversation, and she'd like to hear more. Say hi to her."

"Hey, Tessa. It's great to have the opportunity to talk to you."

"Hi, Braden. I hope you don't mind being on speakerphone."

"No problem. I'm glad Janey called. I hope you found her pitch enticing. I can sure use someone with your excellent credentials."

With Janey carrying most of the conversation,

Braden answered all their questions and posed a few of his own. Not wanting to get their hopes too high, Tessa tried not to reveal her growing excitement. The job did sound perfect. It sounded more than perfect. It entailed every aspect of marketing she loved as well as encompassing areas such as public relations, promotion, website design, and consulting. And after what she'd gone through with Montgomery Group, being an equal partner was almost too tempting to turn down.

Braden came across as intelligent and widely knowledgeable in his field of marketing, and very enthusiastic about the possibility of Tessa working with him. When he asked if she could fly out to Vancouver for an in-person meeting, it suddenly became too real. Nerves hit her hard, and she looked helplessly at Janey.

"There's one thing that'll clinch the deal for sure, Bray," Janey told her cousin, and even Tessa had to wonder what it could be.

"Name it."

"Tell her it's okay for her to wear sensible heels."

That snapped the tension, and Tessa laughed until tears ran down her cheeks when Braden replied that she could wear sneakers, if she wanted. Before they broke the connection, Tessa told Braden she would book a flight for the following week.

Janey gave a whoop of excitement. "I knew this would work."

"It's not a done deal, yet. All I've committed to is a meeting with Braden. There's plenty to be settled before I'd consider making such a huge change in my life."

The front door opened, and Milo lifted his head, letting out a soft woof. He quickly glanced at Janey and wagged his tail, then jumped down to investigate.

There came the sound of luggage on wheels being dragged into the entranceway, then Lauren, looking gorgeous in a silk suit, appeared in the living room with Milo at her heels.

"Hi, Lauren," Tessa greeted her. "How was the one-woman show?"

"Wildly successful, of course." She smiled with the air of a woman who had never entertained a single insecurity.

Tessa wished she possessed an iota of Lauren's confidence and poise. Part of her sister's success stemmed from the way she'd accept nothing less than to be the best. The fact that she was spoilt and willing to use anyone to get what she wanted wasn't something Tessa admired and had no inclination to emulate. A little of her self-confidence sure couldn't hurt, though.

"You should've called. I would've picked you up from the airport."

Lauren draped herself gracefully in the armchair. "Anthony came to get me, the love."

Tessa had to wonder how Lauren would manage without *Anthony, the love*. Agent, personal assistant and general fetch-boy, about the only thing the blissfully gay Anthony deAglo wasn't, and never would be, was Lauren's lover. And Tessa pegged that as the single most significant reason why they'd been able to work successfully together all these years.

Lauren waved a hand in the direction of the near-empty wine bottles. "Are the two of you celebrating something?"

"Yes," Janey agreed, just as readily as Tessa denied it.

Apparently deciding Janey's answer held more interest, Lauren focused on her. "And what are you celebrating?"

"Tessa's new job."

Tessa winced. She hadn't wanted to say anything to Lauren until she knew more about the job, and she didn't want Lauren spilling the beans to their father before Tessa had the chance to discuss it with him—a prospect she wasn't looking forward to. The mere thought of Ellis Caldwell's sharp tongue made Tessa want to cringe.

Lauren's gaze swung over to Tessa, one elegant brow raised. "New job? Didn't you recently get promoted at your current one?"

Tessa reached for Milo, sitting at her feet, and fidgeted with the little bow on his head. "It's a long story, and I'm sure you're tired after your long flight from Toronto. I can fill you in later."

"I want to hear about it now."

"Tessa's going into partnership with my cousin, Braden," Janey answered in a rush of words before Tessa could come up with a more convincing diversionary tactic.

"That sounds interesting. Is this Braden married? What does he look like?"

Despite being annoyed with Janey's big flapper, Tessa almost laughed. Trust Lauren to get right down to the important stuff.

"I'm only considering the possibility." She glanced at Janey. "And last I heard, Braden wasn't married."

"Nope," Janey agreed happily. "And he's a real hunk, if I do say so."

From what Tessa could remember from a brief

encounter several years ago, Braden Kent had been passably handsome, and she had to wonder if Janey was trying to fix her up with more than just a job. No way was she ever going to get involved in another office romance. If she'd learned nothing else from this fiasco with Ben, it was never to mix work and pleasure.

"Braden's looks and marital status has absolutely zippity to do with do-dah. Up and moving to Vancouver isn't something I'm going to decide on in one day."

"It means you'd have to move?" Lauren's face clouded briefly, as though the thought hadn't occurred to her.

"Afraid so. That's why I have to consider this carefully, and I won't make any decisions without consulting you first."

"This is an excellent opportunity for your sister to advance her career, Lauren," Janey said with quiet emphasis. "It'll mean more money in the long run, and she'll be her own boss. No one will ever be able to demote her without cause again."

Tessa winced a second time. Darn Janey and her runaway mouth.

Lauren jerked forward in her chair as if poked with a live wire. "Whoa, pump the brakes for a sec. What's this about being demoted?"

Tessa nodded, swallowing a pang of despair. "Mr. Montgomery demoted me yesterday, and I ended up quitting. It's all some ghastly misunderstanding, but the bottom line is, I'm without a job and without many prospects of getting another unless I find a way to restore my reputation."

Losing her job was bad enough. Being betrayed by the man she loved was unbearable, and Tessa would've given anything if she could drop the subject before she broke down in front of Lauren and Janey. She refused to reveal the additional anguish she carried.

Lauren's finely etched mouth flexed with annoyance. "To hell with that horrid boss of yours, then. I say you take the new job and become horribly rich and famous. What better revenge?"

Tessa's fingers fluttered to her neck. "But, Lauren, that'd mean moving. From this house. Could you handle living here by yourself?"

"Are you kidding? I'd be outta here and into a cute little condo downtown so fast it'd give you whiplash."

Tessa was unprepared for Lauren's reaction. Her initial feeling was one of astonishment, though sadness followed close behind. She'd had no idea Lauren didn't like living here, in the house Tessa loved so much. Lauren tended to be very vocal about her wants and dislikes, yet never once had she mentioned it.

"You'd want to move out? Sell the house?"

Lauren thrust out her bottom lip. "Oh, Tessa, don't look so crushed. I know I'm selfish and self-centered, and I depend on you way too much. So, living in this drafty old mausoleum is my way of making it up to you. Don't kid yourself, it's never been my first choice. You'd take the dog, wouldn't you?"

Tessa glanced down at her precious little Milo. He gazed back as if waiting for her answer. "You wouldn't mind if I did?"

"He's always been more your dog than mine, anyway." Lauren rose to her feet and stretched like an elegant feline, then smoothed her tumble of blonde hair back over her shoulders. "If you'll excuse me, I have a dinner date to prepare for."

Joyce M. Holmes

The only sound for several moments was Lauren's suitcase bumping up the stairs. Tessa couldn't move, could barely breathe. She huddled into the corner of the couch with her arms folded on her chest, each white-knuckled hand gripping the opposite elbow, as her mind spun with bewilderment. How could she sell this house—filled with precious memories of her mother—to complete strangers? The mere thought devastated her.

Janey slid over and put an arm around Tessa's shoulders. "Hey, hon, I have an idea. If this deal goes through and you move to Vancouver, what do you think about me moving in here? You'd be doing me a huge favor. I love the location, and just think of all the space I'd have for Stevie when he spends the weekend. He'd go nuts over having his own room instead of camping on my couch."

Tessa let her breath out in a long, silent sigh of relief. Janey's suggestion offered the perfect solution. Having her dear friend live here would be as good as family. Janey would love and cherish this old place as much as Tessa did.

Her eyes filled with tears. "You'd do that for me?"

"I'd do it for us. It sure won't be a hardship. You know how I've always coveted that garden in the backyard."

A hot tear streaked down Tessa's cheek, and she sniffed.

"Oh no," Janey protested. "Don't make me cry. I'll mess up my mascara, and it's real ugly when that happens."

Tessa began laughing through her tears. Her life might still be in an uproar, but suddenly it didn't seem

244

quite as impossible.

****

Ben arrived at work extra early on Monday morning, stopping in the lobby first to ask a few pertinent questions of the security personnel. When he reached Montgomery Group's floor, he made sure no one was around before gingerly approaching Dallas's desk in the main foyer.

He eased the middle drawer open and examined its contents, careful not to mess anything up. Pens, pencils, notepads. Nothing of interest. With a quick glance down the hall, Ben opened the left side drawer. Compact, hairbrush, lipstick, nail file, chewing gum and mints. Obviously the vanity drawer.

Moving to the other side of the desk, he opened the top drawer. More stationery supplies. Damn. He was running out of time. As he started to close the drawer, a corner of buff paper sticking out of a yellow legal pad caught his eye. Lifting the pad to the desktop, he opened it to where the edge of the paper showed.

His breath sucked in on a hiss as he stared down at a sketch of himself. At the sound of the elevator opening, he grabbed the paper from the pad, shoved the pad back in the drawer, and hightailed it out of there.

Safely in his own office, Ben smoothed the paper out on his desk and sat heavily into his chair. He had no doubt this was the page missing from Tessa's sketchpad, the one she'd accused him of taking.

It was a beautiful piece of artwork, not that he looked beautiful or anything, but the details were incredible. He studied the face—his face. It was as if Tessa had captured his very essence in that sketch. His eyes seemed alive, sparkling with undefined emotion.

Desire? Need?

Love?

Ben quickly squelched that thought. Not love, lust more likely. His smile, cocky and self-assured, reflected his personality too. The person who sketched this portrait had to know him well. Intimately. And anyone who saw it would recognize that fact.

When Dallas chose to alleviate her boredom by snooping through Tessa's sketchpad, she must've come across this sketch and decided that Ben's lack of interest in her stemmed from a relationship with Tessa. And she'd put into motion a plot to remove the competition.

Ben wished he could feel more pleased to have figured it out, but the knowledge that he was inadvertently responsible for what happened to Tessa twisted and turned inside him. To make matters worse, he'd unwittingly backed up Dallas's story by going to Morris to request separate offices for himself and Tessa. A burning combination of rage and self-recrimination rolled through his gut, and he'd get no peace until he got justice for Tessa. He glanced at his watch and saw he still had a few moments to sharpen the plan that had been formulating in his mind all weekend. As long as Janey and Travis were willing to be witnesses, he believed he could cajole a confession out of Dallas.

Fifteen minutes later, he had Janey and Travis seated in his office. "Have you spoken to Tessa?" Ben asked Janey. "Do you know how she's doing?"

"As well as can be expected under the circumstances."

She looked as if she might add more, then

restrained herself at the last moment, making Ben certain Tessa had divulged her suspicions to Janey. The fact that Janey was here, still speaking to him, had Ben thinking she didn't share Tessa's belief in his guilt.

"I'm fairly sure I know who set Tessa up and with your help, I intend to prove it."

"Who?" Travis asked sharply.

"Dallas Christopher."

Janey shot him a look of incomprehension, which slowly cleared to shocked realization. "OMG. I joked with Tessa that I forced her to quit in order to have you to myself. That's why Dallas did it, isn't it? She has a thing for you."

A dull red flush crept up the back of Travis's neck, and he stared holes through Ben. "Is this a mutual *thang*?"

Ben got the sudden impression these two people could turn from ally to enemy on the spot if he didn't handle this carefully. "As you most likely know, Dallas has put me in several compromising situations since I started working here, but I've never led her on, I swear. Last Thursday evening, she showed up in my office and put on her usual vamp act. I basically told her I wasn't interested, and somehow she must've gotten the mistaken idea that Tessa and I were an item. In her twisted little mind, she decided to get rid of Tessa."

Travis shifted his lanky frame in the chair, then leaned forward, tapping a finger on the edge of Ben's desk. "Do you have any proof?"

Ben's gaze strayed to his desk drawer where he'd hidden Tessa's sketch. That wasn't tangible proof, and he didn't want to show it to anyone without Tessa's permission. "It's mostly hunch and circumstance right now. Security could probably find something on video showing she returned to our office after hours the other night, but I'm confident I can get Dallas to admit it without resorting to that."

"Good luck," Janey snorted skeptically, crossing her arms over her chest. "She's a professional dissimulator who's got 'not taking the blame' down to a science. There's no way she'll own up to something this awful."

"I disagree. It won't be easy, but if I play on her massive ego and insinuate I'm thankful she got rid of Tessa, she might believe me." The very thought of doing that disgusted Ben, but if it got Tessa her job back and redeemed himself in her eyes, he'd do or say whatever it took.

Travis removed his glasses, wiped the lenses, looked through them and wiped them again. "I hope Dallas stopped off at the bank on her way to work. Because there's going to be hell to pay if she did this to Tessa." He resettled his glasses on his nose, his expression bleak and determined.

"What do you want us to do?" Janey's tone told Ben she'd taken him at his word and was ready to help.

"Okay, here's the deal. I plan to lure Dallas into the break room, where the two of you will be hidden in the coat closet, and I'll go to work on her. Once she admits what she's done, you guys show yourselves, and Dallas won't be able to wiggle out of her confession."

"It could work," Travis said slowly. "What will you say to her?"

"I have a few ideas, mostly I'll improvise. When's a good time for you to do this?"

Janey and Travis exchanged glances. "Now?"

Janey asked.

"Let's get this over with," Travis growled back.

Wired, on edge, Ben rose from his chair and began pacing. "If you'll head over to the break room, Dallas and I won't be far behind."

When Janey and Travis left the office, Ben took out his cell phone and after a moment of reflection, texted: *I need to see you. Meet me in the break room right away*. He hoped the wording was suggestive enough to intrigue her into following him. Back when Dallas had helped herself to his phone and programmed her number into it, he'd thought her awfully forward and had no intention of calling her. Now he was thankful he had the ability to text her. Texting, rather than asking her in person, eliminated the chance for her to propose they use the privacy of his office. The office would've been an easier choice, with less chance of someone walking in on them, but short of stuffing Janey and Travis under the desks, it lacked a place to hide his witnesses.

From halfway down the corridor, Ben could see Dallas seated at her desk, cell phone in hand. Please, he prayed, let this work. As casually as possible, he sauntered past her desk and gave her a wink that turned his stomach. Without looking back, he made a beeline for the break room to make sure his cohorts were in place.

****

"Ben, this is such a sweet surprise."

Dallas's saccharine tone made him want to puke, but Ben notched his smile up to full industrial strength and turned to face the woman he'd come to detest.

"Thanks for getting here so promptly. I've been

Joyce M. Holmes

thinking a lot about you this weekend." That much was true. He'd spent the entire weekend planning ways to bring her down.

When she tried to put her arms around him, he managed to sidestep her advance without making his avoidance too obvious. He nonchalantly strolled the length of the room, taking care not to look at the closet's partially opened door, and came to a stop with the table between himself and Dallas.

"So, what do you think of this rumor about why Tessa quit?"

The corner of her mouth curled into a vindictive little smile, which she quickly suppressed. "I guess she got what she deserved. Who'd possibly be interested in her advances anyway? She should've known better."

That was her first slipup. Morris hadn't revealed why Tessa had left. Only someone involved, or close to Tessa, would know the truth. Dallas definitely wasn't close to Tessa. Although feeling dangerously irritable, Ben kept his expression under control.

"That's not Tessa's style." He shook his head slowly, feigning uncertainty. "Come to think of it, I doubt Tessa's even guilty. I bet someone set her up," he went on, as though the idea had just dawned on him. "Whoever it was, I'm extremely grateful. It leaves me the promotion free and clear. My career's real important to me, and I'm relieved to have the competition out of the way."

It sickened him to say the words. The gloating expression on Dallas's face sickened him further. But he'd started this, and he intended to see it through to the end. Tessa deserved nothing less from him. "I'd sure like to express my appreciation in person."

Dallas put on an air of astonishment, then abandoned it almost immediately. Her calculating look told Ben she was reviewing her options, trying to balance what she had to gain and lose.

"Exactly how grateful are you?"

Ben gripped the back of the chair in front of him. It took all his effort to keep his voice casual. "Why? Are you saying you're the one who lodged the complaint against Tessa?"

Dallas ran her tongue over her lips and smiled. She seemed very pleased with herself. "Let's say I removed a mutual nuisance." She reached out with her arms opened wide. "Now stop all this tiresome chitchat, and come show me the gratitude I deserve."

A muscle ticked furiously in his jaw. "Oh, you'll get what you deserve." He took a calming breath and asked the question to which he already knew the answer. "Tell me though, why did you think it was necessary to get Tessa demoted, to force her to quit?"

Dallas shook her head, her mouth twisted with resentment. "I couldn't understand why you kept turning me down. It didn't make sense, until I realized you were involved with Tessa. Really, Ben," she said with a condescending lift of an eyebrow. "Why would you even want her when you could have me?" She copped a provocative pose, her hands skimming down the length of her body, caressing her abundant curves.

Ben's temper went from slow simmer to full boil, but a lifetime of containing his anger came to his rescue. "Where did you get the idea I wanted Tessa? I don't want her. I never have." He didn't realize how badly it would hurt to say those words.

Dallas grinned unpleasantly and gave herself a

little hug. "I'm sooo glad to hear that. She's not good enough for you. You deserve much better—you deserve me. You and I are two of a kind—we're both physically sensual creatures who know what we want and how to get it."

Blind anger tore at Ben's insides, a searing hot rage he could no longer contain. "You gotta be kidding, right? Where do you get off making such an outrageous suggestion after what you've done?"

"Why are you sounding p.o.'d?" She was still smiling, although the smile had developed brittle edges. "Let's just forget all about this little bit of unpleasantness, and no one else ever needs to know."

"They already do." Janey's outraged voice came from across the room.

Dallas let out a sharp squeal as Janey and Travis revealed themselves. Her lovely face transformed into something hateful, lips turned back, eyes narrowed to slits. "You tricked me," she shrilled. "If you think this proves anything, you're crazy."

"You're the one who's crazy, thinking you could get away with such a stupid stunt. We heard every sick word you said," Janey continued, her expression thunderous.

"This is a witch hunt," Dallas screeched, her head swiveling from Ben, to Janey, to Travis.

Travis's mouth thinned as if tasting something sour. "Yeah and it worked, cuz we found us one. Although in your case, I'd say the word starts with 'B'."

Janey stalked across the room, coming to a stop in front of Dallas, her hands clenched tightly into fists at her hips, two bright red spots of anger in her cheeks.

"You're going to be sorry you did this to Tessa." Janey wasn't a small woman, but Dallas topped her by at least three-four inches, and Janey lifted up on tiptoes to yell directly into Dallas's face. "And if you mess with my friends again, I'll rip those collagen lips right off your face."

"Try it," Dallas spit furiously, and for split second Ben worried the two women might come to blows.

Travis swung an arm around Janey's waist and hauled her back a few steps. "Forget it, Janey. She's not worth it."

Janey's breath came in gasps, and her face turned pale and pinched. Ben could relate to how she struggled with her tears and anger. He felt quite unsteady himself, sick with guilt for having played any part in this unbelievable farce. He moved forward, purposely placing himself between Dallas and the other two.

"If you'd please escort Janey to her office, Travis, and make sure she's okay, I'll handle the rest of this on my own."

Travis's eyes, behind the glasses, filled with contempt as he glared at Dallas. "Gladly." He draped an arm around Janey's shoulder and tucked her protectively to his side, murmuring softly to her as he led her away.

"Just how hateful are you?" Ben yelled at Dallas when they were alone. "What has Tessa ever done to you to make you treat her like this?"

"She got in my way," she said evenly as though the answer was obvious. Her voice contained absolutely no emotion, and it chilled Ben to the bone.

"So you say, but you never did have a chance with me." Ben tapped a finger to his temple. "And you're irrational if you think I'd be interested in you now. You did a terrible thing, Dallas, and you have to make it right by telling Morris you lied."

She gripped his arm with crimson-tipped fingers. "He might fire me, and I can't lose this job, Ben, please." Her voice caught in a small sob, and huge crocodile tears clung to her eyelashes. "I'm in way over my head with my credit cards. I need my income, or I'll be in big trouble."

He tried but couldn't find one shred of compassion. Dallas had set Tessa up to take the fall for something Tessa would never have done. No tears, no excuses, could change that.

"You have only yourself to blame for this. Did it ever occur to you Tessa didn't want to lose her position either?" He had to tug hard to get his arm free of her clutch. "You live in your own little narcissistic world, only thinking about yourself, and meanwhile you've trashed the life of a caring and talented woman. It's time to 'fess up. Let's go."

When he started for the door, Dallas snagged his arm, sharply pulling him around with a grip tight enough to leave dents. She planted her feet, rocking back on her slender stiletto heels, and he didn't dare break loose of her maniacal two-handed grasp for fear of hurting her.

"Don't do this, Ben." Desperation clawed through her voice and expression, but Ben figured the panic was as fake as the tears a moment ago. "I'll make it worth your while to forget all about this. I'll do anything." Her tone changed abruptly, turning flirtatious. "Anything."

She let go of his arm with one hand to walk her

fingers across his chest. Rubbing her body against him like a cat in heat, she breathed into his ear, "I'll satisfy you right here, any way you want. Come on, Ben. Don't worry about Travis and Jane. It'll be their word against ours."

Ben snatched at her hand and shoved it away from him. "I didn't want you before, and I certainly don't want you now. You turn my stomach."

Abandoning the vamp act, she turned on him, her expression vicious. Sympathy and sex hadn't worked, so now her true colors came out. "You stupid man. I've already told Morris you were the one who fed me the stories about Tessa. If anyone lied about what happened, it was you, not me. He'll believe me."

"I could always show Morris the sketch you stole out of Tessa's sketchpad." The widening of Dallas's eyes confirmed what he'd already figured out. "But that sketch is Tessa's private property, and I'd rather not show it to anyone without her consent. At any rate, building security can give us all the proof we need."

He removed his keychain from his pocket and singled out the little fob employees needed to enter the building after hours. "These key fobs are registered to record the names and times of people entering the building. There are video cameras in the lobby and in the elevators. I bet security could tell us exactly when you came back up to the office for that sketch." He marveled he could speak rationally, he was so furious. "I've asked you to do the honorable thing, and why am I not surprised that you've refused? I'd say, see ya later, but somehow I doubt I will."

With Dallas screeching like a fishwife behind him, he left the break room. He had a man to see about a job.

****

Ben rapped on Morris's open office door, then entered without waiting for permission. "Excuse me, Morris, I'm here to talk about this situation with Tessa."

Morris glanced up from his desk, annoyance showing on his face. "I do not have the time or inclination to discuss the matter of Tessa Caldwell. It is a closed issue, and I should think you would be thankful I dealt with it." With a dismissive wave of his hand, he returned to his paperwork.

Ben's barely leashed anger rose again, and for the first time in memory, it felt good to be righteously angry. Morris Montgomery was nothing but a bully, and he'd tormented Tessa for far too long. Ben was here now, though, and he'd protect her. He'd do for Tessa what he hadn't been able to do for his mom.

With a deliberately casual movement, he pulled back one of the chairs in front of Morris's desk and sat himself in it, crossing one leg nonchalantly over the other. "Too bad, because I'm reopening the issue. I just had a conversation with Dallas Christopher where she admitted she fabricated the entire ridiculous story, hoping you'd fire Tessa."

Morris's shaggy brows headed toward that bald spot on his crown. "You have proof?"

"Dallas admitted to the whole thing in front of Janey and Travis. Even though she'll likely try to deny it, she definitely made it all up, and it's your responsibility to fix this with Tessa."

"I don't pay you to be my conscience, young man." Morris smoothed a palm over his neckwear. "I will decide after speaking with Ms. Christopher what course of action to take. It is of no concern of yours."

With Tessa gone, a full promotion would likely be in the works for him, with accounts of his own. But how badly did he want to stay with an agency that encouraged its employees to compete against each other rather than work together?

He shook his head, his anger contained behind a derisive smile. "You either hire Tessa back immediately, or I'm walking."

Morris frowned in exaggerated concentration. He clearly wasn't used to being so boldly challenged. "You don't mean that."

"Try me." Returning fury thickened Ben's voice. "And while you're at it, the apology to Tessa should be very sincere and include whatever monetary amount necessary to make it worth her while. Because if I were her, I'd tell you where you could shove it."

Morris's lips puckered like those of a sulky child. "Frankly, I am shocked by your attitude, Benjamin. I expected better from you."

Ben uncrossed his legs and leaned toward Morris for emphasis. "I'm sorry if I disappoint you. But the disappointment is mutual. Not to mention what you've done to Tessa. You demoted her without giving her a chance to redeem herself, and even though I've told you who the real culprit is, you still haven't agreed to reinstate her."

Morris nodded, steepled his fingers under his chin and looked exceedingly ponderous. "Very well. I will call the girl some time this week and arrange a meeting with her."

Damn the man, anyway. He was a boor and Ben disliked him intensely. "First off, Tessa is a woman, an adult, not a girl. And secondly, you'll make the phone call today and set up the meeting for no later than tomorrow. Tessa's waited long enough to have her name cleared."

"I will agree to your terms this time, Benjamin, because you are correct, an injustice has occurred. Do not, however, think for one moment that I will accept this type of insubordination from you in the future."

Ben kept his grin of triumph from showing on his face. The only way to handle a bully was to bully him back. On the other hand, if that bully also happened to be your boss, it was wise to pick your fights judiciously. He could afford to be gracious; he'd won this round.

"Yes, sir. And thank you, sir. I appreciate it."

Chapter Thirteen

"Hey, Tessa, it's Ben. Don't hang up. I have something important to tell you."

Tessa was so startled to hear Ben's voice, she temporarily lost the use of her own. He was the last person she expected would want to talk to her. She cleared the nervousness from her throat and said, "I know. Janey already called. She told me it was Dallas who played me for a dupe."

Another sick ache of shame knotted her stomach over the way she'd accused Ben of that crime. Ever since Janey called, Tessa had alternated between waves of relief over being vindicated and gut-twisting guilt for the shabby way she'd treated Ben.

"Ben? Aren't you angry?" He'd acted with tenderness and understanding the other night, asking only that she believe in him. And she hadn't done that. She'd believed the worst instead, and she couldn't blame him if he wanted to rub her nose in it.

"Not anymore. I was furious with Dallas at the time, but you know, it was only anger. I had no urge to act on it. In fact, at one point she had my arm in a death grip, and the first thought through my head was if I tried to break free, I might hurt her, so I didn't try. Even though I was completely furious with her, I didn't want to hurt her." His voice sounded amazed, incredulous.

He'd misunderstood her question, but as Tessa

listened to his answer, she at last began to understand Ben's secret fears. It had shocked him to realize he could get infuriated with another person, yet not have the urge to hurt them. Talk about the sins of the fathers.

"Did you honestly think you might hit someone in anger?" Tessa's heart squeezed at the thought of him having to carry this burden. She'd never in a million years understand what it must be like to live in fear of your own genes.

"I didn't mean that the way it sounded. Of course I didn't want to hurt her," he said with an offhandedness she didn't believe for a moment.

He didn't *want* to hurt Dallas, yet past experience had repeatedly shown him that when his father got angry, he struck out, and Ben had naturally assumed he might behave similarly.

"Are you afraid you might act like your dad, is that it?"

"Afraid? No." Two short, emotionless words that revealed so much.

"You want to know what I think?"

"Not really."

It had been a rhetorical question, and Tessa carried on as though he hadn't interrupted. "I think you are scared. Terrified, probably. Your father hit your mother in anger, and you've been worried you could do the same. This explains so much. I've watched you get angry several times, yet you'd just stand there pretending to be calm until you had all your emotions carefully contained. I used to wonder why, and now I understand. You're afraid of your anger because of your dad's violent temper."

"Please don't overanalyze this."

"You must understand, there's a vast difference between anger and cruelty, and I'm positive you're incapable of harming another person. No matter what you've said to the contrary, you've shown me over and over again that you're a kind and noble gentleman. You could never behave like your dad because you're one of the good guys."

Silence strained across the line. Either she hadn't convinced him or he refused to talk about it. Knowing Ben, it was probably a little of each.

"Look at the way I treated you the other night," Tessa continued. "I completely overreacted, falsely accusing you of such horrible things, and although we both know I was wrong, you haven't ventured a single 'I told you so'."

"What's the point? I knew you were devastated by what happened. So you lashed out at the wrong person, big deal. It's all straightened out."

He was honestly more concerned about her feelings than his own. And that reinforced her belief in his integrity. Her fears and insecurities had almost destroyed her faith in him, while her heart had never stopped believing in his goodness.

Janey had told her how relentlessly he'd gone after Dallas. He could've just as easily stepped back and left the matter alone. Without Tessa around, the promotion would've been all his, yet he didn't even consider that option.

"You're wrong, it's a huge deal to me. And I offer you my most heartfelt apology. I truly am sick with regret because I didn't trust your word. You see, no man has ever been there for me when I needed his support. Not my dad, old boyfriends, my boss, none of

261

them, and I erroneously expected no better from you. That's no excuse for my bad behavior. I was wrong, and I can't express how sorry I am. I also want to thank you for sticking up for me, for being smart enough to figure out the truth behind what happened. I'm beyond grateful."

Tessa half expected him to make a crack about showing him how grateful she was, the old Ben would've done it in a flash. The new Ben, the polite stranger Ben, merely coughed, and Tessa could feel his discomfort radiating through the phone.

"I have to go," he said abruptly. "I just wanted to let you know Morris will be calling to offer you your job back."

"Was this your doing, too? Did you tell him to rehire me?"

"It's the right thing to do," he said impersonally, which didn't answer her question. A click sounded in her ear as the phone disconnected.

Tears welled in her eyes and flowed slowly down her cheeks. She wished with all her heart she could erase Ben's hurtful past and heal him with her love, but offering him her love was pointless, when he would no longer even accept her friendship.

****

Morris stood with his back to the doorway, gazing out the window with his hands clasped behind him. When Tessa knocked, he pivoted at the sound and moved in the direction of his desk.

"Enter, Tessa. Have a seat."

"Good morning, Mr. Montgomery," Tessa said politely as she seated herself. She had to battle with her dread of confrontation, because she sensed this could possibly turn into one of the most difficult confrontations she'd ever had. Her hands squeezed tightly together on her lap, and she unclasped them, discreetly wiping their dampness onto her pants.

Morris licked his lips. He seemed to have some difficulty controlling his eyes. His gaze skittered about the office, finally focusing in middle-space. He coughed awkwardly and linked his hands together on the desk in front of him.

"It has come to my attention that perhaps I was a bit hasty in my actions last week. I now understand someone else's improper behavior caused the misunderstanding."

His sanctimonious attitude irked her, and the temptation to lash out and go on the defensive ran strong, but Tessa intended to stick to the high road.

"I'm relieved the truth finally came out." Amazingly enough, she got those words out without sounding half as snide as she felt.

"Because you were unfairly accused, I feel it is obligatory of me to offer you your position back."

His words created an instant's squeezing hurt—he apparently felt no obligation to apologize for *unfairly accusing* her.

"How kind of you, sir, but I respectfully decline." Ever since Morris had called the previous day to set up this appointment, Tessa had debated which course of action to take. Until this moment, she'd been unsure whether she wanted to take the job back or not.

It'd likely never matter how good she was, she could never succeed on her own terms in this oppressive male environment. Morris wanted her to stay in the background, content with the occasional pat on the head, but she now knew if given the opportunity, she could be a success in her own right. Signing Pearce Jeffries had proven it, and she refused to sit quietly in the corner any longer.

She ignored the sadness that welled up at the thought of not working with her friends and colleagues. She'd considered this carefully, hadn't slept much last night as a result, and she knew in her heart she'd never be satisfied working here again.

Morris's lower jaw unhinged and slowly sank. "Excuse me? There must be a misunderstanding. I am allowing you to return to work with no loss of remuneration or position."

Allowing her to return to work? As though she should be grateful? Unfortunately for him, she didn't happen to be in a grateful mood.

"How generous of you, but no thanks." It grew increasingly difficult to maintain a civil tone. Surely Morris recognized the shades of sarcasm coloring her words.

"You realize, do you not, that cutting off one's nose to spite one's face is a painful and most unsatisfying experience? I strongly suggest you rethink your decision. I had been prepared to offer you a cash incentive for your trouble."

Aggressive and impatient, he spoke in a voice designed to be heard by the deaf, but this time it didn't have the ability to intimidate Tessa. Her dignified restraint collapsed under the weight of his pompous words. To hell with the high road. She was about to take a much different path. A path she'd wanted to travel for far too long. With nothing left to lose, she'd found the perfect opportunity to finally tell Morris

Montgomery where to stick it.

"You would've gotten much further to offer a sincere apology, but I've yet to hear one. 'I'm sorry' must really get stuck in your throat, eh?" Taking a deep breath, she rushed on blindly, anxious to get the words out before her nerve failed her completely. "I've worked for this agency for eight years, and during that time I've conscientiously given you the best I had to offer. I'm not very good at blowing my own horn, and maybe that's been my downfall.

"In place of thanks or praise for my loyalty and hard work, I've had to put up with all levels of condescension on your part. You overlooked me for promotions and generally made me feel unappreciated, if not downright incompetent. You continuously underestimated me. You've labeled me a certain way because of my looks and gender. Well, guess what? I'm much more than a kewpie-doll, but hey, it's your loss."

Annoyance sharpened his features. "You will come to regret this outburst."

"The only thing I regret is putting up with your garbage all these years." Her voice sounded shakier than she would've liked, but she continued on sheer adrenaline. "The only decent thing you've ever done was give me that cruise last fall, and I have a strong suspicion you did so under duress. If I hadn't gotten it, there would've been hell to pay with some of the other senior executives who actually respect my abilities, regardless of the fact I'm a short blonde woman."

His brows drew together in an angry frown, and he knocked his fingertips against one another impatiently, not denying her assertion.

"But you got yours back, didn't you? Hiring Ben

Dunham to share the promotion with me, dangling the possibility of losing that position over my head. And now, trying to make me feel as though I should be grateful because you're condescending to give me my job back. A job I didn't deserve to lose in the first place. Well, I'm not grateful, and like the song says, you can take this job and shove it."

Whenever Morris opened his mouth to interrupt, she simply turned the volume up a notch and continued talking until there was nothing more to say. Then, with a sense of triumph such as she'd never experienced before, she got up and walked out, not giving him a chance to have the last word.

Her first impulse as she carried on down the hall was to let Ben know what happened, and she actually found herself standing outside their office—his office—ready to go in, before she stopped herself. Her fingers reached out, only to rest lightly on the door. Ben was right on the other side of this slab of wood, and Tessa had to fight her overwhelming need to be near him. He probably wouldn't want to see her. She hadn't been able to forgive Morris for the way he'd treated her. What gave her the right to expect Ben to forgive her?

A hollow feeling settled in her heart, and she closed her eyes against the tears welling up. It was best to leave without seeing him. Best never to see him again.

Lifting her chin and squaring her shoulders, she went to Janey's office instead. She plastered a convincing smile on her face and poked her head through the door.

"Hey. Do you have time for an early lunch?"

Janey bounded from her desk and grabbed Tessa's

arm, propelling her into the room. "What happened? Did Morris give you your job back? Or have you decided to go with Bray?"

"Buzz Travis and see if he can join us for lunch. I'll tell you both everything while we eat."

Janey reached for the phone and punched the number to Travis's intercom. "Come on. Tell me now," she wheedled as only Janey could wheedle.

"Be patient."

"Patience is such a boring virtue. Oh hi, Trav. Can you have lunch with Tessa and me?" She pinned Tessa with an offended glare. "She has news, but won't spill until you're here. Of course, right away. Whaddaya think, I want to wait another hour?" She bobbed her head impatiently as she listened to what he had to say. "Okay, meet you at the elevators."

As Tessa stepped out of the elevator with her friends and plunged into the throng of people in the lobby, she realized this would be the last time she'd ever do that here. Surprisingly, the realization didn't depress her. Although she still didn't have a job, quitting had given her a great deal more satisfaction than returning to the agency with her tail tucked meekly between her legs. She was scared, yet also felt a measure of peace with her decision.

****

"Okay, first thing I want to do," Tessa said after the waitress left with their orders, "is thank the two of you for helping to clear my name. I can't tell you how much it means the way you both stuck by me."

"My gosh, you're more than welcome. If this is a thank-you lunch, Ben should be here, too," Janey told her pointedly. "He's the one who figured out what

Dallas was up to. And he was the one who confronted her about it. All Travis and I did was hide in the closet."

"By the way, who was the brunette watchdog at Dallas's desk this morning?" Tessa went on as though Janey hadn't spoken. "I practically had to show ID before she'd let me by."

"She's a temp. Dallas hasn't been seen since the debacle in the break room yesterday." Janey made a contemptuous sound in the back of her throat. "It's my guess she hightailed it out of there before Morris got the chance to fire her."

"I say, good riddance," Travis growled. "That she-devil obviously has a bucket of screws loose."

"Ya think?" Janey nodded, wrinkling her nose in distaste. "She had that whole *Fatal Attraction* thing going on, and frankly it creeped me out. Ben was awfully choked, too. Even though it made him feel rotten, he sure knew what to say to get Dallas to spill her sick guts."

Janey had given Tessa a very detailed accounting over the phone yesterday, yet she obviously felt compelled to repeat it. For Tessa's benefit, no doubt. Tessa fully understood the extent of Ben's involvement in clearing her name, and she didn't care to rehash it. She was tired of talking about Ben. She was tired of *thinking* about Ben, but before she could redirect the conversation, Janey resumed her play-by-play.

"After he went to Morris to explain what had happened, he was considerate enough to come by my office to check on me. He was so sweet about it, too. He even apologized for involving me." Janey propped her elbows on the table and sank her chin into one hand with a sigh. "That's a real hero, in my eyes."

Tessa couldn't bear to hear another word about Ben's heroics. He belonged in her past, and she had to keep him there. At the moment, she had no idea how to accomplish that feat, but not dwelling on him, particularly on how *sweet* or *heroic* he was, would be a good start.

"I would've paid big money to see the two of you hunkered down in the close confines of the coat closet. How comical." Tessa intercepted the look Janey cast in Travis's direction, a look that called to attention how she'd once again ignored the mention of Ben. "So, Travis," she continued, determined to keep the topic light—and off Ben. "What would your wife think if she found out you were hiding in a closet with a female coworker?"

Travis rolled his eyes and grinned. "She'd understand I must've had a darn good reason, of course."

"Of course." Janey snorted and did the eye-rolling thing back.

The waitress arrived with their lunch, pasta for Janey and Travis, and a salad for Tessa.

Tessa stabbed a tomato wedge, but Janey laid her hand on Tessa's arm, stopping her from eating it. "Enough already. Tell us what happened with Morris. Did you get your job back?"

"Short answer. No."

Travis paused in the middle of tasting a forkful of pasta. "He didn't offer to take you back?"

Tessa made a vague gesture. "He offered, I didn't accept."

"Say again?"

"If you want a direct quote, I believe I told him he

could take the job and shove it." She took great pleasure in being able to grin at Travis's drop-jaw expression.

There was a long moment of shocked silence, then Janey said, "I think you better give us the long answer now."

Tessa held up one finger as she popped the neglected tomato wedge into her mouth. She hadn't realized she had an appetite until that acidic tang assaulted her taste buds. Ignoring Janey's glare of impatience, she slowly chewed with appreciation and swallowed.

After a sufficiently protracted delay—a payback of sorts for the ice cream-savoring incident on the weekend—Tessa described what had transpired. Now that the worst was behind her, she could find humor in the way Morris's mouth had opened and closed like a big, ugly guppy.

"He was such a—oh what's the word I'm looking for? Jerk. Yeah, a big sanctimonious bag of jerk will do nicely, and be damned if I could find it in me to remain polite. I just couldn't let him continue to steal my dignity."

"Good for you." Janey gave a quick congratulatory handclap, as always, there to back her up no matter what the situation. "I'm so proud of you for finally taking a stand with him."

"What you're too nice to say is it's about time I found my backbone, right?" Tessa asked with a wry smile.

Janey shook her head. "I'm not criticizing you, honey. You are who you are, and it's what makes you special."

"Okay, but the truth is, no one can make you feel inferior unless you allow them to, and I gave that horrid man permission to undermine my confidence for far too long."

"Morris's problem is he wants to know he's powerful and in control, and it doesn't seem to matter that he loses respect by demanding it," Travis said. "It's not your fault, it's his."

Tessa glanced at him. "I've always shown him respect, and he still didn't respect me back. I honestly don't know how you guys put up with him."

"I made sure he knew from day one that I wouldn't permit him to walk all over me. Being in the art department, not in sales, probably makes a big difference too. According to that old chauvinist, women have no place in marketing. Scribbling pretty pictures, on the other hand, is well suited to our sub-species." Janey opened her mouth and made a gagging motion with her finger. "What a pompous windbag."

Travis took off his glasses, wiped them with a napkin, then rubbed his eyes before replacing the glasses. "I'm sure going to miss you around the office, but more importantly, what do you plan to do now?"

Janey made a fist and tapped Travis's arm. "We'll all miss her, but she has the offer of a lifetime waiting for her in Vancouver, remember?"

Travis looked at Tessa earnestly, blinking behind his glasses. "Are you seriously considering that, Tessa? From what Janey's described, it'd be right up your alley."

Tessa rolled her glass of iced tea slowly between her hands, staring down into it as though she could find the answers to her dilemma in there. "Yeah, well, it's not just down the block."

They continued to discuss the pros and cons of Tessa taking the job for a good half hour while they ate their lunch. Janey was as energetic and encouraging as ever. Travis was more low-key and levelheaded, but no less supportive.

Tessa's heart seemed to shrink as the ramifications of this decision sank in. Good intentions and everything else aside, Ben had become so important to her in such a short space of time, she didn't know how she'd cope with the emptiness leaving him would cause. Never in her life had she felt so utterly helpless in the face of her own emotions.

Travis pushed back the sleeve of his suit jacket and looked at his watch, then picked up his soda and downed the rest of it in one long swallow.

"I have to run. I've got a meeting at a radio station in twenty minutes, and you know what traffic's like." When he stood and reached for his wallet, Tessa stopped him.

"Not a chance, buddy." She dredged up a genuine smile for him. "This one's on me."

"You don't have an income. Let me grab it this time."

"Absolutely not. I can still afford to buy a dear friend a plate of noodles."

"Thank you." He slipped his arm around her shoulders and pulled her close for a hug. "Stay in touch. Promise?"

"I promise." She watched Travis leave the restaurant and worked to get her emotions under control at the same time.

"So," Janey said, poking her in the arm to get her

attention. "Have you made your plane reservations yet?"

With a sigh that didn't begin to express her swarm of conflicting feelings, Tessa said, "Not yet. I'll make them as soon as I get home. There should still be open flights for tomorrow." She sighed again, unable to help herself, and this one was even louder. "Oh, Janey, I'm afraid I might be making a terrible mistake."

Janey's brown eyes were too intent, too knowing. "Because of your feelings for Ben?"

"Excuse me?"

"What? Did I stutter? I said you've fallen in love with Ben. You have, haven't you?"

Tessa drank her iced tea self-consciously, then stared at the glass, only vaguely aware of the hum and buzz of restaurant noise around her. "I don't think I want to answer that question. It's beside the point anyway. Ben can barely tolerate me, and I can't say as I blame him. I don't know, it's probably best for both of us if I move away," she said at last, because she really wanted it to be the truth.

A perverse thought entered her mind. When she began working with Ben, she had resolved if she couldn't get him out of her life, she'd at least keep him out of her heart. Now she had to get him out of her life because she couldn't get him out of her heart.

Chapter Fourteen

Tessa certainly didn't look happy to see Ben once again standing uninvited on her doorstep. Although this time, her expression seemed more pensive than angry.

He peered over her shoulder as Milo came barking from down the hall. The dog reared up on his hind legs when he reached Ben, and danced around him, pawing him and squeaking in excitement. Ben hunkered down to tickle him behind the ears and before he could back away, the little bugger jumped up and lathered his face with his quick pink tongue.

"*Ewwph.*" Ben jerked his head out of reach and scrambled to his feet. "Knock it off, doggie breath."

"Sorry about that. He thinks you're his friend."

She made that sound like an accusation, and it had Ben wondering if she was projecting her own feelings. He had to admit there'd been a serious strain to their friendship lately, and he accepted the blame. He'd thought putting some distance between himself and Tessa might make her less of a distraction. Instead, she weighed even heavier on his mind.

Tessa bent down and scooped the dog into her arms. Milo yipped, straining to get free. "Settle down, Milo. What can I do for you, Ben?"

Ben used a corner of the folder he carried to scratch tensely at the back of his neck. "Can I come in? I have something that belongs to you."

Tessa stepped back and let him enter, then put Milo on the floor and closed the door. "I don't have much time. I'm expecting my father any moment."

"This won't take long. Here you go." He handed her the folder, watching closely for her reaction.

"Where did—how—" Tessa lifted her wide-eyed stare from the folder to look at him, then her chin dropped an inch and her gaze cut away. She closed the folder and made a self-conscious noise. "Where did you get this?"

"I found it while searching Dallas's desk. It's what you were missing from your sketchpad, isn't it?"

Tessa nodded briefly. A shadow of distress touched her face. "I'm sorry I accused you of taking it."

"I'm not looking for an apology. I just wanted to return your property."

And have an excuse to see you.

Ben followed her down the hall to the living room, tried but failed to keep from staring at the sweet sway of her little butt. She turned to face him, and he hurriedly lifted his gaze before she caught him looking where he had no damn business looking. She motioned for him to take the armchair, while she chose the couch for herself.

He nodded at the folder she'd placed on the coffee table. "When did you draw that? And why?"

Tessa shrugged, then focused her eyes on the window. "A long time ago, in one of my weaker moments."

"You drew it from memory."

Her eyebrow rose a fraction. "Do you remember posing?"

"It wasn't a question. I meant you did an incredible

job without having me there for reference. It looks just like me, annoying smile and all."

Tessa's mouth curved with tenderness, and Ben almost forgot his resolution to stay detached. It was damn hard when all he wanted to do was kiss those delicate lips and drink in their sweetness. The woman had the ability to tempt him without even trying, and he fought not to react.

Then he remembered the other reason for his visit, and the heat fled his body. He hunched himself, turtle-like, into his shoulders. "I spoke with Janey earlier. She told me she had lunch with you today."

An *uh-oh* look crossed her face, but she didn't say anything.

"She said you're thinking about taking a job in Vancouver. That you're flying out there tomorrow," he added, doing his best to sound interested, but not anxious.

"It's an option I'm considering. I wouldn't have left without telling you."

Her features remained apprehensive, and Ben got the distinct impression she was shining him on. She'd planned to leave without even saying goodbye. He obviously didn't matter enough to her, to let him in on her plans. That stung. A lot.

"Why *are* you leaving?"

"To make a new start. Vancouver will be a good place to do that. There's nothing to keep me here anymore."

The meaning behind her words hit him with the impact of a hard-swung 2x4 across the chest. "What about your family? What about your friends? What about—" *Me*! he almost blurted, but clamped down hard on that. "Why didn't you take your job back? Morris told me he offered it to you, and you turned him down."

"He should've done a nicer job of offering it, if he sincerely wanted me to take it."

"Damn it. Damn that pompous old ass to hell. Is that why you're leaving? I can speak to him again. You two can arrange another meeting and talk it out."

Tessa rested her head against her open palm, her elbow propped on the arm of the couch. She looked tired and a little sad, but determined. "Look, I don't know if I'm taking the job in Vancouver or not. It's a tempting offer, but either way, I won't be returning to Montgomery Group. I'm not happy there. I haven't been for a long time, and I don't want it anymore."

That stopped him cold, if only for a second. "And this job in another province is what you want? What's so great about it anyway?"

"I'd be partner, for one thing. No more putting up with Mr. Montgomery's b.s.. I'd be working with small businesses, for another, covering a broader spectrum of the market. And the man I'll be working with wants me there and will treat me as an equal, unlike the situation with my previous position."

An electric tickle, much stronger than simple curiosity, zinged down the back of his neck. "How old is this guy?"

Tessa gave him a funny look. "Mid-thirties, I guess. Why?"

"Married? Settled down?"

"I don't see what that has to do with anything."

"It means he's responsible, and the business is stable," he said, pretending to a patience he didn't feel.

What he felt was jealousy, ugly, biting jealousy, at the thought of Tessa working with another man. And worried, because this guy could be an unscrupulous operator who'd take advantage of Tessa financially and professionally, not to mention how he could mess with her on a personal level.

"Not that it's your concern, but Braden Kent is highly intelligent, incredibly talented and the business is flourishing. Satisfied?"

Satisfied? Not by a long shot. Although the jealousy thing continued to eat away at him, at least it didn't appear as if he had to be concerned about her professional welfare. "What do your dad and sister think about you moving away?"

She traced a toe along the leg of the coffee table. "My sister's okay with it. I haven't told my dad yet. That's why he's coming over."

"I'll miss you." He told himself not to go there, but the thought of never seeing her again, never to kiss her, to touch her, was too much.

"You don't have to say that."

"It's the truth. I wish things had gone differently between us because I'm attracted to you, and I value our time together."

He had no business saying these things to her. It wasn't fair. But it was hard letting go of something you didn't know you were hoping for. Tessa was everything that appealed to him in a woman, and he hadn't even realized it until he met her. He had thought he liked his women statuesque, she was a petite blonde. Prior to meeting Tessa, a sexy body had been enough, yet he found Tessa's delicate curves and spunky nature that hid a touch of vulnerability even sexier. He'd only pursued women who were interested in shallow relationships. Tessa made no effort to hide that a relationship without a commitment was the last thing she wanted, and for reasons he couldn't begin to fathom, this made her all the more appealing.

She bent her head and studied her hands. "You told me all you wanted was sex. Even spending the night was too much of a commitment for you."

A sinking regret went through him, weakening him. "Because when I'm with you, I find myself caring about you, and I don't know what to do about it. I don't want to have feelings for you, so I have to go to a place inside me that isn't ruled by emotion." His words sounded cold and cruel. He was trying to explain the unexplainable. Even he couldn't understand it. That's just the way it was. The way it had to be.

He met her gaze, and she searched his face. Searched with undisguised perplexity, with bewildered concern. "That's because you're afraid." The gentle understanding and tender empathy in her voice both angered and touched him deeply.

"No, this is who I am. This is me. I'm not capable of anything more." He struggled for breath as impossible feelings for Tessa ambushed his heart. There was too much emotion to deal with here. He shouldn't have come, and he needed to leave before he did something he'd regret. Like beg Tessa to stay, even though he could never offer her what she needed, what she deserved.

Tessa could see a slight tremor in the hands clasped tightly together on Ben's lap, could hear the hitch in his breath. He looked hurt, confused, angry. All the same emotions stirring inside her. She wanted to fling herself at him, tell him she'd made a mistake and didn't care about her career, only about him.

If he asked her not to leave, she didn't know if she could go through with it. Even though she was completely in love with him, could she risk losing everything that mattered to her career, just to stay near him? More to the point—did she have the strength to leave if he asked her to stay? Could she go, knowing she'd be leaving her heart behind?

Tears floated in her eyes, and she swallowed the despair in her throat. "It's not who you are," she said fiercely, daring him to refute her claim. "Don't you see? You won't let yourself be anything else. You won't allow anyone to love you."

The anguish in Ben's eyes leapt out at her. "Mom loved my father and he put her through hell. What if—"

She wrapped her arms tightly around her waist to keep from reaching for him. "That won't happen. Because you aren't your father. You're nothing like that man, and if you ever have doubts, just ask me. I have complete confidence that you would never express your anger in a violent way."

He threw up his hands, then slapped them back down to his sides. "You can't know that. What went on between my parents was sick. It was wrong. No child should have to watch that. I lived it, and I won't ever make another person live it."

"I believe you. Because you aren't your dad."

"Says who? You? And how do you know what ugliness exists inside me? When I was a kid, I'd get so mad I wanted to pulverize something. What if the man I am is no better than my DNA?"

Tessa pointed at him urgently. "Ah, see. You said

something, not *someone*. Who could blame you for feeling frustrated? You were just a child trying to deal with some very complex issues. You had every right to feel angry. That doesn't make you anything like your father." He gave a derisive snort. He was doing this to protect her—from himself—and it made her furious. She didn't need protecting from Ben, she needed to be loved by him. "You're so damn stubborn, how can I get through to you?" she all but yelled.

"You're a sweet person, Tessa, and you're acting with the best intentions, but this is my life and you need to stay out of it," he said through a clenched jaw.

She jerked to her feet and practically flew across the room to stand in front of him. She'd have the challenge of her life on her hands, but if she could provoke him to react with natural anger, she might be able to prove her point.

"Ya know, Ben, I've seen you cocky and arrogant more times than I care to remember. I've seen you considerate and sweet a time or two, and heaven knows, I've seen you sexy and charming. You can also be witty when you choose. You're so loaded with natural talent, you could sell oil to the Saudis and ice cubes to the Inuit." She met his glare and determinedly stared him down. "Yet, for all that, you seem incapable of selling the hottest commodity of all—*you* to yourself."

His gaze strayed off to the side, and he muttered something savage under his breath. "I'm not doing this, Tess. Please get out of my way so I can leave."

She leaned in, bracing a hand on each arm of the chair. Her breath came hard and a trembling had started in her limbs that she couldn't seem to master. "No, I won't get out of your way. I'm so frustrated, I could spit." She poked him in the shoulder. "How about you, huh?" She poked him harder. "Tell me how you feel. Show me."

He exhaled slowly, not rising to her provocation. "I know what you're trying to do, and it won't work. You can't fix what isn't fixable." His hands came out and spanned her waist, easily lifting her as he stood, then lightly setting her back down once he'd stepped away from the chair. "I'm going home now."

The doorbell rang, and Tessa raised trembling hands to her face, pressing her fingers to her stinging eyes to keep from crying. "That'll be Dad." Darn it, why did the man always have to be so punctual?

"Perfect timing," Ben muttered and headed for the hallway.

Tessa followed close behind, darting ahead just before they reached the door to open it for her dad.

"Hi, Dad. Thanks for coming." She embraced him quickly, pressing her cheek against his, so he couldn't see the shine of tears in her eyes.

"Tessa, dear, nice to see you." Ellis stiffened as he spotted Ben hovering behind them, looking as if he was waiting for the opportunity to bolt. "Oh, I didn't know you had company."

"Dad, this is Ben Dunham, he's..." He's what? A friend? Nope. Not anymore. A colleague? No longer that either. An ex-lover? Way too much information.

"Just leaving," Ben finished for her. He flashed her father a watered-down version of his incomparable smile. "Nice to have met you, Dr. Caldwell."

"Ben." Ellis nodded and shook the hand Ben extended to him. "I'll wait in the living room, Tessa."

Before Ellis had taken three steps down the hall,

Ben brushed past Tessa and out the door. He paused on the stoop and glanced over his shoulder.

"Good luck with whatever you decide about Vancouver." From his tone, it was a matter of complete indifference to him. He gave a curt goodbye nod and walked away, his movements stiff and awkward, hinting at the simmering anger kept under wraps. Anger at her for meddling in his private life and no doubt, anger at himself for allowing the conversation to turn personal.

A pang of regret twisted deep inside Tessa as she watched him walk out of her life. But no matter how much she loved him, she couldn't fix what's wrong inside him. Ben had to do that on his own, and she obviously wasn't important enough for him to want to make the effort. Any dreams or hopes she had for the two of them were just blind delusion. They had no future together. No future, she repeated emphatically, and wanted to cry at the pain of loss that ripped through her at the thought.

With dragging feet, she returned to the living room to find Ellis and Milo sitting on the couch together. She crossed over and joined them. Milo had pulled a disappearing act as soon as Tessa and Ben started raising their voices, and Tessa was relieved that her dad's presence had coaxed him out of hiding.

"Looks like Milo's been missing you."

Ellis gave Milo another pat, then turned his attention to Tessa. "I wondered if maybe you'd invited me over to meet that young man. Does the fact he knows I'm a doctor mean the two of you are close?" There was an annoyingly speculative tone to his voice.

Tessa drew a breath to steady herself, only to

release a humiliating whimper. Her eyes filled with tears so suddenly, she had no hope of stopping them. "I, uh, no, we, he..." Then to her horror, her face contorted, screwing up with terrible pain, and her tears turned to helpless sobs.

"Tessa? What is it?" Her father patted her stiffly on the shoulder, clearly ill at ease with her unexpected show of emotion.

Instead of reassuring him she'd be okay, her blubbering grew louder. Her father's arms awkwardly enveloped her, pressing her to a shoulder that smelled of some indefinable scent she'd always associated with her dad and doctors' offices.

"There, there, now." More nervous pats that did nothing to soothe her.

When the storm of tears slowed, she pulled away. "I'm fine, really," she managed through her snivels. That was the second suit jacket she'd cried all over in the past few days. She'd liked the smell of the other one much better.

Stop. Stop thinking about Ben.

She fumbled for a tissue and accepted her dad's large white handkerchief instead. "Thanks, Dad. Don't worry, I'm finished crying on your shoulder."

"Did that young man upset you? He looked distressed when he left."

Tessa used the handkerchief to mop up her face and blow her nose. "I'm just stressed out, and we need to talk. It's not about Ben."

She refused to get onto the subject of Ben. What she had to tell her dad would be hard enough without confessions of a broken heart thrown into the mix. She had been downright dreading this moment for days. In her mind, she had practiced a hundred different ways to break the news. Hard as she had tried, she hadn't found an easy way to tell her father she might be leaving. Tessa wanted his approval, very much wanted to please him, to make him proud. At the same time, she'd promised herself not to be intimidated, not to let his wants dominate her needs the way they had so often in the past.

She sniffed again and gave her nose one last swipe. "I have something important to tell you."

Ellis leaned back and crossed his legs, folding his arms over his chest. "Do I want to hear this?"

"Let's find out." Tessa drew in a breath for courage. "I'm thinking of taking a new job. In Vancouver."

His eyes widened with concern. "I don't understand. The last time we had dinner, you were all full of news about your promotion and some big account you'd just signed. Why would you want to quit at this point? Isn't that what you've been working so hard for all these years?"

"I've been thinking about a change for a while. There's been a, uh, development at Montgomery Group, and the more I contemplate this move, the more it feels right."

"You aren't acting like yourself, Tessa. First sobbing your heart out, then telling me you're going to leave a perfectly good job to move to a distant city? What's going on?"

"It's been a tough week, Dad. I no longer have that perfectly good job." Explaining only the absolute necessities, she told him what had happened at Montgomery Group. "Now, this wonderful prospect in

Vancouver has come up at the exact time I'm looking for a change."

Her father shook his head, disapproval forging deep, hard creases across his forehead. "There's a difference between running away and starting over. So there was a misunderstanding and things got a little tough for you, it's all behind you now. Go back and talk to your boss. Tell him you've changed your mind. Why toss aside everything you've accomplished here in exchange for something that might not be a sure thing?"

So much for hoping he'd understand and give his support. She should've known he'd point out the reasons why she shouldn't go. "I choose starting over. A fresh start will be good for me."

"It's not necessary. Pulling up stakes now just doesn't make sense. You aren't going about this rationally, and that has me concerned. I'd expect something rash like this out of Lauren, not you. You're too levelheaded to rush into a venture blindly."

Tessa rubbed her temples. Useless arguments always resulted in a headache. Hurt, frustration, too many emotions she didn't care to define, churned inside her. "I'm sorry, Dad, but I've spent my entire life answering to other people, doing what they expected me to do. It's time to do what's best for me. I'm not saying I'm moving to Vancouver tomorrow. I'm saying it's an interesting proposition, and I'd be cheating myself if I didn't check it out thoroughly."

"I understand you feel the need to do this. I just want to make sure you're doing it for the right reasons."

Tessa was about to offer a last explanation, but she sensed her father hadn't finished with her yet. It was one of those loaded silences that meant he had more to say.

"I've always admired your steadfast determination and integrity, sweetheart. I guess I should trust you not to rush into anything blindly." The words held a tone of grudging approval. "Besides, it isn't my place to tell you not to take a healthy risk. To be fully alive means taking risks, I should know because I've tended to only choose the safe and narrow path."

"You?" Tessa turned to look more fully at him, shocked by this admission. "What do you mean by safe and narrow? You've had a wonderfully interesting career."

"The question is, what did I give up in place of it?"

Tessa blinked. "I don't understand."

"Shortly after your mother died, I was offered a surgical teaching position at a small hospital up north. It was a stellar opportunity with plenty of challenge. But it scared the heck out of me. I'd have had to uproot you girls, start over in a new place." Ellis ran his fingers along the arm of the couch, his gaze following the movement. "In the end, I said no. Although I've had a more than successful career, a part of me always wondered what kind of difference I might've made if I'd taken that job when I had the chance."

"My gosh, I never knew." For the first time she really looked at her dad as a person, as a man who'd had his own set of hopes and dreams, and had experienced the pain and anguish of having some of those dreams die right in front of his eyes. Losing his beautiful young wife, and having to raise two juvenile daughters alone, must've been terribly difficult for him. "Do you still miss Mom?" she asked, feeling the ache of longing for her mother's arms, yearning for the comfort only a mother could offer.

Ellis looked up from his contemplation of the couch's silk damask upholstery, his brow furrowed. "Of course I do. Why do you ask?"

"Because I miss her, too. I miss talking to her." She could use a dose of her mother's soothing practicality to get her on track. "And I miss talking about her. You never want to talk about her."

He lowered his head slightly in acknowledgement and folded his hands on his lap, but said nothing.

"I've always wondered if you blamed yourself because you couldn't help her when she got sick, even though it wasn't your fault." She saw in his eyes that she'd hit on the truth. "You don't think we blamed you, do you?"

"How could you not have? I was the big fixer in my little girls' eyes. Whenever one of you was sick or injured, Doctor Daddy made it better. Then your mommy got sick, and Daddy could only stand by and watch her die. It was a horrible, helpless feeling, and I never wanted to feel like that again."

All these years and he'd never remarried. Now Tessa realized why. He loved his wife so deeply, and it had hurt so badly when he lost her, he couldn't bear to take that risk again. So he'd chosen the safe and narrow path. And here she thought he'd strictly focused on his career. She'd used him as a role model for her own career aspirations. To have an important, successful career, you had to make sacrifices in your personal life.

"Oh, Daddy," she sobbed and pulled him close for a hug. "Lauren and I love you so much, and we admire you even more. Not once would it have occurred to us to blame you, and you shouldn't ever have blamed yourself. I have enough medical knowledge to understand that when those viruses attack a vital organ, there's little that can be done without an immediate transplant."

"Although I understand that here." He tapped his temple. "It's hard to convince here." He tapped his chest.

"I know that feeling." Oh, boy, did she know that feeling. "Sometimes the head and heart are really at odds with each other, aren't they?"

She caught a faint smile, a relaxing around his eyes. "So, why don't you tell me about this exciting job prospect?"

With enough enthusiasm to do Janey proud, Tessa launched into a detailed description of the job with Braden Kent. She continued on to tell him how eager Lauren was to move into a condo downtown and how Janey was no less eager to move into the house.

"I almost believe Janey when she says some things are fated, because everything seems to be falling perfectly into place." Everything except the one big thing that meant the most to her. Her bottom lip quivered, and she sternly firmed it.

Nope, not going there.

Her dad rubbed his knuckle against her cheek and smiled. "Okay, this is me, backing off, baby. If you feel moving to Vancouver is right for you, go for it and give it your all."

"Thank you, Dad. That means a lot."

And, just like that, she made her decision. Unless the job ended up being a complete dud when she checked it out, she *would* go for it and give it her all. This time she'd also try to find some balance in her life.

She'd *thought* she loved Colin, and it had hurt when she lost him. She *knew* she loved Ben, and the idea of never seeing him again was beyond incomprehensible. But he couldn't or wouldn't love her back, so as painful as it was, her only choice was to move on.

Two strikes against her didn't mean she should turn her back on the next pitch. Rather than go through life alone the way her father had, she resolved to open up both her mind and her heart to any new possibilities Vancouver might have to offer. She could start by taking small risks. Stray off that safe and narrow path occasionally. Believe in herself. Have some confidence.

Confidence that she could succeed at a new job in a new city. And confidence that she could find love again.

If only that last thought didn't hurt quite so much.

Chapter Fifteen

Ben floated in a twilight world of intermittent consciousness, reminiscent of the recovery room after his appendectomy. Half-awake, half-asleep, not sure if he was dreaming.

Somewhere in the distance, thunder grumbled bad-temperedly, penetrating his reverie, signaling a storm on the way. With the sound, an unexpected bleakness shuddered through his insides, making him wonder what was wrong with him.

Tessa's face stabbed at him through the darkness. *Tessa*. The storm reminded him of Tessa and how much he missed her.

A glance at his clock told him it was only 6:30, way too early to get up on a Saturday morning. He thumped his pillow with frustration, wanting to go back to sleep, yearning for that state of oblivion where he could escape his thoughts. He rolled onto his side, tried to relax, flopped over onto his back. No use. He was wide-awake now, his mind dwelling on Tessa.

She would leave a huge, gaping hole in his life when she moved. And he didn't know how he'd fill the void. He'd set out to seduce Tessa, but somehow he had fallen into his own trap. He hadn't meant for this to go beyond a flirtation, a dalliance. Definitely nothing heavy or serious.

He never intended to fall in love, but he could no

longer push aside his feelings. He knew damn well she was under his skin and had been since he'd first met her. For five long months in Vancouver, he'd wanted her. And in the following months since she'd come back into his life, he'd wanted her even more. Even after she left, he'd continue to want her, and he needed to come to grips with his emotions. Not to analyze them, just to accept they were real.

He was completely in love with Tessa Caldwell.

Instantly his old misgivings and self-doubts came crowding out of the shadows. What good would it do to admit the ache in his chest was love? Love changed who you were. It made you vulnerable. Tied you down. He had only to remember what love had done to his mom. From what he'd seen, it could seriously mess you up.

He rubbed his burning eyes, while his thoughts continued to run unchecked. Fleeting snapshots of his parents. The arguments. The violence. The sickening scenes of forgiveness—until the next time. Ben covered his face with his hands, trying to block out the images.

Go away. Go the hell away. I don't want you in my head. I don't want you ruling my life anymore.

He breathed deeply, steadily, imposing a calm over himself as was his habit whenever his emotions threatened to overtake him. Remembering the past always brought anguish and frustration and anger. He was self-aware enough to realize he'd become trapped in the net of his memories. Shackled to his past.

He knew who had the key to release those shackles. Someone who could free him from the prison of his memories.

How far would he go to keep Tessa? That question,

and too many others, ricocheted around in his mind as he untangled the sheets from his limbs and hauled his butt into the shower. How much was he willing to risk to keep her in his life?

Tessa wasn't the type to play around with, and a man with shallow feelings had burned her once before, so if he planned to commit to her, it'd have to be all the way, and forever.

His mind shied away from that thought, and then came hesitantly back to examine it more carefully. He tried to tell himself the notion was crazy—marriage was exactly what he didn't need, what he couldn't have, but he'd gone beyond being able to reason with himself. He couldn't bear not having Tessa in his life. It was pointless to deny his attraction for her. She was in his heart, in his blood. He never expected to love so deeply, yet it had happened anyway, and he wasn't sorry.

He rubbed his body down with a towel, then padded into the bedroom to pull on jeans and a T-shirt. He got breakfast over with, then tackled his Saturday chores. All too quickly, he ran out of diversions. The cupboards needed stocking, and he decided on a trip to the grocery store. Instead of going to his car, he went out on the street, heading in the direction of Tessa's house.

If she had returned from Vancouver, they needed to talk, no matter how difficult that conversation might be, or how much he dreaded delving into his private fears.

Storm clouds were moving in across the mountains from the northwest, darkening the skies. Distant thunder rumbled, and the first fat drops of rain landed on his head and shoulders as he walked.

His thoughts filtered back to when he'd first met

Tessa. The memory of her blinding fear during the thunderstorm at sea went down his spine like cold water, and a sense of urgency drove his feet faster down the sidewalk.

Minutes later, Tessa answered his knock, Milo tucked securely under her arm. "Showing up at my door unannounced has gotten to be a bad habit with you."

He hesitated, measuring her for a moment. He'd made such a mess of things, he couldn't blame her for sounding annoyed.

A sudden jagged fork of lightning spiked across the sky. Though she seemed to brace herself for the following clap of thunder, its arrival still made her jump and press a hand to her throat. He felt an overpowering need to protect her, to hold her and keep her safe. He took her arm, instead, and ushered her inside, closing the door on the gathering wind and rain.

"The radio guy said two fronts collided," he said to make conversation while they walked the few steps down the hall to the living room. "It's a freak spring storm."

"This is Calgary. Thunderstorms pop up any old time they feel like it." She didn't offer him a seat or anything to drink. She just stood there, clutching that silly little rag of a dog and watching him warily.

"Hey," he said, sticking his hands in his pockets awkwardly. "You might be interested to know I spotted a moving van at your old friend's place yesterday." He didn't want to let on he'd been driving down the street looking for any glimpse of Tessa. She'd really think he was lame, or worse, borderline stalker. "Judging by the stuff they were hauling from the van, it looks like you got your wish and kids will be living there again."

A small smile touched her lips. "Really?"

"Maybe not the loads you'd hoped for, but at least one or two."

"That's great." She finally gave in to Milo's squirming and put the dog down. "I'll have to tell Mrs. P about it next time I see her. It'll please her."

Milo came over to sniff his leg, wagging his tail happily. Surprised to realize he was actually happy to see the little rascal too, Ben bent down to ruffle his fur. He glanced up at Tessa. "You saw her then, while you were in Vancouver?"

"I made a point of it. She's in a good facility and seems to be doing well. I think she recognized me, at least I want to believe she did."

He rose to his feet, feeling edgy and wishing they could dispense with the small talk. "I'm glad you had the chance to spend time with her. How did the rest of the trip go?"

"Good, very good. I've decided to take the job." She nodded and rubbed her hands against the sweats she wore. Faded pink and baggy, they hung enticingly low on her slim hips. "The finance terms for the buy-in are attractive, and Braden Kent will be a gem to work with. There'll be no need to defend myself as a woman with him."

She didn't sound snide. She sounded as if she just wanted to let him know how things stood.

He'd half-expected this and thought he had his face under control, but couldn't prevent the slight flicker of alarm that widened his eyes, nor the brief flash of panic that tightened the corners of his mouth. He hardened his features into an indifferent expression, his best form of defense when he needed to protect himself from vulnerable emotions.

"I see. Well, it's all good, then."

She raised her small, resolute jaw. "Yes, I think so. It'd be hard to pass up that sort of opportunity."

The crisp firmness in her voice told him she meant it, making his chances of changing her mind slim as a dipstick. It'd be selfish of him to even try. Tessa was better off with the new job. Morris was a difficult man, and if she asked for her job back, he'd make her pay for her insurrection in a thousand different ways.

Oh, God. How was he going to let her go?

Ben's insides jangled with excitement as a sudden idea struck him. What was stopping him from moving to Vancouver with Tessa? Calgary was a nice enough city, but he missed Vancouver, missed the warm weather, missed his mom. The thought of going back to the city he loved, to see his old friends again, to be close to his mom. Be with the woman he loved. Damn it, why not?

The room darkened as sheets of rain poured from the angry skies, driven and tossed by the wind. Lightning flared and thunder crashed over the city, diverting Ben from his wandering thoughts. Tessa rubbed her hands briskly over her arms, and he wanted them to be his hands, his arms, warming her and comforting her.

"I don't want you to move without me." He forced the words out, making a stupendous attempt at control.

Tessa froze to the spot, staring at him as though she couldn't believe what he'd just said.

He worked off his nervous energy by pacing the room, using his hands as he spoke. "We know we're compatible. We've shared an office, worked successfully together. We've shared a bed, more than once, with phenomenal results." He paused and took a breath, realizing what he said next would change the course of his life forever. A hell of a lot hung on the question he was about to ask. And on Tessa's answer.

"Can I share the next phase of your life? I know, uh, you've never given any indication you'd like me to move with you, but I want to. Hell, I-I can't let you walk out on me. Not now..." He let his words fade away, aware he was stupidly rambling.

Tessa put her hands to her temples, clearly in shock. "What? What are you saying exactly?"

He stopped pacing and stood with his shoulders hunched defensively. "I thought we could take a shot at being a couple."

Her swift intake of breath and wide eyes told him he'd caught her off guard. Silence hung between them, loud and long.

"Uh, Tess, you aren't saying anything. Please say something?"

She watched him for a moment longer, as if trying to gauge his sincerity. "You aren't the committing kind. You've told me that all along." Her voice betrayed surprise and bemusement, but not a hint of the happiness or excitement he longed to hear. "You prefer your pleasures without strings. The only time you've mentioned love, was to say it wasn't for you."

That much was true, he'd always thought love wasn't for him, but he had changed somehow. He was different on the inside, and he could never go back. Something turned over in his belly at this realization, something warm and as exciting as it was scary. For once, instead of trying to hide his feelings, he let them show openly on his face.

"Damn, I'm bad at this. Nothing's coming out right." He shuffled his feet and made a nervous sound, like an idiot. "It's all so clear in my head, but I guess I can't explain how I feel because I've never experienced this before." A hot ache grew in his chest, and he closed his eyes against the unexpected tears that hit him. He'd never told a woman he loved her, not counting his mother, and that was totally different. He'd thought he never would, yet now he couldn't wait to get the words out, and he found himself talking almost compulsively.

"I knew you were someone special right from the start, and I shouldn't try to take up with you. I just couldn't help myself. I never wanted to love anyone and have always battled not to fall in love, easily winning every single battle. This time I lost, and it wasn't even much of a fight." He lowered his head for a moment, then looked up to try again. "I love you, Tessa. I didn't mean to. I didn't want to. Yet somehow I let myself fall in love with you."

The words floated between them, suspended in the air, and for a moment, neither of them so much as breathed. Then, to his surprise, she wheeled around and crossed the room, stopping in front of the window. Her arms were wrapped around her waist as though holding herself together.

He came up behind her and placed his hands on her hips, resting his chin on the top of her head. The feel of her sweet little body nestled against his sent heat flooding through him. The shifting response in his crotch forced him to ease back a pace. This was not the time for that type of reaction.

"You're responsible for me, remember? You saved

my life. You can't up and desert me now," he joked, trying to defuse the escalating tension.

A clap of thunder exploded directly overhead, and rain beat noisily against the window. Tessa jumped, but instead of seeking comfort in his arms, she pulled away. He caught the look in her eyes before she turned her back on him. Although he had no idea what she was thinking, he sensed it wasn't good.

Knowing his happiness was dependent on someone else terrified him, and the old fears began advancing along his arms and legs, tying up his belly in painful knots, twisting around his heart. She didn't want him. He'd opened up and offered her everything, and it wasn't enough. He had the sensation of falling through space and lunged for the only lifeline within reach. Honesty.

He moved in to take up a position at her elbow. "I've screwed this all up and said everything the wrong way. I couldn't have been less romantic if I tried. I'm speaking the truth, though, when I say you mean everything to me, Tess. I couldn't contemplate marriage until I could trust myself. You gave me that ability," he continued, carefully feeling his way along unfamiliar emotions. "You've given me the power to feel. To trust in myself, after spending a lifetime of not allowing myself to feel, of not trusting anyone, especially myself. I want to return the favor and prove to you that you can trust a man. You can trust me."

She shifted a bit, clearly uncomfortable. Her uncertain glance settled on him for a moment, and then bolted away.

After a very long, very strained silence, he reached out, swinging her around to face him. Her tear-filled gaze met his, stealing the breath from his lungs. The next words he spoke were incredibly important. The biggest sales pitch of his life.

"I love you," he said softly. "I don't know how it happened, but it did and I'm glad. I'm so incredibly glad."

Her eyes were so full, when she moved they overflowed. She shook her head and tears flew off her face like rain. Both laughing and crying, she said, "Are you sure you're not just saying that because I'm leaving?"

He held her face in his hands and kissed her under both eyes, tasting the salty drops on the tip of his tongue. "I said I love you, and I mean it. I always have, I guess, except my history got me all mixed up and stupid. It needed something like this, the risk of losing you, to make me realize it. I'm scared of rushing into this, but twice as scared of losing you."

As soon as the words were out, he realized he'd somehow said the wrong thing again. Without moving, she seemed to withdraw from him. Her face was pale and wide-eyed, her mouth quivering. Fat tears rolled down her cheeks, and she pushed them away with the side of her thumb.

Ben let go of her and took a step back. "I guess we still have some issues to settle, huh? Are you unsure of me, after all? You're worried I might turn into my father?"

She looked directly at him, her eyes flashing like fire. "That has never been an issue. I trust you." She stretched out her hand and touched his cheek, and he immediately shifted to press his mouth to her palm. She just as quickly drew her hand away. "From the bottom of my heart, I know you'd never hurt me. At least not that way."

"But you think I might hurt you some other way?" He couldn't prevent the desperate edge to his tone.

She continued to stare at him, her brow furrowed in thought, but her mouth softened. "I don't know. You've always offered me honesty. No lies, no promises. Nothing beyond what you wanted."

Incandescent lightning skittered across the sky, trailed by an avalanche of thunder. Tessa's lips drew together in an agonized expression. She was actually trembling.

Ben pulled her against him. "It's okay, I've got you."

He held her close, caressing her hair, soothing her with gentle words. Instead of relaxing, she stiffened in his arms, her body language screaming, *Let me go, I don't want this*. The play of emotions over her face read just as plainly. She might say she trusted him, but she didn't. She was afraid.

Living in the shadow of her flamboyant sister had taken a toll on Tessa. It simply amazed Ben how she could be so talented, so beautiful, yet so unsure of herself, and he silently cursed that jerk of an ex-boyfriend and every other person, especially Morris Montgomery, who'd made her feel inferior, for robbing her of her ability to trust.

"Why are you so afraid? You say you trust me, yet your actions say you don't. You think I'm going to hurt you, don't you? You've told me I'm a decent person so many times you nearly had me believing it. But you didn't mean it. Damn it, Tessa," he shouted in spite of himself, furious with himself for falling for her lies. For allowing himself to care this much. "You're afraid of me."

What the hell was he thinking, yelling at her? If Tessa seemed afraid of him before, she looked absolutely terror-stricken now. Anxiety began eating away at his gut like acid, and his mind screamed for him to do something, but he couldn't move. He stood frozen in indecision, torn between his need to reassure Tessa and his urge to escape before he made matters worse.

Panic such as he'd never known welled up inside, and he spun on his heel, striding for the door. Walking away was what he did best and was exactly what he'd do now.

"Ben, wait."

His shoulders clenched protectively at the sound of her voice behind him. He glanced back before turning to face her.

She sent him a pleading look that he didn't understand. "Don't go. Please, please don't go yet."

Okay, that he understood. He closed his eyes in thanks as relief flooded through his body. There was hope for them yet. He took two tentative steps toward Tessa. "Tell me what I can say, what I can do to prove my love. Anything. Just please don't look at me with fear in your eyes. I can't take that."

"Tell me why you weren't happy when I signed Jeffries."

That was the absolute last thing he expected her to say. "Are you kidding me? I was thrilled for you. I couldn't have felt more excited and proud if it had been my own success. You did a great job, and you did it all by yourself."

She shook her head, biting hard on her bottom lip. "That expression on your face after I told you about the presentation, it looked angry or some other equally strong emotion. I saw it again the night I accused you of selling me out. And again, a moment ago. What does it mean?"

His forehead beaded with cold sweat. The idea of explaining his emotions made him a little frantic, but he'd promised her honesty, and he was damn well going to give it to her.

"When you told me Morris threatened to bust you from your position I felt so awful, I literally almost cried. Your pain became my pain, and I didn't want to feel it. And confessing that I was on the verge of bawling like a baby over someone else's misfortune wasn't something I'd ever willingly do. The same goes for the day you quit. It broke my heart when I heard what you'd gone through." He swallowed hard. Tears burned his eyes, and he tried to laugh, but it didn't come off very well. "And right now I'm scared as hell I'm going to say something or do something to mess things up with you forever."

Her lashes swept down across her cheekbones. "I forgot you didn't know about Mr. Montgomery's threat. I thought you were disappointed because I landed the account without you." She spoke so softly he had to lean forward to catch the words. "That maybe you were so angry with me, you hated me. Same with the other time."

"I've never hated you. That'd be impossible. I've been angry with you, most definitely, but not then. You've made me plenty angry by pushing me to face my feelings when all I wanted to do was hide in my

303

safe little emotion-free bubble. And if I had a brain in my head, I'd be thanking you for that. Is that why you're afraid of me?"

"What? No. I've never been afraid of you. I have complete faith in you, in your integrity, your honesty. You aren't your father, and I'm not your mother. Their mistakes are their own. Our mistakes would be our own, too. It's those mistakes I'm afraid of."

Her tongue came out and moved from one corner of her mouth to the other, and she met his gaze squarely. "I'm worried you feel pressured into rushing this because I'm leaving. Then one day you'll realize I'm not what you want, that I'm too old for you or not attractive enough or something. You'll take a look around and find someone younger, prettier, more suitable for you. There's no doubt in my mind you could pick and choose from any number of women far more beautiful and interesting than me. And I don't know how I'd bear to give you up once I had you."

Ben burst out laughing as a final tiny fear slid away from his heart. The way Tessa gaped at him, her mouth opening then tightening in anger, told him it wasn't the most sensitive thing he could've done, but he couldn't contain his relief. Admitting his fears, telling the truth had lifted an oppressive weight from his shoulders. For the first time in memory, the gnawing anxiety he lived with on a perpetual basis had shrunken to something minuscule and unimportant.

"How can you say that? Our age difference is negligible. I'm in love with you, and I don't want to be with anyone else. You're my perfect match, and I want to spend the rest of my life making you happy." He had an indefinable feeling of rightness, saying those words.

Tessa took a deep, shaky breath. "If you love someone, you have to be willing to make a leap of faith, so I'm ready to take the risk, ready to leave that safe path." Her cornflower blue eyes glowed with emotion as she took a final step forward. "I love you so much, Ben."

Her words sucked the air from Ben's lungs. With a groan, he crushed her roughly against his chest and closed his eyes, abandoning himself to the surge of emotion that swept through him. After the briefest hesitation, Tessa flung her arms around his neck, clinging as if she'd never let go. Her head fit perfectly in the hollow between his shoulder and neck. They fit perfectly together in every single way.

"I couldn't bear to leave you, but I didn't think you wanted me."

Her tone clogged his throat with sadness. "Oh, baby, I want you. I really, really want you." This was everything someone in love should feel. Tenderness, excitement, passion, so much more. "I love you and I want all of you. Always."

Her low moan was wildly exciting, and he captured her lips with his. Their tongues tangled together in a dazzling, blinding blaze of sensation. Somehow, they made it up to Tessa's room. After two clumsy tries, he managed to shove Milo into the hallway and get the door closed before the little dog darted back into the room. When he turned around, Tessa had her clothes off.

Her spectacular nakedness sent a flood of stark desire coursing through him, while at the same time the fragility of her beauty filled him with tenderness.

She was an enchantress, and she had him under her

spell.

"Beautiful," he murmured, his voice so husky it was barely audible. She shook her head in swift denial. "Yes, you are. You're incredibly, exquisitely"—he took two steps closer to her—"arousingly beautiful."

She smiled, and that smile sent heat searing through him. He could hear his pulse pumping in his ears, could feel his breath catch in his lungs. Unable to control his desire, he tugged his clothes off in record time.

Tessa's eyes widened at the sight of his healing scar. Little sparks of fire flew along his nerve ends as she tenderly ran her hand over the spot. "I wasn't thinking. Your incision—"

"Is fine," he growled as he eased her down on the bed.

His hands explored the soft lines of her back, her waist, her hips. Her lips were supple and responsive against his. Within the space of a heartbeat, what began as a gentle kiss, soft and tender, turned into something urgent, passionate, demanding. Their tongues met in a hungry, stabbing dance until the need to breathe forced them apart.

If he wanted to make this last, he had to slow things down. Way down. Taking his time, he explored the delicious length of her body, tasting his way from her throat to her collarbone, pausing to cherish one breast, then the other, caressing her with lips and tongue.

Tessa squirmed and giggled, interrupting his tour of pleasure en route to her belly button. She pulled him up against her, then rolled him over onto his back. "It's only fair that I get a turn."

She traced the long muscles of his torso from his waist to his pecs. Her palms rubbed languorously over his chest, stroking him. When her nails scraped gently over his nipples, he shuddered, his breath coming out as a groan.

"You like that?" she asked with a tease in her voice. Oh yes, he most definitely liked that.

Her fingers went from his shoulders to his thighs in a long shivering caress that almost destroyed the little control he had left. Her hand smoothed over his thigh, her breath a warm flow across his waist. She carefully kissed the length of his scar, then she became all searching fingers, warm mouth, soft skin, rubbing against him, dominating him, tormenting and torturing him. His entire body screamed with need as he surrendered helplessly to the temptation of her touch.

Flames flickered in his veins, fire burning fiercely beneath her caresses. He groaned, his breath hissing between clenched teeth. His desire raged against the restraint he imposed on himself, and he strove to conquer the cresting release he strongly craved and yet badly wanted to delay.

His last controlled thought was that they needed protection. Practically blinded by his blistering need, he stumbled from the bed and fumbled with his clothes, searching for a condom. He cried out in relief when he found one, and five sets of thumbs clumsily attempted to open it.

He cursed, afraid if he wasn't careful, it would tear and he might not have another one. Then a small pair of hands took the packet from him and delicate fingers deftly rolled the condom into place.

"Ah, hah, hah," he panted. Even that light touch

had almost teased him beyond his endurance. Then he gave up trying to speak, to think. All he could do was feel.

And it felt so damn good.

****

An enjoyably long time later, Tessa stirred languidly and glanced up at Ben. He watched her as though she was a dream and he was afraid to wake up. Love flowed through her like warm honey as she contentedly nestled against the strong lines of his body. Filled with an amazing sense of completion, her instincts told her something extraordinary had occurred, not only for herself, but for him too. They'd connected with a beauty only a man and woman in love could bring to each other.

"That was magical," she told him. "I love you beyond words."

He leaned back against the pillows, his eyes soft green and clear, free of the shadows that haunted him. "You're amazing. Absolutely amazing, and I'm sorry I didn't admit my love sooner."

She kissed him lingeringly to quiet him. "You don't have to apologize."

He bit lightly on her lip. "Are you kidding? Look at how much time we've wasted, when all along we both wanted the same thing. Each other. Only each other."

Rain pounded the roof, and thunder rumbled close by, but here inside her bedroom, all was tranquil, safe. Her mind touched on the memory of her mother, as it always did during a storm. She missed her and always would, but Ben's love had filled the empty spot in her heart left by her mother's death, and she knew her memories would no longer leave her aching and craving something just beyond her reach. She'd found that something—that someone—and he was lying right next to her.

Speaking softly, without hesitation, she told Ben the rest of the story about the night she developed her fear of thunderstorms at Sylvan Lake all those years ago. He said nothing while she spoke of the loss of her mother, but his arms tightened around her and his lips pressed lovingly against her temple.

"Because of you, I'll be okay now," she told him as she finished her story. "In fact, I might even become partial to storms. You've made me strong enough not to shatter into a thousand pieces with every crash of thunder."

His gaze was as tender as a caress. "We make each other strong enough to face our demons."

She settled on her side, facing him, her elbow bent to support her head. "You'd really do it? You'd ditch what you have here at Montgomery Group and move away with me?"

Ben crossed his arms behind his head. "A condition of my transfer states that if either party isn't satisfied with the situation any time within the first three months, I can return to my old position in Vancouver. I happen to find myself completely unsatisfied with the situation. I don't like the way Montgomery treats his staff, and I hate the thought of not working with you any longer."

If he returned to Montgomery Group in Vancouver, he not only wouldn't be working with her, he'd be indirectly competing against her. An idea began to take hold, and Tessa put her fingers to her mouth, a smile growing behind her hand. She couldn't wait to discuss with Braden the possibility of Ben joining their firm.

Braden had mentioned that they'd need to expand before too long. He'd be a fool to turn away the likes of Ben Dunham, and one thing Braden wasn't, was stupid.

She held Ben close, feeling his muscles come alive beneath her fingers. "Everything will work out. Somehow." She giggled. "I feel it in my bones."

Ben leaned up on his elbow. "When do you start this new job?"

"In about a month."

The old devilish gleam returned to his eyes. "That's enough time to plan a wedding, isn't it?"

"A *what*?"

"A man should propose in a romantic setting with a diamond ring and a bottle of champagne. Well, at least with some clothes on." Tessa grinned, but Ben's face remained serious. His earnestness came across tender and endearing. "I want us to get married." His voice cracked on the last word, and he cleared his throat before continuing. "I love you, Tessa Leigh Caldwell, and if you'll have me, I'd be so proud to be your husband."

She rose up to meet his lips as he bent to kiss her. "And I'd be honored to be your wife." She felt lightheaded, euphoric, giggly. "I can't stop smiling."

"It's my intention to keep it that way. I plan to love you and make you happy forever."

"Don't make promises you can't keep."

"I was lied to my entire childhood, and damn near every promise made to me ended up being broken. I swore I'd never do that to someone I cared about. So when I promise you something, I mean it. I'm gonna love you and cherish you and make you smile for the rest of your life."

Tessa believed him. She didn't feel old or insignificant. She didn't feel skinny or flat-chested. She lifted Ben's hand and placed it on her small breast, watching the rapt expression come over his face as his hand caressed her eager skin, his fingers teasing and taunting her responsive nipple. She felt as loved and adored as his words, his eyes, and his touch told her she was.

"That sounds delightful, sweetheart. I think you've spoiled me already." She pulled him on top of her, rubbing her body seductively against him, pressing her hips up against his growing heat. "Because I'm craving some of that love, and I want it this minute."

Laughter rumbled from his chest to hers as he deliciously and delightfully made good on his promise.

A word about the author...

Joyce Holmes lives with her husband and very small dog in the beautiful Okanagan region of British Columbia. An empty-nest mom, she treasures family time, especially with her two precious little grandsons. Hiking, biking, boating, and photography are pursuits she enjoys when she's not dreaming up stories in her head or planning her next great adventure.

http://JoyceHolmes.wordpress.com

Thank you for purchasing
this publication of The Wild Rose Press, Inc.

If you enjoyed the story, we would appreciate your
letting others know by leaving a review.

For other wonderful stories,
please visit our on-line bookstore at
www.thewildrosepress.com.

For questions or more information
contact us at
info@thewildrosepress.com.

The Wild Rose Press, Inc.
www.thewildrosepress.com

Stay current with The Wild Rose Press, Inc.

Like us on Facebook

https://www.facebook.com/TheWildRosePress

And Follow us on Twitter
https://twitter.com/WildRosePress

www.ingramcontent.com/pod-product-compliance
Lightning Source LLC
Chambersburg PA
CBHW050656290626
47170CB00015B/619